Knot For Keeps

Melissa Huxley

Copyright © 2023 by Melissa Huxley

All rights reserved.

No part of this publication may be reproduced, distributed, or transmitted in any form or by any means, including photocopying, recording, or other electronic or mechanical methods, without the prior written permission of the publisher, except as permitted by U.S. copyright law. For permission requests, contact melissahuxleyinfo@gmail.com.

The story, all names, characters, and incidents portrayed in this production are fictitious. No identification with actual persons (living or deceased), places, buildings, and products is intended or should be inferred.

Book Cover by Melissa Huxley

Editing by Erin Newman

Hello There!

Thank you for reading *Knot their Burden*. This book is written in British English which is a weird language in it's own right at times - but if you feel like you've found an error please drop me a message at melissahuxleyinfo@gmail.com I would greatly appreciate it!

For a full list of trigger and content warnings check my website melissahuxley.com

CHAPTER ONE
Lavender

Life at a Haven was many things, but it was never boring.

"He offered me a mansion, like that would make up for his blatantly rude behaviour?" Fawn sighed, running her hands gently over her impossibly neat blonde curls. She never had a hair out of place, it was infuriating.

We were sitting around the counter in our dorm's common space, an open bag of pretzels between us while we lamented.

"My last offer didn't include any property, not even a pack house! The pack was living with their parents and said they were going to wait and see if I *deserved* a family home; after I had been their omega for a few years and given them sons of course." I scrunched my nose at the memory. I had a habit of attracting the less-than-stellar packs. Then again, my misfortune was nothing compared to Fawn's.

I could understand *me* being rejected or judged. I looked like I had just come out of a flea market; being adorned with numerous gold rings and necklaces, alongside my wild brunette waves with the ends dip dyed a patchy purple. Despite the messy nature of my chest-length hair, I was still pleasantly surprised at the outcome of that three-in-the-morning impulse decision.

I tended to wear mismatched clothing, whatever was comfortable as well as bright and fun - rather than adhere to the latest fashion trends that just weren't my style. I was currently wearing leggings and a large flannel sweatshirt that probably belonged to a giant once upon a time given its size.

Fawn on the other hand was flawless, she always looked pristine. Her style was sleek and classy, like a genuine princess. She wore delicate, expensive jewellery and almost always wore heels. Both polite and respectful, she was the model omega and I was baffled she hadn't been snatched up by a pack already, despite all the big packs being attracted to her.

She had been in talks with the last three or four big money, old-school wealth packs that had come through the Haven, but it never seemed to work out. Her last potential pack had looked like it was going to, but two days after leaving with them she returned, oddly silent and resigned, unwilling to talk about it.

"You know..." Fawn grinned, lifting a handful of pretzels to her mouth. She wasn't even being careful about crumbs, a surefire sign she was still stressed. "You could always go on *Date an Omega.*"

I laughed, taking another pretzel. "I don't think I'm *that* desperate just yet." I grabbed a small throw pillow off a nearby bar stool and lightly tossed it at her perfect face. "I'm no spinster yet, and let's face it, a pack needs to see all *this*—" I waved my hand dramatically, gesturing across my whole body, bunny slippers and all, "—before they make an informed decision."

Fawn just laughed, not a hair out of place despite the

projectile. "It's not for me, either, but you never know!" She glanced down at her watch. "Shoot! I have to go."

Another part of her ladylike demeanour? Fawn refused to cuss. I, however, loved it.

"Pack meeting?" I asked casually.

"No." Fawn grimaced. "Meeting with the Haven lawyers about the pack I went home with. We're still dissolving a lot of the contracts and frankly it's a mess."

"Oh no, that sucks. If you need anything, just pester me!" I knew she hated confrontation. Typical Libra.

"Haven't you got a call with Archer tonight?" Fawn asked, raising her eyebrow. "No disaster could pull you away from that."

"I do!" I couldn't help but grin. Archer and I had struck up a conversation a few months ago and became fast friends.

"Then you better get going. You really need to introduce me to this alpha, I can't believe he wasn't on my roster. I thought I had every pack on my roster." Fawn frowned.

"Perks of being a Haven princess? Having every pack at your disposal?" I asked.

She sighed deeply, dramatically resting her hand on her forehead. "It's the burden I bear!"

I snorted. "A burden you must carry alone. Now go, get to your meeting!"

"Okay, but I wanna hear more about Archer, it's been *months* and you've hardly told me about him. I want to know more about the alpha that's caught your attention!"

"*Mine!*" I tried to growl playfully, but broke into a fit of laughter instead.

Once in the safe confines of my nest, I piled a bunch of my favourite plush soft pillows against a wall to use as a back rest. My nest was where I felt calmest, all omegas made their nests comfortable and safe. Tapestries decorated every wall and soft fairy lights gave the space a dim glow that just made me feel at peace.

Quickly swiping through my tablet I deleted any notifications that weren't relevant and opened the video call app. Archer and I spoke via text most days, but after a few weeks of messaging he had suggested a video chat and I decided to go for it. I was so happy I did. We got on like a house on fire and the video calls had been a weekly thing ever since.

THREE MONTHS AGO

> How much does a polar bear weigh?
> Enough to break the ice!

The amusing message popped up on my screen one evening while I was shovelling pasta into my mouth at dinner.

I had frowned at my tablet, who was this person? Usually alphas could only message us once we approved their profiles, and I didn't recall approving this one. His cheeky message had caught my attention though.

> Hello stranger, I don't recall approving you…

> I should be offended that you don't remember me, but I was also surprised to find you pop up on my screen as available to message.

> Hmmm, computer glitch?

> A happy one for me, unless you want to block me. I wouldn't blame you, I'm a terror, at least according to my pack.

I smiled, my forkful of pasta halfway to my mouth. Usually alphas were immediately telling me all their positive traits, like how much they could give me and how amazing they were, all in an attempt to make me interested and pick them to talk to. It was actually quite the turn off.

> A terror? How so?

I replied, finding myself eagerly awaiting an answer, the food an afterthought.

> I steal all their gummy bears.

I grinned, shaking my head as I typed my answer. He was clearly mischievous.

> Oh no, that is a grievous offence. Are we talking the cheap off-brand gummy bears, or the nice branded ones?

> I am a classy gentleman, only the top name brand for me.

> I'm jealous. My favourite brand of gummy bears was discontinued last year, the brown sugar ones, and I still crave them with a vengeance.

> Ouch! If you let me know your name, I could always see if I could find and send you some. It's weird chatting with Omega1327. I'm assuming you have a name?

> Those gummy bears are GONE. Trust me, I've searched the internet a million times over at this point. You don't mess with an omega and her sweet tooth. And the name's Lavender. What's yours?

> Lavender, that's pretty. I'm Archer.

I noted his name, swiping from the chat to the alpha profiles. Glancing through quickly to try and find it, surely his pack was in here somewhere?

> I'm trying to find your profile and failing! You could be a serial killer for all I know.

> Don't worry Love, I'm a cereal killer, not a serial killer :D

I snorted with laughter, making a few people glance over at me. I probably looked insane, grinning maniacally at my tablet. What could I say? Dad humour was hot.

> Look under my pack name, Rowe. Our pack head is a grumpy moron called Gage.

Flicking back and searching just for the pack name I got a hit. Pack Rowe. Four members with a good reputation. Small town, hard working alphas from the looks of it. A butcher, a computer analyst, a security expert and a veterinarian. They must have saved for a while to afford the Haven fees, which probably meant they were serious about looking for an omega, which made me smile.

There was only one picture on their profile, which was a little odd. It was four alphas squished together wearing fake moustaches. The one on the far left with shaggy blonde hair was taking the photo. It was a far cry from the usual professional photos, I suspected the cheeky alpha I was currently talking to may have instigated this, and butterflies erupted in my stomach at that idea.

> What do you know, there you are! You look adorable in your picture by the way, which one is you?

I replied. They were an official pack, available to talk to and they had a sense of humour, clearly. Immediately I found myself sucked into the conversation.

> Dark hair and glasses. I think the 70's moustache look suits me well

> You can totally pull it off! Though you're looking a little Richard Chase with it...

> Richard Chase?

I cringed. I'd typed before I thought. Usually I would avoid the gorier topics I liked to talk about, but taking a moment to look at the screen I decided to throw caution to the wind and just say the things I wanted to say. What was the worst that could happen, I would be blocked? That had already happened plenty, so I wasn't afraid of it.

> Serial killer, nicknamed the Vampire of Sacramento because he drank his victim's blood.

> Well I don't want to be giving off that impression! How on earth do you know about 70's serial killers?

> True crime isn't a hobby, it's a lifestyle. The freakier it is, the more intrigued I am. I go to sleep watching murder documentaries.

> That sounds kinda fun, recommend me some?

My eyebrows were so high they were almost touching my hairline, and my pasta was long forgotten about. No alpha had ever reacted like that, usually they made a few comments about the topic matter being too dark or inappropriate for omegas. No one had ever asked for documentary recommendations.

> I can give you a whole ass list. What are you feeling, serial killers, cults, or kidnapping?

> Tell me your favourite, most interesting one.

I thought for a moment. I could ease him in with a simple, easy case. Or I could throw him in at the deep end, he did seem interested after all...

> The Zodiac Killer, any documentary on him.

> Done.

I wolfed the last few bites of pasta down before returning to my nest, my eyes never leaving my tablet. I had even physically bumped into a guard at one point, and after a quick apology continued to my nest, engrossed in conversation until I fell asleep.

The next day he messaged me again.

> They never caught the guy?!

A grin so wide it almost hurt broke out on my face. He had actually watched it and was messaging me back about it!

> I know! What I would give to find out his identity.

> I say the cop was a good bet.

> But the evidence said otherwise.

> This is painful. Tell me more to watch...

Ever since that day, we had been in constant communication, mostly speaking about documentaries and a little about day-to-day life, but it just felt so easy to talk to Archer, like I could one hundred percent be myself.

Just over a week after we started talking a box had appeared on my kitchen counter. A delivery one of the Keepers dropped off for me, yet I hadn't ordered anything.

I had opened the box cautiously, worried that my family managed to slip a parcel by the Keepers and I was about to open a box of bibles or letters telling me I was a terrible daughter and a disgrace; only I was shocked to find six party size bags of brown sugar gummy bears.

Picking up a bag I turned it over in my hands. It was the exact type of gummy bear I had been craving for weeks. Taking another look in the box I found the note.

Told you I would find some.
-Archer

Dumbfounded and happy, I ripped into one of the bags there and then, and ever since there had been a steady supply of discontinued gummy bears being delivered for me.

CHAPTER TWO
Lavender

Looking over at the clock I smiled. He would be calling any moment now. Leaning over to grab a can of soda, I heard the telltale chime of an incoming call the moment I looked away from the screen.

Quickly accepting the call, I couldn't help but smile again when Archer's face appeared on screen. His hair had grown out a lot in the last few months, flopping over his face and brushing against the top of his glasses.

"Hello Lavvy girl." His eyes lit up as he took me in, gently running a hand through his hair.

"Hey Arch, you look exhausted. Work still kicking your butt?" I asked. He had bags under his eyes and was a touch paler than normal.

"Of course, this coding project is determined to kill me."

"It's getting late, you should sleep. Don't exhaust yourself further on my account, it's not like I'm going anywhere!"

Archer snorted. "Not happening, this call is the highlight

of my week Lav. It's not worth missing for an extra hour of sleep."

"Flattery."

"Flattery and bribery are the only ways I have to win you over! I've got to use what I can. Do you still have plenty of gummy bears by the way?"

"I'm almost out." I pouted, holding up a half empty bag.

"Oh that's no good. I'll send some more. There are some limited-edition gummy bears I saw today, watermelon and blue raspberry ones!"

"They sound so good, but brown sugar is where it's at."

"Very true."

"How did Kane's latest job go?" I asked. Archer's packmate had been away for a few days working a private security job.

Archer smiled. "I'm surprised you remember that. It went really well. He's tired, extra grouchy, but home safe and well. Gage ordered enough Mexican take out tonight to feed an army."

"Ugh, stop. You'll make me jealous."

"You could always join us." Archer raised his eyebrows.

"I think the Keepers would frown on that."

"Too busy being locked in your tower?"

"It's a hard life of luxury." I giggled.

"How's Fawn doing?" I had told Archer about my roommate when she had returned from her pack house. At first I'd panicked, thinking Archer would want to start talking to her, but instead he had shown genuine concern.

"Good, and she thanks you for finding the discontinued eye cream. She's convinced you're a wizard."

"Abracadabra!"

I snorted. "You're such a moron. Why do I keep talking to you?" I asked.

"The food."

"Ahh yes, the food. Oh! You'll never guess who emailed me today - my mother." I shuddered.

"I thought you had her blocked?"

"I did. Yet somehow, the religious nut still manages to find ways to let me know just how big of a disgrace I am. She's convinced I've ruined my life by getting that pesky education."

"The Keepers should do something about her." Archer frowned. He knew all about my family. I had spilled my guts one evening when I was feeling hormonal, sad, and lonely. He had listened and been so understanding.

"It's not all that bad, at least I have gummy bears!" I laughed, holding up the bag I was currently eating.

"Oh, it's a life of luxury then! Any new documentaries to recommend?" He changed the topic with ease, knowing talk of my mother could drag me down a bit. "I've finished watching the last series you told me about. Seriously, why the dude decided he wanted to murder people and throw them down the drain is beyond me."

Every week I gave Archer new true crime documentary recommendations, and every week he watched it and we discussed it during our calls.

"I think serial killers don't really follow normal logic. I did watch a good series on a whack job religious cult up north that was interesting, I'll send you the link. How do you even find time to watch all these, I thought you had loads of work?" He had a full-time job and a pack, so didn't exactly have copious free time. I, on the other hand, had a pretty light schedule as I was hardly talking to any packs at the moment. I had finished my last university class a month ago and was just waiting for my final grade to come through.

I didn't feel the need to rush into finding a pack. I didn't want to focus on material things, I wanted the vibes to be right. One of the first packs I had gotten to know had been horrified I was getting an education, so they had swiftly been removed from my roster. The pack I chose needed to know me for me, and like me for me. The last thing I wanted was a pack who just chose me because I was an omega.

Archer's grin grew somehow wider. "I've got plenty of work, but sleep is for the weak, and you keep recommending such amazing documentaries. Plus, I'll always find time to chat with you; you're the best sort of bad influence and I never want it to stop."

"Well it's just your luck you ended up messaging the omega who would distract you with gore-filled true crime, your productivity will never be the same!"

Was he only talking to me? I had been thinking about that an increasing amount. He never mentioned talking to others, and he seemed so busy I doubted he had time for anyone else, but I still wanted to know. Usually it was omegas who spoke to multiple packs, although it was generally all pack members, rather than packs talking to multiple omegas or a singular pack member talking to an omega.

"I'm not complaining," he said warmly; I liked the tone of his voice a little too much.

"I can't say I'm complaining either. Did you try that cheese popcorn yet?" I asked. I'd told him about the best brand they stocked at the Haven which I adored, and insisted he try it during our last video call. He had messaged me earlier in the day to say he had grabbed some from the grocery store and would try it that night while on camera because he wanted me to see his reaction.

"No! I said I would wait, let me go grab it. I left it in the kitchen." He stood up, and I took a moment to appreciate the lean muscles of his torso and arms. The dark grey T-shirt he was wearing was tight, and moulded to every muscle, making it easy for me to salivate over.

I shook myself out of the haze. "You know if you don't love it, I'll have to block you and never speak with you again!" I called as he retreated.

"That's rich coming from the woman who hates orange soda!" he called as he left the camera's view.

"It's too citrusy!" I told him loudly as he stepped away, leaving me with a view of the sofa and windows while he made his way to the kitchen. I doubted he'd heard me, but we'd had the orange soda discussion several times before. In the past I tried to crane my neck and see any identifying details as to Archer's home, but unfortunately his space, while well curated and masculine, was pretty nondescript.

Popping a few gummy bears in my mouth, I pulled out my cell phone and started scrolling through my notifications. There was an app where all the girls in the Haven tended to share pictures, and Fawn had uploaded a picture of her latest expensive bag. That omega had a closet that probably cost more than a mansion but it brought her great joy, so who was I to judge?

Another girl, Dalia, had posted about meeting a pack. My stomach flip flopped. I had subtly asked Archer once about meeting but he had just said his pack was drowning in work right now.

I wasn't daft. We had been talking for months, yet there wasn't even a hint of a meeting on the horizon. He had told me a few details about his packmates, their jobs and funny stories —like when Theo accidentally let a feral cat loose in their pack house and then they had to spend days trying to catch the grumpy baby.

Why would Archer tell me all these things if he had no intention of ever meeting me? Perhaps he was just taking my lead? I had made it clear early on that I liked to take my time, but several months in, it would have been nice to actually have spoken to or seen one of his packmates on a video chat, let alone discuss the possibility of meeting one day in the future. They would have paid a lot to join the Haven for the ability to talk to and court omegas, so why weren't they eager to meet?

I didn't want to rock the boat, though. I was enjoying what we had now, and I'd do everything to avoid endangering that. I looked forward to our chats more than anything, they were practically the highlight of my week.

A muffled, off screen conversation caught my attention, pulling me away from my phone. 'Was Archer talking with someone else? I didn't think so, even though I couldn't distinguish what either person was saying neither of them sounded like Archer, I knew the tone of his voice pretty well.

Minutes passed, and the muffled voices continued. I felt rude, listening in, even if I couldn't understand a single word they were saying. After another minute of weighing my options, I decided to say something.

"Arch?" I called out. The mumbling in the background stopped abruptly at that. A large man stumbled onto the screen, throwing himself gracefully into Archer's vacated chair, glaring at me. His blond hair was cropped short, he wore a dark grey shirt with the top button open and slacks. He was even larger than Archer, which I struggled to comprehend. Even in my startled state, I noticed that he was beautiful, in the handsome rugged way.

Heat pooled in my stomach for a brief moment and I thought about what it would be like to kiss under such a sharp jaw.

"Who are you?" he demanded with a growl. I froze, the anger in his voice enough to raise my heart rate. This was one of Archer's packmates, I recognised him from the profile photo. I think he had said this was Gage.

"Uh, Lavender?" I said my name like it was a question. "I was just chatting with Archer; but he went to fetch snacks. Sorry, if he's busy with other things I'll just log—"

"What did you hear?" he barked, glaring at me. Even through a screen, he was intimidating. Power oozed out of the man's every pore. His eyes were hard and I couldn't look at him for too long without feeling that instinctual panic a prey animal experienced when faced with a predator.

I flushed, scared, but something in me also bristled at his tone. "N-Nothing! You're being quite rude." I stumbled over the words, my indignation the only reason I could get them out in the first place. That, and the fact I was safe behind a computer screen. In person I would have most likely cowered: damn omega biology.

"Tell me!" he barked again. The hair on my arms stood up and any courage I had failed me. My heart rate skyrocketed as tears welled up. With shaking hands I quickly tapped on the screen, ending the conversation.

I took a few deep, gasping breaths, running my hands through my hair making it undoubtedly messier. Yes he was desirable, but a lot of alphas were, and that didn't give them the right to act like brutish assholes towards anyone. I couldn't even think of a time an alpha had spoken to me so angrily, occasionally there were snide comments and insinuated insults, but never outright anger. The guards would toss an alpha out on his ass if he ever spoke to us like that.

Gage was the head of Pack Rowe and he definitely fit the archetype of bossy, angry leader. Just the sheer power of his voice had me shaking like a leaf even though I was safe in my nest.

I knew there were questionable alphas out there; I wasn't naïve. Only a few weeks prior Sage had stayed with me briefly at the Haven after she had escaped from some bad alphas, seeking sanctuary with us until they could reunite her with her own pack. Stowing my laptop away, I took several deep breaths. A hot bath, some fresh pyjamas, and my nest would calm me down.

I couldn't sleep.

My skin itched with restlessness as I tossed and turned. The alpha's face was stuck in my mind, his strong bone structure, slicked back blonde hair cropped in almost a military style. His eyes had been the deepest brown eyes I had ever seen.

Why couldn't I get him out of my mind? It had only been an hour or so since the disastrous call, but this unsettling sensation felt like it wasn't going away anytime soon. He looked so much more imposing on camera then he had in the singular, humorous photo I had seen on their profile.

Even in my brief moment of panic I had noticed the defined muscles in his arms and neck. His neck was muscular, for god's sake. Archer was adorable, and I knew I was highly attracted to him both emotionally and physically. But Gage, with that low gravelly voice. *Fuck.* He had such a presence of power and, frankly, was a grumpy asshole. I was calling it, he was a Leo.

Rolling over once more and giving my pillow a thump, I groaned. Why was I so wired? My skin felt electric. I had been restless before, but this was something entirely different. I had been pointedly ignoring the dampness growing between my legs, but with a sigh, I accepted my fate.

Horny. I was fucking horny for an alpha I had seen for all of twenty seconds and knew the bare minimum about. If any other omega told me they were feeling like this, I would tell them it was fate, or destiny. That sort of stuff was real, I knew it, but I had zero faith in myself to accept it was a possibility for me. Listening to my gut on fate would probably end badly, I would follow a serial killer into a van labelled "free candy" thinking it was my destiny when really I was just craving some delicious sugar.

Rolling over so I was on my back, staring up at the twinkling fairy lights and tapestries I used to decorate my nest, I threw the blankets off my legs and let my hand snake down into my sleep shorts. Heat rose in my cheeks as I felt just how wet I had become.

Omegas were highly sexual and I was no different, used to taking care of myself. I had a whole box of goodies stashed away in the nest for moments like this. Heck, I dove into my box of goodies most days, but the reason why I was diving into that box was making me blush like a schoolgirl.

Deciding my hand wouldn't cut it, I rolled over, reaching to the wall of shelves on the far side of my nest with several boxes dotted on them. It was a knotting sort of night. Knot toys were shit imitations apparently, if the omegas who'd had heats with alphas were to be believed. Thankfully I didn't know any better, so the knot toy was pretty damn fun for me.

Usually I would let my mind wander to a romance book plot, or I would load up some adult entertainment on my tablet. Tonight, though, I found myself thinking of two alphas in particular.

What would it feel like to have two at once? I had imagined

it, all omegas did, but the thought of both Gage and Archer sent my blood pulsing.

Gage was the head of the pack, so he would naturally be more bossy, more demanding—characteristics he'd already demonstrated. Would he just take what he wanted? Gripping my hips tightly as he plunged into me repeatedly? Or would he be the slow, dark and dominating type?

Archer I thought I had a fairly good read on, he was sweet. He was the kind of alpha who would take things slow and steady, but there was something lingering under the surface that made me think that when it came down to it, he would ruin me in the best way. Like I wouldn't be able to walk for days kind of way. What was the term I'd heard? Pleasure dom. Yes, that sounded like Archer.

Grabbing my favourite neon pink toy, I settled back onto the sheets. It was the kind of silicone toy that vibrated and had an adjustable knot. It was one of the best sellers for omegas.

Twisting the end of the toy, the familiar hum of vibrations filled the nest. Thankfully all our nests were soundproof, otherwise we would all be hearing all manner of things from one another.

Knowing I needed a fast release, I bypassed foreplay and gently brushed the toy through my folds. I gave myself a moment to adjust to the sensation before softly sliding the toy deep. The knot wasn't inflated at all yet, so it slid in easily. *Fuck. I really am horny.*

What would Gage's gravelly voice be like, right against my ear as he knotted me? Would he be the kind to praise? I was a sucker for praise, though I refused to admit it. I would take that tidbit of information to the grave with me. It gave people a kind of power over me I didn't like. If my alphas could turn me into a puddle of goo with a few words they probably wouldn't hesitate to do it regularly.

Kicking the toy into high gear I started to picture myself pressed between the two alphas, on my hands and knees, Gage behind me while Archer filled my mouth. A loud moan slipped out of my lips as my legs started to shake.

I came embarrassingly fast. Yes, omegas were pretty much hardwired to come, but not in less than ten seconds.

Throwing the toy to the other side of the nest, I turned over, panting as I snuggled down into the blankets.

Usually when I did *that* my mind stayed purely on fictional characters I had read about, or I made up some faceless mystery alpha to help fulfil my need. I had never thought about actual people, and while a part of me was embarrassed, I reassured myself that I was never going to meet these alphas, so their faces —and other parts—were totally fair game for my fantasies.

Thumping my pillow a few times to make it just right, I burritoed myself in my many, many blankets. I was unconscious just moments later.

CHAPTER THREE
Archer

I was out of the room for just a few minutes. My popcorn had mysteriously moved, and for a moment I thought Theo had absconded with it and so I'd have to throttle him. He always stole the good snacks and sodas. I could have really used a mini fridge in my room or office, but that would mean actually remembering to order the damn thing. Although then I would want to research the best fridge possible and it would end up being a week long distraction. Gage wouldn't like that.

Lavender was waiting, so I hurried. She looked just as stunning as always, even when wearing a set of green pyjamas covered in bunnies. Her hair had been its usual chaotic mess; she'd done a dip-dye job in a moment of frankly adorable impulsiveness, but it had almost grown out so now there was only an inch of purple left. It was still beautiful to me, though. It matched her eyes. Those lilac eyes were mesmerising, and almost as on the nose as her name. A lavender smelling omega called Lavender with lavender eyes? I loved it.

She had already removed her various rings and necklaces. Lavender tended to collect thrift store jewellery and wore multiple items. She had once told me she never wanted something expensive because knowing her, she would break it within a week. She tended to lean toward less of a refined look and more of a chaotic, Bohemian one.

Our first few interactions had been very light-hearted, we discussed food and TV shows, which was how I discovered she was fascinated with true crime and would binge documentaries for fun.

Eventually we got to know each other better and started to discuss more. I told her about my pack—or at least the basics, who we were and the jobs we *used* to do. I avoided telling her about the more criminal turn our lives had taken over the last few years.

After finding the popcorn in a random cupboard I made my way back to the den, goods in hand.

Kane's hulking back was in the doorway to the den. *Shit.* Was he antagonising Lavender? I hadn't exactly been open with my pack about how much I had been talking with her. Why did I decide to call from the den? I should have stuck to my room like I normally did.

Hearing my approach, Kane looked at me, eyebrow raised, turning to let me in.

"Hey guys, what—"

Gage was sitting in my recently vacated spot. My laptop shut in front of him. A furious look on his face. *Double shit.*

"Who the *fuck* were you talking to?" he growled, gesturing to the laptop.

"It was just Lavender—please don't tell me you scared her off. I just went to get popcorn," I groaned.

"Who the fuck is Lavender?" Gage growled.

"She's... uh, the omega I spoke to briefly when I was hacking into the Haven computers a few months ago to look for records of any omegas going missing."

"You're *still* talking to her?" Gage asked in shock. "I knew you'd had a conversation with an omega because you thought she was cute, but we agreed it couldn't continue!"

"Yeah, we're friends. I'm allowed to have friends, aren't I? Don't tell me you scared her off, Gage."

"Don't glare at me Archer, you were meant to be done with anything related to the Haven months ago. Why didn't you tell us?"

"Because you would tell me to stop, and there's no harm in just talking with a friend."

Gage pinched the bridge of his nose. "Why the fuck did you leave a video chat open if you're not in the room?"

"I was just grabbing a snack." I know Gage was just being protective. It's who he was, but fuck me, it felt stifling at times.

"Your little omega just fucking overheard me and Kane discussing how we're going to *purchase* a fucking omega on the black market," Gage snarled.

My face dropped. "Shit, are you sure she overheard?" That would *not* be good, that could ruin *everything* we had been working toward for years. All of our sacrifices would be pointless if we were caught before we managed to find Juniper and bring her home.

"Hopefully not, she could cause a lot of issues by saying just a few words," Kane interjected. "She's a Haven omega, Arch, surrounded by guards who she can run to and tell everything. Can you hack into her computer and make sure she isn't messaging anyone? How much does she know about us?"

"Not much, I used our old jobs when telling her about us." I shrugged. "I can hack in, make sure she didn't overhear anything." I dropped the popcorn onto the table and opened my laptop which Gage had slammed closed, typing away.

"What if she talks to someone in person?" Kane asked coolly. "There's no way to know or trace that."

"We'll have to stop her." Gage frowned, looking at my packmates. "Why the hell did you let this go on for so long, Archer? She can't be allowed to talk to anyone."

"How?" Kane asked again. "How can we make her physically stop?"

How indeed.

"Arch, can you do this?" Gage asked.

"Are you asking if I can, or if I am willing to?" I asked, a bite to my voice.

Gage shrugged. "Both? You clearly seem attached to this omega if you've been talking to her for so long."

My only answer was to throw a disgusted look at Gage and continue typing. It would be easy enough to get access to Lavender's electronics—I had done it many times before. Every time we had a video call, I did it. My pack never would have been allowed into the Haven, let alone registered on their computer system, we weren't a respectable enough pack.

Theo threw himself down on a nearby armchair while I typed. Gage stood over me, arms crossed and Kane lurked somewhere in a corner like he usually did. Mere moments later I was opening the audio feed.

"It's late," I commented. "She may be asleep." We tended to have our conversations late in the evening when she was winding down for the day, usually wearing pyjamas, like today's, ones that looked ridiculously comfortable and with a mug of something warm like tea or hot chocolate. Omegas had a sweet tooth and Lavender was no different.

"Well if she was going to talk to anyone about an illegal

omega sale, it would be tonight. She wouldn't sit on this, especially if the timeline was unknown. Either way, we should listen in for a few hours." Theo leaned forward and grabbed my discarded bag of popcorn off the table, opening it and taking a large handful before shoving it in his mouth.

The speakers crackled as sound started to filter out. No one was talking and there was a low hum emanating from there.

"Is she brushing her teeth or some shit?" Theo asked with a frown.

"Is that feedback?" Gage asked. "I thought you could avoid that."

Before I could open my mouth to give him a snippy reply a low moan filled the room. I stilled, my eyes on the screen. There was no video, but that sound was pretty fucking telling. No one said a word, everyone was too startled by what we had just heard, and our brains were starting to catch up when another small whimper filled the room.

Fuck. It was obvious what she was doing, how many times had I imagined what she sounded like? How many times had I taken things into my own hands in the shower and let my mind run wild?

Theo burst into laughter. "Is she having fun?! Hell yes, I see why you like her, Archer."

"Shut up," I snarled, glaring at the manically grinning Theo who looked like his day had just gotten a whole load better.

"Turn it off," Gage ground out, not even looking at the blank screen, like he was worried he would see something dirty.

With shaking hands I quickly closed the window, and the only sound was Theo still giggling from the armchair.

"I don't think she's talking about us," I finally said, looking over at Gage.

He looked ahead, his elbows resting on his knees. "In that case, back to the plan."

"Which is?"

"Figuring out how to break into a god damned Haven."

CHAPTER FOUR
Lavender

After making myself cum, I slept amazingly for all of an hour until the bitter and angry tone of the alpha invaded my sleep. Unable to settle, I eventually gave up at around six in the morning and crawled out of bed. Checking my phone for the hundredth time, I grimaced. No messages from Archer. Ceasing all communication with me must have been in his best interest. His pack leader clearly disliked me and there was no way in hell I could be in a pack where the pack leader despised me. That would be a terrible position to be in. Archer was probably just being pragmatic. Not that he'd even hinted at us being pack, but a girl could dream.

I threw on some gym shorts and an oversized T-shirt. In a moment of insanity I had agreed to attend a cycling class with Fawn first thing, something I was now heavily regretting after a night of minimal sleep.

As I was up first I waited in the common room, scrolling

through my phone, deleting any family messages. They kept managing to get through no matter how many times I blocked them. I wasn't going to give the time of day to people who believed omegas shouldn't have opinions or have a single individual thought and should instead just bow to their alphas' will. Those messages went straight in the trash.

Scrolling through some gifs and links from friends, I made myself a herbal tea. Fawn was a fairly early riser, so I knew I wouldn't have to wait too long for her to appear. I was halfway through the mug when Fawn bounded out of her room in a pair of leggings and a sports bra, her blonde waves up in a chic, effortless messy bun. If I attempted that hairstyle, I would look like I stuck my finger in an electrical outlet.

"Hello Lav! I thought you wouldn't be up for a while, breakfast?" she asked happily as she practically floated over to me.

"Yes please, I want *all* the pancakes."

Fawn frowned. "What's wrong? Pancakes are your sad food."

I cursed myself internally. Of course she remembered that, she was too damn observant, and I was predictable. "It's nothing too important. I think Archer and I won't be talking anymore."

"Oh no, why?" Fawn asked, sitting next to me on the sofa, her soft rose scent flooding me.

"I don't think his pack leader likes me." I shrugged.

"Well, then he's a total idiot if he doesn't. I'm sorry about Archer though, I know you were getting close to him."

I laughed. "It is what it is, plenty more alphas to choose from, I could be drowning in knots if I actually wanted to."

Fawn snorted. "Isn't that true? I don't know why you

don't get some heat helpers in—aren't you due for another heat soon?"

"A few weeks," I nodded. Unfortunately, I was blessed with particularly brutal heats I couldn't suppress. The first time we had tried my kidneys had several issues—there was something in the suppressants my body didn't like. I was fine with all other medications, but somehow I pulled the short straw and got a suppressant related sickness, leaving me with no choice but to ride out my heats.

"Are you sure you can handle it?" Fawn frowns.

"I'm sure—I've been doing it for years."

Fawn looked thoughtful for a minute, sensing that I didn't want to linger on the topic of my heats. "How about we do our hair after cycling? I kind of want pink hair, the same way you have the purple."

"You want to change your hair?" I asked in shock. "What happened to: *I'll never change my beautiful hair?*"

"I don't know," Fawn sighed. "I just want to do something different. I'm sick of always trying to look perfect."

"You'll still be annoyingly beautiful with pink in your hair, you know that? I won't question it though! I say let's do it!"

A cycle class after a breakfast of pancakes was probably not the best idea. I felt like I was going to explode. Tired and a little grumpy, my legs trembled with exhaustion as I stumbled into the shower. Why did people choose to start their day this way? I wanted nothing more than to crawl back into bed and sleep.

After I had stood in the shower daydreaming for twenty minutes before shaking myself back to reality and actually washing myself, I threw on another pair of leggings and an oversized shirt.

While roughly towel drying my hair my phone buzzed loudly on the counter. My feet made slapping noises on the tiles as I padded over to the counter to check it.

It was an email notification. Notifications from the Haven weren't uncommon, it was how we kept track of appointments, the packs we were talking to, if we had any food requests, and any parcels we had delivered.

Fawn's phone was always buzzing as the mailrooms received copious gifts from her many, many admirers.

Parcel for Lavender Wood awaiting collection in the southeast mailroom. Collect in person now or we'll deliver it on rounds tomorrow.

I frowned at the screen. We often had to go to one of the mailrooms to pick up parcels, or the Keepers would drop them off early during their rounds. Early being like five in the morning so I was never awake for that. Parcels just appeared in the common room for me occasionally and I didn't complain.

It was only midday though, and I didn't recall any recent online purchases so I was rather curious. The only thing it could possibly be was another package of gummy bears, Archer may have sent some before cutting off contact.

Well, even if Archer didn't want to talk with me, I may as well get my gummy bears. Grabbing the first hoodie I could find and some flip flops I decided I could use a short walk. Waiting until morning to satiate my curiosity felt impossible.

Fawn had already left for a pack meeting, looking impeccable in skin tight blue jeans and a blouse tied at the collar in a bow. It baffled me how she managed to pull herself together so fast.

Walking outside, I shivered and pulled my hoodie tighter around myself. It was uncharacteristically cool for an early fall day. For some reason this parcel was in one of the lesser used mailrooms about a twenty minute walk away. I had never actually been there, but I knew where it was, there was no point pestering a Keeper or a guard.

The Haven was almost like a university campus, consisting of several buildings and gardens surrounded by one perimeter wall. Everything within the fences and walls of the Haven was a safe space where we could roam freely with zero worries.

The southeast mailroom was in a corner of the compound not often frequented by the omegas, it was mainly the Keepers and other employees of the Haven. Due to there being less omega footfall here the paint was slightly faded and the grounds weren't as pristine as the rest of the compound, but it was still secure. The large brick and barbed wire walls protected us from outsiders.

There were cameras everywhere, their blinking red lights a comfort, knowing I was being watched over. Pressing the buzzer to the small mailroom, I waited a moment.

"Hello?" A disembodied voice came through the speaker.

"Hi, this is Omega Lavender, I got a notification that one of my parcels was sent here?" There was no answer, I waited a moment, looking around the small building. It was far more cramped and low quality than the typical omega areas which had state of the art everything. The computers were at least a few years old and the grass outside could have used a trim. I was about to turn around and walk back to my dorm when the door opened, revealing a confused-looking guard. He was young, probably only twenty, his features were soft, almost childlike and his red hair was cut close to his scalp in a no-nonsense style.

"Uh, Hello, Miss… Omega. We didn't send you a notification for mail, all omega mail gets sent to the central receiving office," he stammered. He didn't seem like he was too used to talking with the omegas, maybe he was more of a behind the scenes employee?

"How odd, I thought they all got sent there too, but look —" I lifted my phone to show the guard my screen. He read it, his expression only growing more confused. I shrugged with a smile, not wanting to stress him out any further. "It must be a mistake, no worries. I'll head back and check the central mailroom tomorrow, to see if my item is there. Thank you, though!" I doubted this was part of his regular job. I chalked it up to a simple communication error. My parcel would find its way to me eventually, if there even was a parcel in the first place.

The guard straightened his uniform shirt. "Uh, do you want an escort ma'am? It's getting dark. I don't think you're meant to be wandering around without an escort." The guard looked around, nervously shifting from foot to foot. The action made my arm hair stand up. Something didn't quite feel right. *You've been watching too many true crime documentaries, you dingbat!* Why was he so nervous? Was he that new to the job? He smelled like onion, hardly an appealing scent. While yes, we did often have escorts I didn't want to be walked back home by a baby beta guard who smelled like a vegetable. He was sweet enough, but I didn't want his scent on my clothing. Most guards wore scent dampening products so it wasn't so obvious and in our faces.

"Thank you, I'm okay though. I know the way back well, I've been here many years. You can't leave your post," I assured him.

"Very well... ask a guard to radio me once you're back, so I can be sure you returned safely."

I nodded. It could be stifling, not being trusted to walk twenty minutes alone, but I knew it was out of concern for our wellbeing. "We have Donovan as the guard on our floor, I'll get him to radio you once I'm back."

I watched the guard consider and then accept my answer. I didn't mention that when I waved goodbye to Donovan I simply said I was going to collect mail, so he would have assumed I was going to the normal room. With a final smile and a wave, I turned to leave.

I had only taken two steps when I heard a thud behind me, I spun to see the guard crumpled into a heap on the floor where he'd been standing mere moments before.

"Oh! Are you okay?" I asked as I ran over to the guard, kneeling beside him. *Of course he isn't okay, he just hit the ground like a sack of potatoes.* He was deathly pale, eyes closed. Was he sick? Brushing the hair out of the guard's face I noticed just how clammy his skin had become. With one hand I grabbed my phone from my pocket to call for help. My free hand reached out and felt for a pulse, relieved to feel it, slow and weak.

We had brilliant medical facilities at the Haven, so if I could get the other guard's attention he would be in good hands.

His radio! It was on his hip. Leaning down I fumbled around for the radio, yanking it from his belt. I had been so distracted and singularly focused on the guard, I hadn't heard someone moving behind me.

A hand covered my mouth, stopping me from calling out as I thrashed in my assailant's arms. A harsh, chemical smell assaulted my senses, making me gag even with my mouth covered. A sharp sensation stabbed at my neck. Flailing against the unknown man behind me was no use, he was clearly bigger than me and already my head was spinning. Through the thick scent I could barely smell faint hints of leather, like someone had tried to use scent dampener. It only took a few seconds for my arms to slump by my sides, eyes closing, slipping into darkness despite my desperate attempts to stay awake.

CHAPTER FIVE
Lavender

Groaning, I rubbed at my sore eyes. *Why am I so tired? Did I stay up too late? Why did my head feel like lead? Was I coming down with something?* With a huff I cracked my eyes open and took in the unfamiliar surroundings. This bedroom wasn't my nest, far from it. Instead of my bright colourful walls I was faced with pale cream ones with floor-length slate grey curtains and matching bedding. Bedding I didn't recognise, but was snuggled up in. Sitting, I ignored the spinning room and looked around, taking a deep breath. There were no particular scents I could detect in the room, so this likely wasn't someone's bedroom. There was the faint chemical smell that felt oddly familiar. The room was so barren, it didn't look like any room I had ever seen in the Haven. No omega liked to keep a possible nesting area so barren.

The smell was also on my clothes. Grabbing the hem of my oversized T-shirt and bringing it to my nose I noted the very leathery smell.

I filtered through my memories, trying to figure out where I was when the events outside the mailroom came back to me, the poor guard crumpled on the floor and the pain in my neck. Reaching up tentatively I felt my neck, a spot on the side felt sore and bruised. *Was I drugged?*

My mind went into overdrive thinking through all the possibilities. Why was I kidnapped? *Who* kidnapped me? The sickening feeling in my stomach only got worse when I recalled what had happened to Sage, an omega who had been kidnapped a few months back. She had been drugged and locked in a cell, and worse was going to happen to her until her pack saved her.

I didn't have a pack to save me.

My thoughts raced knowing of outcomes I had read regarding kidnap victims. I knew my true crime obsession would come back to bite me in the ass one day. I thought it would simply be because a pack found it weird, not because it made me freak out over possibilities in an actual kidnapping situation!

Clearly I wasn't in the Haven anymore, but where could I be? There was no way I could have been taken from the Haven without a million alarms going off as cameras watched my every move. The guards must know I was gone, and would be coming for me, surely?

I wasn't in a basement or a cellar, and while the room didn't scream serial killer, I had listened to enough podcasts to know they could be unpredictable fuckers.

Pushing the comforter off my legs I stood up, swaying as I did. The carpet was lush under my bare feet. *Where the heck are my shoes? I'm going to want them.* I needed to figure out where I was first, then get back home somehow. I took a step towards the door and my stomach rolled painfully.

Okay, maybe vomit first, then escape. I shot through the open door to the ensuite bathroom, falling to my knees with a thud that I would certainly feel the next day. Swiftly emptying my stomach into the toilet, retching as my eyes watered. The sound of me being sick was so loud I hadn't heard, or smelt, anyone coming up behind me.

"Shit, she's sick." A voice called out, and I felt someone kneeling beside me, gently pulling hair away from my face and rubbing my back. The hand felt large, but I couldn't find the will to care, my body was burning up and my head throbbed violently. "Shh love, you're okay." A deep voice soothed in a low, purring tone I felt in my core. A sweet smell assaulted my senses, like candy, and while it wasn't the most comforting thing in the moment, it was a lot better than the aroma of my own vomit.

Instead of answering the unknown man I kept vomiting, my stomach cramping painfully with the effort. The man's voice cursed softly. "Gage gave her a half dose, she should be fine within a few hours." Another unknown, deeper voice spoke behind me.

"Does she fucking look fine? A full dose is meant to take down big ass alphas." The man rubbing my back growled. He growled like a freaking alpha, not that I was particularly familiar with alpha characteristics, but there was something about him that couldn't be beta, I just knew it. Part of my brain was stuck on that voice, it was kind of familiar, but that was likely the drugs talking. Lifting my head up with a moan I took in the man next to me, familiar floppy dark hair and blue eyes stared back at me, forehead creased in worry. My stomach sank as he looked intently at me.

"Archer?" I spluttered, head swimming with shock. Archer, *my* Archer, the sweet man I had been video chatting with for months was right next to me. He wasn't wearing his glasses and I could see the concern marring his features. The face I had obsessed over for weeks was right there, and the sweetness assaulting my senses was him, *his* scent. Alpha.

"Hey Lavvy girl." He smiled ruefully, looking over my pale face with concern.

"You fucking smell like gummy bears?" I snarled, my vision blurring. The universe was playing a fucking joke on me, it had to be. It was faint, but even in my state I was intensely drawn to it.

Unable to keep my thoughts straight I tried to pull away, I needed to be away from Archer. Moving to slide back from the toilet, my vision clouded with dark patches and I slipped back into an unconscious slumber.

CHAPTER SIX
Archer

Lavender was right in front of me, looking me dead in the eye with a hazy expression. She was pissed, but I guess that was to be expected. She opened her mouth to say something but she swayed, slumping forward.

I cursed, grabbing Lavender so she didn't face plant into the toilet. Her face was pale and sickly, her usually bouncy waves were tangled and sticking to her head from sweat. As bad as the situation was, I couldn't help my excitement that Lavender was in the same room as me, the sweet little omega I had been talking to for months was here.

She hadn't been joking when she told me she smelled like lavender. The soothing scent was like a balm for my soul, sweet and with a hint of vanilla, calming me to my core and pacifying my raging emotions. Gage hadn't allowed me to go to the Haven with them, he had been worried that my emotions would cloud the situation and I might have acted irrationally if I smelled her distress. He was right of course, the sound of an omega in distress was difficult for any alpha to ignore, and when stressed their scent often took on an acidic or burnt tinge: yet if it was an omega they knew and cared for, like I was starting to care for Lavender, then their sounds of distress could be downright painful.

I had been waiting in the hallway when they had arrived home, I couldn't just sit around. Kane had been carrying her, a tight look on his face. The sight of the familiar face I had looked at so many times in our video calls, unconscious and thrown over Kane's shoulder stung in a way I didn't expect. My rolling gut made it clear that I wasn't okay with this situation in the slightest. Kane had deep, angry scratches along his arms. They were clearly from Lavender and I couldn't help the feeling of pride swelling in my chest

***.

Lavender didn't look good at all, she was shivering and her face was tinged green. "Gage, should we call the Doc? This doesn't seem right." We knew a doctor that could keep his mouth shut for the right price, and if she needed it we would pay.

"Give her a few hours, make sure she drinks and rests. If she's not better tomorrow we'll call the doc and make sure she's okay. Just give it time for the drugs to leave her system first."

"That shit is meant to take down alphas, what are you doing giving it to an omega?" I asked with a growl, Lavender was still slumped across my lap as I knelt on the bathroom floor.

"What would you have had me do, Archer? I couldn't exactly use the stuff we recovered last month. Fenton was using that to drug the omegas he sold and they all had serious complications like organ failure! At least with this stuff we know what it is and we know it's not been mixed with rat poison or something." Gage's eyes didn't leave Lavender's prone form. "I wanted to hurt her as little as possible. If I had time I would have found something better."

That I believed. Gage was a good man, it's why we all followed him. He had a hardass attitude but I firmly believed that for the right omega he would be a softie.

"I just need to remind myself that this shit is temporary," I said.

"She'll be home before the weekend," Gage agreed.

"I'll put her back to bed." I slid my arms under the limp omega, lifting her with ease. Despite the strong scent of sickness that clung to her I could still make out the floral notes of her true omega scent. Beautiful and comforting. Her parents clearly had a sense of humour calling their child with a lavender floral scent, Lavender. As a baby her scent would have been muted, but amplified when she presented as an omega. She felt so small in my arms, I had to tamper down my protective instincts.

Lavender wasn't mine and she never would be, no matter how much I wanted it.

I had only met Lavender because I was following Gage's orders. He asked me to hack into the Haven databases, no small feat, and see if they kept any information on potentially kidnapped omegas. Sage Rivers had recently gone through the same Haven after a kidnapping ordeal, and we wanted to see if there were any potential leads to who kidnapped Juniper several years ago.

Lavender's profile had just been there, and I had decided to message her out of sheer curiosity. She had captured my attention pretty much immediately and I was hooked. She was beautiful, but that was normal for omegas, yet there was something so damn captivating about her smile. It felt like stopping was an impossibility, and I enjoyed my time with her so much, I found myself hiding our chats from my pack.

Unofficially, my pack was spoken for in Kane's eyes. Despite him not being *officially* part of the pack, I saw him as family, we all did but he believed so fiercely that his sister was meant to be part of our pack, that he had always resisted officially joining, choosing instead to live on the sidelines in limbo. It was a shame he couldn't see we didn't feel that way about Juniper, things could be so different.

Carrying Lavender back to the room Kane had put her in originally, I grimaced at how bare it was. This safehouse was only temporary, but still the barren open space would probably make Lavender feel even more uneasy.

The king bed dwarfed her as I laid her in the centre and pulled the comforter over her. She rolled over and nestled into the blankets instinctively. She was still wearing her jewellery, multiple bracelets and rings on each hand, a lot of it handmade with beads and feathers. She didn't sleep with them normally, I had watched her take them off many times during our late night video calls, so I gently pulled off each ring, placing them on the bedside table so she would be comfortable.

"This has to work." Gage frowned as he looked down at her. "We'll finish this job and return her back to the Haven. We can keep our distance from her, the scent blocker Kane gave her is clearly doing its job. I can smell her but it's hardly noticeable unless I really focus thanks to the chemical stink and the sickness. The issue is it won't last and then she's going to smell potent."

"We need to ensure she stays healthy while she's here," I pointed out. Kane had given Lavender a drug to knock her out but it also muted strong and potent alpha scents so it was working on Lavender despite her being an omega. We all took scent dulling drugs as well; covert work would be really hard if our scents were strong and easily distinguishable. "Juniper would never forgive us if we hurt an omega...any more than we already have."

"What else do pretty little omegas need?" Theo asked, walking into the room, a bottle of water in hand which he placed on her bedside table. "I heard the sight of your face made the omega pass out. I know you're ugly, but that's gotta sting." He laughed at me. His lanky blonde hair fell to his chin, and I could see the tip of a scar protruding from his hairline, its very presence a reminder of how much the last few years had cost us. Theo had been injured more than the rest of us on our little crusade. We chose this, but Lavender didn't. I had to keep her safe. "Kane's been reheating some leftovers if you want to grab some for her."

"Thanks. None of us have really spent time with an adult omega, so we need to figure out what she needs." We had lost our pseudo-sister Juniper when she was still a teenager, so our knowledge was limited. Did omega needs change once they reached adulthood? Or were they the same as teenagers, only hornier?

"We'll ask her what she needs when she's awake," Gage said, his eyes still stuck on Lavender's sleeping form.

"She really is quite pretty, isn't she?" Theo mused as he looked down at Lavender, sitting gently at the end of the bed as she curled up into a ball, clutching the blankets to her chest.

"She's stunning when she smiles. Or when she's chewing me out over my candy choices."

"Candy choices?"

"She thinks that gummy bears are superior to chocolate," I laughed, then sighed looking over Lavender. "One of us should stay with her. She's going to be disoriented when she wakes up."

"I will," Theo said. "No offence, but your face made her pass out. Maybe with a stranger she won't feel so betrayed. Plus, I'm the most handsome of us, it's only fair."

"I didn't betray her," I growled.

"You weren't exactly truthful with her either, were you Archie?" Theo raised his eyebrows in a clear *you know I'm right, dumbass* expression.

I deflated. "No, I wasn't."

"Go check all the security. I'll shout if she wants you," Gage reassured me.

I thanked him and got up slowly, taking one last look at Lavender before leaving, wanting nothing more than to stay. Lavender was mine. Well, she was certainly more mine than any of my packmates.

I watched as Theo grabbed an extra blanket and threw it over her so only her closed eyes could be seen peeking over the top before he flopped down into an armchair in the corner of the room, eyes on the omega as her chest slowly rose and fell. I couldn't deny my instincts as an alpha, I was hardwired to care for and protect omegas, sure I could go against that instinct and many did, but it just felt wrong. Omegas were more maternal and caring by nature. Whereas alphas were designed to protect their omegas to help foster the strongest packs. I couldn't lie to myself, I wanted Lavender, but she deserved so much better than my pack.

For the better part of three years my pack had been a mess, torn apart by the loss of an omega who wasn't even officially ours. We were now tainted, dirty. We had committed crimes and even killed.

We were a disaster no omega should be forced to endure.

CHAPTER SEVEN
Lavender

The next time I woke my head was still pounding and I felt like I had a mouth full of cotton balls, but thankfully I could think a little clearer. My whole body ached, and I was covered in a thin layer of sweat and grime. My stomach was only slightly nauseated, which was an improvement, there was no need for a mad dash to the bathroom. Sitting up I pushed the comforter off and looked around, my eyes landing on the alpha sitting on an armchair next to the bed, phone in hand, lazily browsing on his phone.

"Morning!" he said, his eyes wide and his grin almost manic. "You must be hungry—tacos? Kane makes a mean taco, well reheats a mean taco should I say. I think you scared the shit out of Archer passing out on him like that." He smirked, slipping his phone back into his pocket.

I looked at this strange male like he had suddenly sprouted another head. He was handsome enough and clearly an alpha.

Long blond hair just reached the top of his shoulders and his face had a boyish quality.

"You're Theo, aren't you? The vet?" I asked with a frown. He was larger than me, but not as large as the other alphas I had seen the first time I awoke. He wore casual clothes, black sweatpants and black T-shirt. His shoulder length blonde hair was thrown back into a messy bun with a few strands hanging loose.

"That's right! Looks like our dear Archie told you about us."

Running a hand through my hair I grimaced.

"Why am I here?" I asked in a small voice, hugging my knees to my chest. I wasn't daft, I knew it would be difficult to escape if this house was full of alphas. Still I needed to learn as much as I could about where I was, and who I was with, without making it obvious that I was panicking. "Is this all because of Archer?"

I did my best to keep my voice even but I wanted to scream, shake, and cry all at once. The feeling of being displaced gnawed at me and I wanted nothing more than to crawl into the warm comfort of my own nest.

Theo simply smiled, scratching his chin. "Yeah, I won't lie, it kind of is. Gage will talk to you about that soon though—this is just a temporary situation. You'll be home in no time if all goes to plan and you can go back to your legions of adoring packs vying for your attention."

Looking at him, I took my time to answer, trying to grasp what he had said. This situation was temporary? How? "You broke into a Haven which should be impossible. Why would you do that just to release me a day or two later? I mean I'm not complaining, but this place isn't exactly homey."

"You're surprisingly calm, aren't you?" Theo appraised me.

"Far from it, but it's better to find out facts before I freak out entirely." I shrugged. I had been sneakily eying a large metallic lamp on the bedside table, waiting for the right moment. From the smell of it, there were no other alphas nearby, though their residual scents permeated the room, blending in a delicious way that had me resisting the urge to drool foolishly. There was a chemical tinge to the smell as well; scent blockers. Clearly they were doing a terrible job because I could discern everyone's scent, from Archer's sweet sugary scent to the lemony pine smell of the alpha sitting next to my bed.

Were I not in such a dire situation I would have been revelling in these scents. I had never gotten to the point in a courtship where scent cards were exchanged, so the smell of alphas were foreign to me. The chemicals did ruin the experience somewhat, though.

Theo chuffed in laughter. "Smart girl. Are you hungry?" He repeated his earlier question I had ignored. "I can go grab you some food—are you feeling better?"

"Yeah, just a little fuzzy."

"We gave you a half dose of a drug that would knock out an alpha so you're probably going to be feeling it for a while. Take it easy, grab a shower, eat. We'll leave you to recover for now." He jumped up and bounded out of the room, his footfalls heavy on the carpet. The second the door closed after him I heard the telltale click of the lock.

These alphas were giving me whiplash. They were talking to me so nicely, yet they had kidnapped me. Archer so gently held my hair out of my face, yet they drugged me. Looking down at my hands I saw that my rings had been removed and placed in a tiny dish on the bedside table.

None of this made sense.

Jumping out of the bed, I ignored my vision spinning and ran to the window, the next obvious choice, and it was naturally locked—but it was worth a check. They could have dropped the ball and left it unlatched. Taking stock of the room I noted how plain and empty it was.

There was nothing I could really use as a weapon, other than the lamp. Walking over to it, I picked it up experimentally, pulling the cord from the wall. Shifting it from hand to hand, I noted it was impressively weighty for a bedside lamp, and it was clearly my best option unless you counted a pillow which I doubted would serve me well. Wrapping the cable up in my hand I went over to the door, putting my ear against it to listen for any signs of movement. Theo said he was getting me food, so he would be back soon. Positioning myself on the non-hinge side of the door I plastered myself to the side of the wall and waited, dragging a bedside table over for me to stand on and gain some much-needed height.

It didn't take long for Theo to return. I could have heard him from a mile away as he whistled. He definitely wasn't the reserved or subtle pack member, that was for sure.

"I got tacos! Now shall—" he declared, opening the door, only to be cut off as I brought the lamp down with all the force I could muster on the back of his skull. Theo, clearly shocked, let out a grunt of pain, falling to his knees with a thud. The plate of delicious smelling Mexican food shattering on the ground as he did.

I didn't wait to see if he got up, hopping down, I took off down the hallway, silently praying I didn't encounter any other pack members. Their scents were stronger as I ran past what I assumed to be a common area. All the smells mingled together made my brain short circuit, so I did my best to run down corridors where their scent wasn't as potent. I needed to find an exit, maybe a back door? The house was large, and looked like a show home instead of a pack house. Running through a doorway to my left I stilled as I took in the room before me. The two other alphas were sitting on sofas, deep in conversation. Their heads swivelled in my direction the moment I appeared. The giant one with the buzzcut glared at me while the blond one immediately jumped up.

Shit. This was not what I needed. I turned on my heel and fled in the opposite direction, ignoring the sounds of them chasing after me. I needed to find a way out and fast. They were massive compared to me, and their stupid genetics meant they could easily outrun me if need be, plus it didn't help that they had the advantage of knowing the layout. I was prey running from a predator, and I could smell the panic and perfume coming off me. *Calming lavender perfume won't do shit right now. Even a giant amethyst up their asses wouldn't calm these alphas down.*

The hallways all looked the same, bland, devoid of artwork or anything that could help me figure out where to go. Up ahead I could just make out a doorway, and hope filled my chest. I was going to get the hell out of here! As my hand extended to reach for the door handle, I felt a solid arm snake around my midsection, lifting me clean off my feet.

"No!" I exclaimed, scratching at the arm, trying to pry it loose, but it was solid with thick bulging muscles and the smell of dark leather. It was the buzzcut alpha, Kane.

"*Fuck me*, calm down wildcat," he growled while I was hauled backward, towards the room I had just run from. My only reply was to claw harder, even trying to bite the arm holding me back. "You don't wanna be biting me," he chuckled. *Chuckled.* I couldn't believe this asshole was finding the situation funny! The deep, leathery smell assaulted my senses and every part of me wanted to roll over and show this man my stomach, to beg for rubs. I had to fight every one of my instincts to keep on scratching and fighting whilst my inner omega wanted to go floppy, submit, be good for the big alpha. For some reason my instincts were telling me these alphas were safe, which considering they had kidnapped me was complete bullshit.

Stupid omega hormones.

"Let go of me goddamnit!" I snarled, raking my nails across his skin, doing my best to inflict some damage to his stupidly hard muscles.

"No!" he growled, his steps never faltering despite my attempts at self-defence.

Gage was standing in the hallway, watching us with a pissed look on his face. "How the hell did she get out of her room?" he asked the brute holding me as he hauled me into the common area they had just been sitting in.

"She hit me with a lamp!" An excited voice exclaimed from the direction I had just fled. "I knew she was special, Gagey! Can we keep her?" Theo was cradling the back of his head, a look on his face that I could only describe as love-struck.

This was too much. My head was swimming and I felt nauseated again. I slumped, no longer fighting the arm around me. I was stuck, at least for the time being. Three alphas versus one omega? I didn't like those odds.

Their combined scents were cloying at me, dark, leathery, pine and sweet at times. there was a chemical tinge to the smell as well; scent blockers. Something in me was so drawn to them. Everything about them screamed safety to my instincts, though my logical mind screamed that I was an idiot who needed to escape or I would be chopped into itty bitty bits.

"She's shaking? Why is she shaking Kane?" Theo whined.

He was unhappy that I was distressed? I had just clocked him with a lamp. Had I entered topsy-turvy land? Forget being in retrograde, mercury had full on left the building in a fiery ball of doom.

"Come on, let's sit down in the den. Theo, I need to check that head wound. Kane, keep an eye on her." Gage looked me over. "If Kane lets you down, are you going to behave or try and run again?"

"No promises," I growled, even though my little omega growl was pathetic compared to theirs and the corner of his mouth lifted. I must have looked deranged, but I was beyond caring at this point.

Gage's grumpy, sarcastic Leo ass could get bent for all I cared.

"Okay, princess, you need to behave, I don't want to make you," he told me pointedly. I glowered at the nickname, but I wasn't exactly in a position to complain.

"Let me go," I hissed. We were just standing in the middle of the room, me held aloft by the brute. Gage nodded, looking over my head so I assumed some sort of silent communication was happening there. Kane dumped me unceremoniously on a sofa and I scrambled to sit up.

Leaving me with the grumpy barbarian standing over me Gage walked over to the fridge grabbing an ice pack and gesturing for Theo to sit down so he could check his head. Theo didn't question him, plopping down on the sofa and looking up at his pack leader adoringly as he looked him over for any injuries.

"Well, you'll live, but it'll hurt like a bitch for a few days. There's a cut on the back of your head, it's not deep, but it'll sting. There's also a pretty impressive bump."

"I don't mind. I'll wear my wounds with pride, Gagey.

She's got fire." He smirked at me, and I shrank away. His eyes crinkled when he looked at me.

What on earth was happening? Did they drag me into this room so they could show off Theo's injury? Kane was still standing over me keeping a very close eye on me. My skin prickled under all the attention.

After another moment of silence, I couldn't contain myself. "Can someone tell me what the knotting hell is going on?"

Gage took a moment before looking away from Theo's head to me. "I suppose you need a few answers, maybe then you'll stop trying to murder my pack." Gage sighed, walking over and sitting opposite to me. "You're gonna stay here for a day or two, that's it, and then we'll return you home."

"Why?" I asked, looking him dead in the eye. He was handsome, even I could admit that. That jawline was just as sharp in person as it had been on my tablet screen, and a part of me still wanted to bite it. Their entire psychotic pack were handsome, but serial killers could be handsome, I mean just look at Ted Bundy.

"What you heard the other night was confidential—we can't risk you telling anyone."

My brow furrowed. "Overheard?" Did he mean the mumbling on the video call before he decided to be a dick to me? I ran a hand through my hair, deep in thought. "You mean when I was on a video call with Arch? Is that why you kidnapped me?!" I asked, eyes wide. Of all the daft reasons to kidnap an omega…"What you heard was…delicate in nature and you don't know the full story. Now, it's not your fault. Archer is to blame for that, but at least for now, we need to make sure you don't tell anyone what you overheard."

Only I hadn't heard anything. I debated whether I should

tell him that. Did knowing this mystery information give me power, or put me in more danger?

"Okay…" I trailed off, not wanting to give them any more information.

"You're going to stay here, just temporarily. We will stay out of your way and give you whatever you need to remain comfortable. In a day or two when we finish our job, we'll let you go back home, and all this will be forgotten."

"Just like that?" I asked cautiously. "I know your names, I've seen enough true crime to know it doesn't usually go that way if the kidnapped party knows too many details. Usually, they end up chopped into itty bitty bits at the bottom of the river, or clogging up a drainpipe."

Gage let out a bark of laughter with an expression of sheer disbelief. "Archer said you were a macabre one."

I lifted my chin as I replied, "I like to think I'm realistic."

"Worst case scenario kind of girl, eh?" Gage asked with a humourless laugh. "Look, we can be realistic, you know a lot about us, and could easily report us. We aren't going to hurt you though and we are only doing the things we are doing to save someone we love. I'm sure you can appreciate that." He didn't look away from me as he spoke. "You know none of the finer details of our operation and Archer is so damn good at hiding our tracks that even if you did report us, it would be highly unlikely that any authorities would actually find us."

I broke the intense eye contact to stare at my feet, taking a second to gather my thoughts, which was impossible to do while having an extreme staring contest with an exceptionally hot alpha.

"Why should I believe you? I had a friend kidnapped by a rogue pack recently, and it wasn't pretty."

"This isn't what we wanted at all. Listen to your instincts. Do you really think we want to hurt you?"

I looked over at Kane, who still stood over me, glaring. Arms crossed, making his muscles bulge under his too small T-shirt. Between the sheer muscle mass and the buzz cut he radiated a dangerous energy. "Him, maybe," I admitted.

"You just knocked our packmate out with a lamp," Kane growled.

"You would do the same in my situation." I shrugged at the grumpy giant.

"Oh, I'm not complaining," Theo interjected. "I like her fire. Though Kane would never resort to something so normal as a lamp. He'd be all fists."

Gage ignored Theo's words and answered me, "Regardless, you're not going anywhere right now and you need to rest. We gave you some pretty strong drugs and you can't be feeling all that good."

He was right, I was feeling lousy, but didn't want to admit that. Everything felt overwhelming and I just wanted to be curled up in my nest, ignoring the rest of the world, only my nest was nowhere in sight, all I had was that sterile, cold bed.

"Yeah, I still feel a touch dizzy," I admitted, cursing myself for letting that slip. Why did I just tell them I was feeling weak? Stupid, moron move.

Gage stood up and strode over to a mini fridge on the far side of the room, grabbing two bottles of water and a protein bar. "You need to eat," he told me gruffly.

"I did try to bring her food, but thanks to her stunning moves, it's all over the bedroom floor," Theo whined.

"I'll get Archer to pick it up," Gage said.

"Where is Archer?" I asked with a frown. It hadn't even

occurred to me that he wasn't in the room, I had been far too distracted by the adrenaline rush that was my escape attempt.

"He's around," Gage offered simply. Archer had dragged me into this, and I wanted to avoid him at all costs, but a small part of me was keen to see him again. "Working on some computer things. I thought it best he stayed away for a while, knowing you were likely mad at him."

"I am," I agreed. I was fuming, he had gotten me into this situation. If he had never looked at my profile I would still be safe at home, going to exercise classes with Fawn.

Gage nodded. "You'll see him because this house is only so big, but we'll try and keep our distance. We are all on scent dulling meds, and we gave you some but still..."

"Yeah, they don't really seem to be working well, I can smell all of you."

Gage did a double take. "Wait, you can smell us?"

Theo's giddy laugh almost drowned his voice out.

"Yeah, it's weak, but I can easily distinguish you. You smell like whisky, kinda smoky. Kane is leathery, Theo is pine and lemon and Archer smells like fucking gummy bears."

Gage looked shocked, his eyes widening further as I listed each of their scents.

"Well...uh." He scrambled to gather his thoughts. Could he smell me? I picked up the bottle of water and cracked it open, taking a few slow sips. "Okay, we'll keep out of your way, and hopefully the scents shouldn't be too much. Kane? Can you escort her back?"

Kane just nodded in lieu of an answer.

Kane followed behind me as I made my way back to the jail cell of a room. It wasn't difficult to recognise the path I had run down. Kane was carrying my half drunk bottle of water and protein bars so I just hugged myself with one arm and chewed my fingernail in stress.

Fawn would slap my hand if she caught me chewing my nails, but I was on my own and besides, I think in this situation she'd forgive me.

As we reached my doorway I noticed all the spilled food was already picked up. Taking a step into my room I turned back to Kane.

"Tell your packmate, Theo, that I'm sorry I clocked him with the lamp." I looked up at him with a frown. "I didn't really hurt him did I?" I grimaced. As mad as I was at these men, I didn't want to hurt anyone. I liked watching shows about serial killers chopping people into itty bitty bits, but I cringed at the thought of killing a bug.

"Why are you apologising?" Kane questioned with a raised brow as he placed the snacks on my bedside table.

"Karma is real, and that little stunt probably earned me some negative juju."

"He's got a thick skull, he'll be fine," Kane grumbled. "And don't feel bad for protecting yourself. It's impressive you got the drop on him."

"Thank you." I smiled gently at him. He didn't reply. He didn't seem like one for conversation and he was clearly done with this one.

The remnants of the lamp had been cleared away; all evidence gone. Kane merely walked me to my door, closing and locking it behind me once again. With a sigh, I sat on the bed next to a pile of clean clothing, men's T-shirts and leggings. There was only the faint smell of laundry detergent on them, no alpha scents, though I couldn't decide if that was a blessing or a curse. Despite my urge to get away from these alphas, some deep buried part of me wanted to roll around in their scents, curling into them and resting my head in the crook of their necks, drinking in the delicious smells—part of me was getting wet just thinking about it.

If I didn't know better I would think I was already entering preheat, but luckily I had at least three weeks to go. I was like clockwork with my heats.

Grabbing the clothes I decided to grab a shower, the adjoining bathroom had a lock, so I felt comfortable stripping my clothes off and getting under the boiling hot spray. Staring at the tile wall I took a moment to let the last few hours sink in. I had been kidnapped from my home by four strangers. Alpha strangers who smelt so damn good, but also exuded an air of danger I couldn't miss.

As the reality of the unknown, of my situation, sank in I started to tremble, and in the safety and solitude of the shower I finally let a single tear fall. Then another until I was sobbing, one hand clutched over my mouth in an attempt to reduce any noise I made, praying the sound of the shower would drown it out.

When would I get to go home, to my nest? To Fawn and my friends? I was a lone omega here and while I wanted to trust the alphas—I didn't know them. In fact I thought I had known one of them, Archer, but the realisation that I had been taken for a schmuck and knew nothing about him only made me sob harder. The alpha I had spent many nights talking to was pure fiction.

I could only act so brave for so long.

CHAPTER EIGHT
Archer

I knew I wouldn't like hearing her cry, what I didn't realise was that it would hurt like my heart was getting ripped out of my chest. My bathroom and Lavender's shared a wall, so I sat on the cold tiled floor and listened to the deep wracking sobs on the other side.

It was me who caused this and I hated myself for it.

When we had started speaking it had been a dangerous slope, but I just couldn't find it in me to pull away. Something about her had just enthralled me. She kept making TV show suggestions and insisted on reading me my horoscope several times—she had guessed I was a virgo. Then there was the way her nose scrunched when she spoke about maths, or the little dance of happiness she did when she tried a new snack she liked. Lavender just radiated a warmth I couldn't resist . In a short period of time Lavender had become the highlight of my week, and I was too weak to give that up.

I should have let her forget me and move on with her life.

Despite her insecurities, I knew there were plenty of packs interested in her, she would have moved on eventually. Risking everything, I had thought with the non-logical part of my brain when I logged on week after week. I was good at covering my tracks, but fucking around in the computer systems of one of the largest government organisations in the country for any longer than necessary was just asking for trouble, but I did it anyway so I could keep talking to Lavender.

Gage didn't bother to knock. He took one long look at me sitting with my back against the tiled wall and strode in, sitting on the edge of the fancy free-standing bath tub.

"She has quite the swing," he admitted with a rueful smile. "That shit actually hurt Theo's thick skull." He looked at me, and in the silence, picked up on the noise. "Is that? Shit. Is she crying?!" he asked, looking at the adjoining wall, face aghast.

"Yep," I confirmed. "I'm feeling like the biggest ass ever."

Gage took a deep breath before moving to sit next to me. "You didn't know talking to her would lead to this. It was a dumb idea, but you had no way of knowing."

While he was my pack leader, Gage was also my closest friend since childhood. There had been a time when we would tell each other everything, but as the stress and responsibility of our life choices weighed us down, the chasm between us seemed to only grow larger.

"Surely this situation doesn't sit right with you? Gage, we've spent the last three years saving omegas, and now we've got one we kidnapped locked in a spare room! This... it just feels wrong in every sense of the word."

"Of course, it doesn't, Arch. But she's safe here, by keeping her out of the way and unable to talk to anyone we're one step closer to finding Juniper. You know you mean her no harm and I won't hurt her either. Kane would rather cut off a limb than let any pain or suffering come to that omega. And I think Theo is head over heels for her... She'll be fine."

I snorted. "That concussion was pretty much foreplay to Theo."

"He's changed so much. Sometimes I swear he's the exact same kid who stole my shoes in fifth grade, and other times..."

"He's improving." A year ago we had been chasing down a lead, things had gone wrong and sadly Theo had been injured. He had been drowned almost to the point of brain damage. Ever since he had moments where he was just not himself. Before he had been the most caring soul I had ever met. He went to school to heal puppies! Then after his accident it was like a switch flipped and a darker side of him slipped through on occasion.

"He is. I can't lose him, or any of you for that matter."

"You won't," I said, looking at the wall behind us, still able to make out faint sobs. "We put her in the wrong room. You should have put her in the smaller room."

"Why?"

"She hasn't got a nest, somewhere she can hunker down. Omegas tend to like smaller spaces—I've seen Lav's nest. It's all fairy lights and hippy tapestries, with enough pillows to open a goddamn bedding shop."

"And here she's got one comforter and two mediocre pillows."

"Yeah, if she wasn't going to be going home soon I would say we need to get her more. As it is I doubt she'll be comfortable for the next day or two, but there's not much more we can do."

"Do you think she believes we're going to let her go?" Gage asked. "Or do you think she's scared something far worse is going to happen?"

"Maybe. She's so fucking smart, Gage. Sharp as a tack. I just wish I could have met her in a different way."

"She sounds pretty great, everything you've said about her seems nice. She sounds a lot like Juniper, or at least how I imagine Juniper would be today."

I snorted. "In some ways, but in other ways they're chalk and cheese. Lavender loves stuff like zodiac signs, even though she hardly believes it. She started studying astrology after she got away from her crackpot parents, mainly as a form of rebellion. Also Lavender can talk for hours on how to dispose of a body because she's watched so many true crime documentaries."

Juniper had been so gentle, even someone getting slightly injured on a TV show would stress her out. Documentaries like Lavender's would only freak her out and give her nightmares for weeks.

Gage ran a hand through his hair. "She fought like hell though, I didn't expect that."

"She took some self-defence classes even though omegas aren't encouraged to take them. Plus she watches so much horrific true crime I'm sure she's picked up a few self-preservation tips and tricks from that."

"If she were my omega I would be damn proud of her for that trick with the lamp," Gage chuckled, then his face dropped, "Not that we'll ever have an omega..."

"One day, maybe." I replied. Kane would go mental at the idea of us finding an omega. I had never felt romantic feelings for Juniper, she was like a little sister to me, but Kane had been so convinced that we were the pack for her it was why he was resisting joining us so badly.

The look Gage gave me spoke louder than any words.

He believed it would never happen.

CHAPTER NINE
Theo

I was insane.

That was the only reasonable conclusion that could be drawn from the fact I was taking more food to the little omega right after she had bashed my head in. What's more, I was *excited* to see the little spitfire again. Gage told me to be careful not to spook her. Spook her? Who was he fucking kidding? The beauty had whacked me good and proper with that lamp, and I had zero doubts she could do it again.

I had never been so hard in my life. She could be rough with me any time she wanted.

"Come in," her soft voice answered my knock.

She was sitting in the middle of the neatly made bed with her legs crossed and her arms hugging her middle, like she wanted to shrink in on herself. Dark circles rimmed her eyes, and her gaze was vacant.

"I'm not armed, Kane took the other lamp away," she assured me. Her hair was ever so slightly damp and she was wearing fresh clothes, including a *man's* shirt. The only mens clothing around here were ours. Doing my best to look subtly, I recognised the logo on the chest. It was Kane's. It wouldn't have smelled like him as it was clean but the sight of her wearing it, on a bed and smelling fucking delicious was almost too much for me.

She took the plate cautiously, and looked me over before tentatively taking a bite. She was small. Were all omegas so small? It had been so many years since I had seen one, other than the two or three bruised and beaten ones we had recovered from various shitty situations, and that was only from a distance.

"What day is it?" Lavender asked, her voice quiet and subdued. I didn't like it, where was the firecracker that had whacked me with a lamp and made me hard as steel?

"Friday, you were out for about twenty hours this time, your body really needs the rest." We had taken her almost three days ago, and her absence was surely being noticed by now.

A small moan escaped her mouth as she took another bite, and I shifted from foot to foot, trying to make my erection die down before she noticed it. Had omega sounds ever affected me *that* much?

Clearing her mouth she spoke, "Thank you, for this. I don't know when I last ate."

"Archer said you lived on a diet of gummy bears and chocolate, so I'm glad you at least ate something proper."

She frowned. "I never want another goddamned gummy bear again. He's ruined that treat for me for life."

"Ah, yeah, we teased him a lot growing up for smelling like candy. Archer's loss, I say. You're a smart spitfire. I like you, you're the most interesting person I've spoken to in days. If Gage would let me, I'd keep you."

"Keep me?" Her brow furrowed.

"Like a pet, but not a pet?" Then again, keeping her as a kinky pet could always be fun. Gage would never allow it though, spoil sport.

"I think your logic is slightly flawed," she said, never taking her eyes off of me, like she was being cautious. She didn't think I would actually hurt her? Did she? I wanted her to hurt *me*, and make me cum harder than I ever had.

"Yeah—" I nodded, "—it is, which is why daddy Gage would never let it happen, even though we could have so much fun! We could have all sorts of adventures," I finished in a whining tone.

I expected her to be nervous, I knew I wasn't being the most logical, so when she burst into laughter a warm feeling spread throughout my gut.

"Okay Donald," she laughed.

"Donald?" My name definitely wasn't Donald. Did she hit her own head with a lamp?

She tilted her head to the side. "Donald DeFreeze. He led the group that kidnapped Patty Hurst and brainwashed her."

"Sounds like my kinda guy, should I start calling you Patty?" I asked with a grin.

"DeFreeze died at thirty in a firefight with the police."

"Oh no, that won't do. I plan to be old and wrinkly before I die in a big fancy explosion." I put my hand on my chin in an exaggerated gesture of being deep in thought. "I'll have to watch some more stuff and figure out a better comparison!"

"Archer mentioned you and Gage both like documentaries," she said. She was still sitting cross legged, but she was no longer hugging herself. She was slightly more at ease and that pleased me.

"What else did he tell you about the pack?" Did she like

what she had heard about us? I wanted her approval. I knew I didn't need it, but something in my hindbrain was insisting she needed to like us. Kinda hard to do when we kidnapped her, but fuck it, I liked a challenge.

"Not much, names, that you were a vet, he worked with computers and that Gage was training to take over his fathers business and Kane worked in security, though I'm starting to doubt that now. Though he never told me what business Gage's father was in," I admitted.

"His folks own a butcher's shop, it's been in his family for years. My pack are good people, we are just a little rough around the edges. Soon they'll be in the rear-view mirror and you won't have to think of them again. Or any of us again, tragic as that may be." I pouted, and even though my tone was playful I did feel a pang at the idea of her leaving, which was laughable because why would she want to be near us?

"You're being so nice. Why? I clubbed you with a lamp!" Her tone was exasperated.

"To be fair, I would have done the same in your position—you're a resourceful little thing. I can't blame you for trying to escape, and it was the sexiest thing I've seen in years. The boner I got, *ugh*." I smirked at her, thrilled at the slight blush that rose in her cheeks at the mention of my cock. "Seriously, you can do *anything* you want to me, I'm down!" I laughed before letting my face drop and becoming serious. "I *will* stop you from leaving until Gage clears you to go though, because I refuse to let you go when you know information that could be dangerous to my pack if it got out. They're my family. None of us have it in us to hurt an omega."

Clearly this alpha would have done anything to protect his family, I understood his threat, yet I wasn't sure whether I should be turned on by that or looking for another lamp.

"Yeah, they always tell us at the Havens that alphas are hard-wired to protect the omegas. That we should never fear them."

"That seems a bit idealistic."

"It is—just a few weeks ago my friend, Sage, went through hell at the hands of some rogue alphas. Just because the Havens only let reputable packs through their doors doesn't mean there aren't bad ones out there."

"We've learned the hard way that there are bad folks out there. We lost someone close to us, and it's never been the same since."

"I'm so sorry, it's horrible to lose anyone, let alone a loved one."

"Is it," I agreed with a sigh, taking the now empty plate off Lavender. My hand brushed against hers for a moment, and my hindbrain went into overdrive from the simple touch. *Grab. Claim. Keep her.*

Images flooded my brain of her on top of me, choking my cock as she took what she needed. Maybe she would grab my throat, or I would grab hers. Fuck, she had just the right amount of fire and softness, she would be so much fun.

I took a step back and nodded at her. "Rest, you're still gonna be recovering from the drugs. I'll bring one of the TVs in here later if you want so you can watch something, or I'll talk to Gage and see if you can camp out in one of the dens." I wanted her to be happy, and if I could do anything to make it happen without pissing off or endangering our pack, I was going to do it.

"Thank you." She smiled.

"You'll be home before you know it, and until then we should all keep our distance, the scent blockers *really* didn't do their job." The room was full of the alluring lavender and vanilla scent, it was delicious, but it wasn't a completely in your face omega scent yet.

Lavender stilled, probably taking stock of her situation and understanding that her sweet floral scent was coating every surface of the room. Or that I, and every other alpha in this house, wanted to drown in it, personal feelings aside. Giving her one last tight smile, I left, locking the door behind me.

Jesus fucking Christ. No one has any right to smell that damn good. It had taken everything in me to keep a respectful distance from Lavender.

CHAPTER TEN
Gage

Theo had come to bed after that first night and he couldn't stop talking about Lavender. He was obsessed. I was sitting up in bed checking through a few phone notifications when he came skipping into the room. Skipping. Like a goddamned school girl. Usually he just slithered in without saying much. The first few nights we had spent together after his accident were completely silent, he would just creep into my room and slide into bed without a word. He couldn't handle being alone at night anymore.

"Oh Gage, she's perfect. I wanna keep her forever!" Theo cooed, jumping into bed and wriggling down under the covers, pulling them up to his chin.

"We aren't keeping her," I reminded him. He looked over at me with a pout. I resisted the urge to groan, the last thing we needed was Theo forming an attachment.

"But Gagey!" he whined. "She's pretty *and* she smells nice.

Don't lie to me, you've had a permanent hard on since we grabbed her, haven't you?"

I had, her scent was a fucking aphrodisiac and I couldn't control my physical reaction. That was beyond the point, though.

"No," I kept my voice firm.

"You're no fun. I want to play with the pretty omega!"

"We have enough problems as it is," I said as I set several alarms to go off throughout the night at regular intervals. "We should sleep, we are going to be up every two hours to make sure that omega hasn't given you even more brain damage."

"Ugh!" Theo turned onto his back with a dramatic eye roll. "Spoilsport. Why are you even bothering to set alarms? I wake us up every few hours anyway."

"Sometimes it's only once or twice a night—I'm just being cautious. Come here." I grabbed my keychain torch and flicked the light in his eyes, checking his pupils. Doc had told me to do that regularly and if one didn't react to the light, shit was probably serious.

"Is it bad I want to be near her?" Theo asked.

"No, it's just biology," I said, though I didn't know if I believed that or was just trying to convince myself.

"Can't I at least play with her a bit?"

"No, we are going to give her space and get through this as quickly as possible. If we manage to finally make a sale and buy an omega from Fenton we will be one step closer to finding Juniper."

"I don't want to give her space," Theo admitted, staring at the ceiling.

"Tough. I'm in charge."

"Okay Daddy," Theo smirked, though he didn't look at me as he spoke.

A smile tugged at my lips when I turned off the bedside lamp. If the injury hadn't posed a real threat to Theo given his past, I would have been impressed at Lavender's fight. As it stood, she posed a real threat to my family—and I refused to let her harm us.

Two days later it was obvious that my pack was a mess. The pretty little omega had turned us all on our heads. The entire safehouse smelled like a floral explosion and none of us were immune. While we weren't going rutting crazy over the smell, it was still obviously clear it was an omega scent and fucking delicious.

Archer was moping around the den, unhappy that Lavender was unhappy. He never vanished into his own room though. The safehouse was pretty sterile, so I didn't blame him as his room was pretty much just an empty shell. Yet I got the feeling that wasn't the reason, more that he wanted to be around in case Lavender popped her head out again. Kane was pissed, he wanted her gone yesterday, he had been stomping around and was even more surly than usual.

Grabbing a bottle of water I walked down the hall, taking a deep lungful of air before unlocking and walking into her room, not bothering to knock.

She was sitting in the bed, but at the sight of me entering she scuttled back towards the headboard, startled. Her hair was messier, wild, and her eyes hooded with sleep. She must have only woken a few minutes beforehand.

"Here," I said roughly, throwing the bottle at her. She caught it, surprised.

"Uh, thanks, I guess," she mumbled.

"Did you tell *anyone* what you overheard?" I asked, getting straight to the point. I don't know why I was asking her again, both me and Archer had already asked.

"No! I already told you!" she growled, but it was a cute growl, like an adorable kitten. "Even if I did speak to someone, why would I tell you? You kidnapped me! I'm not going to risk you taking anyone else because you're a bunch of deprived criminals!"

I froze. "So you *did* talk to someone?" I stalked up to the edge of her bed so I loomed over her. I couldn't hurt her, I didn't have it in me, but she didn't need to know that.

Lavender scrambled off the bed, glaring at me as she put some distance between us. "I didn't. I thought we covered this?"

I ran my hand roughly over my head, growling in frustration. "I want you gone, as soon as possible."

"I'd leave right now if you let me," she fired back, her tone full of snark as she glared at me, her earlier worry gone, replaced by pure fury.

"You're fucking with my pack's heads, I don't like it. Archer is acting like someone pissed in his cereal and Theo wants to follow you around like a fucking puppy."

"That's not my fault! You need to keep *your* pack under control. I didn't ask Archer to reach out to me! How is this in any way, shape, or form *my* fault? You need your head checked." She went to move away but I grabbed her wrist pulling her to me.

"Whatever it is you're doing, *stop*," I snarled, my face inches from her. Her nose flared as she took in my scent, pupils blown wide as she looked up at me.

Light notes of lavender flooded the room, along with the sweet scent that I had only heard about; perfume and slick. My body reacted before my mind could, pulling her closer until our chests crashed together. My hand fisted in her hair as I kissed her. *Fuck.* Why did she taste so good? I let go of her wrist, my hand trailing over her waist and up to her breasts, moving on autopilot.

Instead of pushing me away her hands fisted in my shirt, pulling me closer. She was kissing me back, her lips incredibly soft. Sweet vanilla and lavender assaulted my senses.

My hand clenched tighter in her hair and on her hip, eliciting a needy whimper from her as the smell of her slick became so potent it was almost unbearable. I pulled her in even tighter and the temptation to press her into the wall and feel every luscious curve of her body was heady.

She tasted like vanilla and mint, she must have found the spare toothbrush I had snuck into her bathroom before she woke up.

What the fuck am I doing? I jumped back, pulling us apart. We both panted hard, just staring at each other. Lavender's pupils were blown and she looked almost feral with wide glassy eyes. Her omega instincts were riding her hard, and my alpha ones were responding. There was no scent of fear in the air, just sweet slick. It clung to my clothes and my body was thrumming with desire.

I had been so distracted looking at her face and drowning in her scent that I hadn't noticed her hand rear up until it slapped me across the face. She packed a punch, my face stung from the impact.

"Careful, darling," I warned. "You forget who's in charge here." I stalked forward, backing her up against the wall I had wanted to press her against just moments earlier. The sting from the slap didn't hurt too badly. She was challenging me and the alpha in me wanted to assert my dominance, to prove to her I was stronger.

She looked up at me defiantly, but the smell of burnt sugar was starting to infiltrate her scent. Good, the last thing I wanted was for her to realise that I wasn't capable of hurting her if she didn't behave. Fear, as much as I hated it, was my best motivator right now.

"Get out," she snarled.

"Tonight we will finish all this, and you can leave tomorrow."

Taking one last deep breath of her floral scent, I stepped back, turned, and left, unable to take the fear.

What the fuck was I doing? I was meant to be leading our pack, and instead I was making out with an omega. One who wasn't meant for us, like a horny teenager.

My phone buzzed, I pulled it out of my pocket and made my way to the kitchen. It was a text from an unknown number with an address by the docks. That was where the buy was going to happen tonight. If we could take down this trafficking operation, we would be one step closer to figuring out where Juniper was.

As soon as this meeting was done we could take Lavender home. Twenty-four hours and it would all be done with. We would drop Lavender somewhere near the Haven and lurk long enough to ensure she got back safe and sound.

Kane was sitting at the kitchen island, reading something on his tablet when I walked in.

"We have an address for tonight," I told him.

He turned to face me. "I'll get the gear then. You, me and Theo, yes?"

"Yes, I don't trust Theo here right now. Archer will at least keep his distance. She'll probably spend all day sleeping off the drugs. It's 3pm and she's still half asleep."

"Okay, I'll get everything ready and let Theo know." Kane

looked at his tablet before glancing back at me. "Should we drug her again? That way she won't be causing issues when we're busy."

I shook my head. "That'll only scare her further."

"We can slip it into her food, she probably won't even realise," he rationalised.

"She's still sleepy from the last dose, it's probably not safe, I don't want to risk her having a reaction when we aren't here to keep an eye on her."

Kane grimaced. "Okay, Archer will have to behave then."

Considering I failed to keep my own distance from her, I highly doubted Archer's ability to.

CHAPTER ELEVEN

Kane

The docks were fucking freezing. Naturally of all the places for a seedy purchase of a human being, Julius had picked here at two in the morning. The few surrounding lights were a dull hazy yellow and there was fog coming off the water. Visibility was shit, and that pissed me off.

The omega had been fast asleep when we'd left, Archer had stayed behind to keep an eye on her in case she woke up and used the time alone to enact another escape attempt. He could help with any computer stuff remotely as well, if need be. He hadn't voiced any complaint at being left behind; clearly wanting to be near her.

"Do you think Archer will be able to handle being with her on his own?" Gage asked me. Frowning as he looked over the foggy water, his hands tucked into his pockets. "He's quite attached, as is Theo. You or I should have stayed, but we needed to be here." I knew without even asking that one of his hands was clasped around the Glock in his pocket. He was hyper aware of our surroundings, me, Gage, and Theo all were—it was a crucial part of our dealings. We were the only ones here, there was no sign of Julius. His phone was going to voicemail, so there was nothing we could do but wait. I *hated* waiting.

"I hate that she got mixed up in this," Gage said.

"I'm not!" Theo piped up, grinning madly.

"I blame Archer, his curiosity led to this situation. He's usually so much more level headed. Hopefully she's still asleep, otherwise he may be distracted and let her run amok." I wouldn't admit it out loud, but I could see the appeal of the angry little omega. Her fight and escape attempts had been pretty impressive. I had no doubt that were she to go head to head with Archer, she would be the one to come out victorious.

I still had the marks on my arm from where she had sunk her claws into me while trying to escape. There was a pang of emotion when I thought about the scratches healing over, but I tamped it down. The alpha in me wanted to preen over the fact an omega had marked me, but I needed to be thinking with my brain, not my knot.

Gage avoided my eyes. "I guess he's lonely and craving female attention. We can't begrudge him wanting to talk to someone for that."

"He won't be lonely once we find Juniper. The ass can keep it in his pants until then," I growled. My sister would be their omega, if it was the last thing I did. Reuniting her with them was my sole reason for continuing at this point, they could look after her, help her heal. She had adored them, and confided in me years ago that she liked Gage. I would make this work for her.

Gage turned to look at me. "Archer wasn't tossing Juniper

aside. He needed an outlet, and I think Lavender was that. They were never meant to meet in person. Had we not taken her she would have stayed at the Haven and gone on with her normal life."

"Juniper deserves better."

"Better? Kane, she was never our omega, nor had we plans for one, and yet we have torn our lives apart to find and save her. Archer gave up a lot. Yes, Juniper didn't deserve to be taken, but don't take your frustration out on Archer. He's trying, we are *all* trying. It's been years, let him have this small thing."

I wanted to shout *no*. Archer shouldn't have even been thinking of another omega, let alone regularly speaking with one. Gage's pack was derailing, and he couldn't even see it. When he told me about the meeting earlier I could smell him. He had been with her, and the smell of arousal clung to him. Both hers and his. They had clearly touched.

"Fuck me it's cold. My dick is going to disappear for good if we don't warm up soon!" Theo moaned, rubbing his hands together. "Gagey, this really isn't the fun kind of blue balls, why are they so late?"

I checked my watch. 2:30am. That didn't bode well, he was thirty minutes late.

"They're late. Significantly late," I said.

"Maybe they've been caught up? I imagine transporting cargo of that nature could be problematic and lead to a whole host of delays." Gage frowned, ignoring Theo's previous comment.

"How long do we wait?" I asked. "We need this to work, Gage."

"I'm well aware of that, Kane. Fuck. How long can we wait?"

"As long as it takes."

"Fine. You can warm my balls up later then, Gagey," Theo grumbled petulantly, shuffling from foot to foot.

It was no secret that Gage and Theo had a flirty thing going on—those two spoke to each other like they were an old married couple who loved fucking like rabbits. Juniper had bet me a hundred dollars before she vanished that those two would end up hate fucking at some point, but it was never going to happen. They were family, best friends—friends who shared a bed every night because Theo couldn't contain his nightmares. Nothing more.

We didn't know much about what happened to Juniper. One day she was home, the next she was gone without a trace. Two years ago, we hunted down a trafficking ring operating in our hometown. The ringleader was still in the business and we needed to find him. It was the only thing we had to go on to find Juniper.

The sun was rising by the time we gave up waiting. They hadn't shown, and we were no closer to finding my sister, or the bastards who had taken her.

CHAPTER TWELVE
Lavender

I woke gently, comfortable despite the lack of blankets and pillows. The sun had clearly started rising and pale orange light filtered through the slate grey curtains. I didn't remember going to bed. I must have been truly exhausted, the emotional nature of the situation taking its toll. Rolling out of bed I padded over to the sleek, modern bathroom and did my business. I made quick work of brushing my teeth, thankful I didn't feel quite as grimy anymore.

By the time I went to bed again, I would be home, safe in my own nest and this place with its bizarre pack would just be a distant memory. Fawn would probably be going insane with worry, she was that kind of omega. I hated the idea of her being upset I was gone, she was likely working herself into such a stress filled state because she cared so deeply.

I was rinsing my mouth when I heard the door open. Going still, I listened as someone walked into my room. *Please don't be Gage,* I thought to myself, I didn't want a repeat of yesterday. Well, part of me did, but I wasn't going to listen to my horny omega brain.

Taking a deep breath, I poked my head around the door, seeing the large alpha who had restrained me when I did my little jailbreak was standing in my room. Kane, I guessed from the general surly appearance. His hair was buzzed super short, but it only made his facial features look stronger. His arms were thicker than my thighs—no wonder I had been pathetic at fighting him. He looked like he could take me out merely with the strength of his pinky finger.

"Gage needs to talk to you," he grumbled, turning back to the door, pausing when I didn't follow and giving me a cold stare.

"Why?" I asked after him, hating how my voice shook. Everything about this alpha screamed pissed off, and I didn't want to be on his bad side. Gage probably just wanted to talk about the logistics of going home...but something about Kane's angry aura set me on edge.

Instead of replying he took two long strides over to me, grabbing me by the upper arm and physically dragged me out of the bathroom and bedroom with little effort. A warm leather scent engulfed me whilst his vise-like grip stung and I had no choice but to follow.

"That hurts!" I cried, letting a low, pathetically sad whine slip out. The sound made his steps falter for a brief second before he continued on, his grip just a touch lighter.

"You should have listened then," he said as he pulled me down the hallway, back to the familiar den where I had seen the alphas sitting together during my escape attempt. It was sparsely furnished. There was no way they lived here permanently.

The whole pack was there, Archer and Theo both sitting

down, Gage pacing around. They looked terrible; like they hadn't slept in days. Gage had dark circles under his eyes, and they were bloodshot.

"Kane. Be gentle. Don't take our shit mood out on her," Gage ordered.

Archer's hair was sticking up in various directions, something I knew for a fact was a result of him running his hands through his hair constantly when he was stressed.

The mood was sombre, and I didn't know if I should speak. I didn't want to anger or upset anyone further.

"Our job went sideways, the person who was meant to turn up didn't," Gage ground out frustratedly, pacing like a caged animal.

"Oh... I'm sorry?" I asked, rather than spoke.

"Lavvy," Archer said from the armchair. "Come sit down," the dejected tone of his voice set me on edge. I was about to refuse when Kane gently pushed me toward the armchair and I resisted the urge to laugh at Kane's sudden softer manhandling, clearly Gage was the boss of the group. The overwhelming scent of alpha muddled my senses, yet I didn't feel the urge to panic and run. In fact, I wanted nothing more than to curl up on the laps of these strange alphas and bathe in their scents. My instincts were screaming comfort and security, even though the situation was far from it.

"I'm still going home today, aren't I?" I asked quietly. The despondent looks on their faces gave me the answer I needed.

Still, I didn't want to accept it. I looked at Archer. "Arch?" He couldn't look me in the eye, staring at the floor instead.

"I need to go home!" I said louder, a desperate edge to my voice, looking between the downtrodden men.

"We want to take you home, and we will, it just can't happen right now." Gage spoke from behind me.

Standing in the middle of the room, surrounded by alphas, I was starting to feel claustrophobic, like the walls were closing in. I was meant to be home today, back to my nest, not another night in that sterile, cold room.

I sank into a nearby armchair, my knees weak. Had they ever intended to take me home? Was this all part of their plan, to give me false hope and keep me complacent? Goddamnit, I was so freaking gullible. It didn't matter if their auras were calm or they gave off good vibes, my instincts were clearly broken.

"I can't. I need to go home!" I whined, an actual omega whine that hit every alpha in the room in the gut, Several of them winced at the sound. An omega's whine was painful to them, alpha instincts demanded they care for omegas, protect them, keep them safe, warm, and loved.

Out of the corner of my eye I could see Archer openly wincing at the sound.

"Lavender…" Gage kept his voice low and gentle. "This will only be for a few weeks. I promise, you will go home, it's just going to take a bit more time."

"Weeks?!" I exclaimed, shaking my head. "No no no no, I can't do that—I need to be back in the Haven—I'm due for a heat within the next two weeks!"

Gage frowned.

"We can get you medications to stop your heat from coming and keep you safe. We won't go near you. You have nothing to fear from us," he assured, looking off into the distance in thought.

I opened my mouth to speak, but Archer cursed loudly before speaking, "She can't take blockers, Gage, they fuck with her kidneys." I glowered at Archer, regretting how much I had told him on our late night video calls. Why had I been so trusting and chatty? Karma was chomping on my butt at this point.

"I really need to watch what I say to strangers on the internet." I frowned at Archer. I had gone through a particularly brutal heat alone a few months back and had to explain to Archer why I had missed several video calls.

"So you've gone through heats with alphas before?" Gage asked. Not liking where the topic was going, I opened my mouth to answer, and again was cut off by Archer. Stupid stalker pen pal. He needed to take a long walk off a short pier.

"No, she does them solo, but she looked like a fucking corpse after the last one."

"Shut up, Archer," I growled. " I would like to maintain at least the *illusion* of privacy."

"Don't Havens have trained alphas for these situations?" Theo asked. "I'll happily volunteer as tribute, you know, for a good cause." He grinned at me. There was no venom in his words, only playful excitement.

"Quiet," Kane snarled at him.

"I didn't want to deal with any of those knotheads." I shrugged. "You see why I can't stay?" I implored, looking at Gage with wide eyes. "I won't say anything about you guys, your names, looks, or anything but I need to be safe and in my nest by the time my heat hits. No one can resist heats or ruts, and you promised no harm would come to me!"

Gage cursed, looking between his packmates and me curled up on the armchair, eyes wide with fear. "Lavender, we can't. We're stuck between a rock and a hard place here."

"Take her back to our house," Kane spoke, standing next to the armchair I was on. "We have the space for her to nest and be far enough from us that we won't smell her, or vice versa. I don't fucking like it, but we can't exactly stay here, can we?"

I shook. That sounded so far from ideal, my stomach turned. Heats were mind fucks, they made an omega so desperate for alpha cock their senses became muddled. Many times I regretted my choice to do it solo when in the midst of a bad wave of heat cramps. Heats were only manageable because of copious toys. the guards wouldn't let an alpha near me unless I had approved of them prior to the heat, an omega in heat was like a drunken sorority girl, totally unable to consent. Some omegas opted to ride out their heats with alphas, and all the more power to them. They came out of their heats exhausted but clearly happy and satiated, whereas I came out the other side looking like an animated corpse. I just couldn't bring myself to get into a situation like that with someone I didn't have a strong connection with.

"You can't ask her to be somewhere unknown for a heat. That's cruel, Gage," Archer defended me.

"Well what do you propose we do?" Gage asked with a grimace.

Archer seemed lost for words. He probably didn't have a better solution either and knew that they couldn't release me until they had completed whatever this job was.

"Let me go home?" I questioned pointedly.

"I'm sorry, Lavender." Gage sighed. "The pack house is the best solution for now, and I know it's not ideal, but given the situation I think it's the best we can do. We'll leave in an hour or so. There's no point in waiting around." He looked away as I wiped at the tears on my face. I didn't deserve this, he knew that. Gage sent some sort of unspoken signal to the rest of his pack, and everyone started moving, packing up computers and any other personal items.

While the alphas sprang into action, I just sat still, my mind running a million miles a minute. What was going to happen to me now? I wasn't safe. There was no way I was going to get out of this unscathed. An unbonded omega, going into heat in the same building as a bunch of unbonded alphas? It was a recipe for disaster.

I hadn't moved from the armchair forty minutes later when Archer stood in front of me, scarf in hand. "I'm sorry Lavvy girl, we are going to have to blindfold you, we can't have you seeing where we are going...or able to take the blindfold off." I looked at his hands, he also had cuffs on him. Fuck that.

"No," I bit out. Restraints and a blindfold? That didn't exactly scream *safe* to me.

Archer sighed. "It's this, or we knock you out again. You've had so much crap in your system the last few days I'm sure it'll be much better for your health if we don't. Hurting you is not our intention." His eyes roamed over me, stopping on my upper arm where Kane had manhandled me. A dark bruise in the shape of his rather large hand was already forming.

"That's nothing," I scoffed. "My midsection is covered in bruises from him grabbing me." Despite my best efforts a few tears leaked out, running down my cheeks.

"I'm sorry," he repeated, his words gravelly as he refused to meet my eyes.

"I fucking hate you for this," I sobbed. His face fell at my words, hurt flying across his features, but I honestly couldn't give a damn.

"You don't mean that, Lavvy girl. It's me."

"I wish you had never reached out to me, you and your gummy bears can get bent."

Archer shook his head, a sad look etched on his features. He took a step forward with the blindfold and I shrank back. He hesitated.

"I have to," he said quietly.

"Not you," I ground out. I couldn't bear the thought of him touching me. "I don't want you going near me. Let the grumpy one do it."

Kane was standing in the kitchen, packing some things and able to overhear us. He looked up, glancing between me and Archer with an unreadable expression on his face.

"I trust him more than I trust you," I said. That was totally a lie. I didn't trust that big grumpy fucker in the slightest, but my words had the intended impact as Archer's face fell. A small part of me also couldn't handle if Archer physically hurt me, and another part wanted him to hurt like I was from his betrayal. In my mind he had been the perfect potential alpha partner when in reality he was clearly some kind of fucked up.

"Fine." Archer strode over to Kane and roughly shoved the blindfold and restraints at him. "I'm going to help Gage."

A tiny part of me didn't like that he was upset, but I had spent all my childhood worrying about what others felt instead of myself—one of the perks of being raised by whack job religious nuts—and in this situation, my feelings were far more important.

Kane walked over to me, his face unreadable.

"I'll blindfold you, and if at least one of us has a hold on you, then we don't need to bother with the restraints."

I nodded. "Okay, are we going now?" I resigned myself to the fact that this was happening. I didn't mind a scrap, but I would have to be certifiable to think I could get out of this situation via brute force. I resolved myself to go with the flow and bide my time until a better opportunity appeared.

Kane nodded and didn't say a single word as he placed the blindfold over my face. His touch was so soft and caring, it was such a stark contrast to the behaviour I had seen from him before.

A large hand gently cupped my elbow as Kane led me out of the room. His leathery smell was becoming familiar.

The flooring changed and fresh air invaded my senses as we walked over what felt like gravel. Car doors opened and I let out a little squeak of fear as I was suddenly airborne, but a split second later I was sitting in a seat with a seatbelt being pulled over me and buckled. I could tell by the slightly leathery smell that it was Kane on the rear driver's side, Archer on the other.

"Okay, time to get comfortable, it'll be an hour or two."

It looked like I was going to be the filling of a grumpy alpha sandwich for the duration of the drive. The back seat of the vehicle I was in wasn't that large, so both Archer and Kane were close, their thighs touching mine.

"I'm meant to keep this on the whole time?" I asked with a whine. The small space combined with the lack of sight and two alphas was wreaking havoc on my senses. Their smell coated every surface, and I felt myself pining for more, mortified when I felt myself getting slightly damp—like some freaking newbie omega who was hankering for a knot.

I crossed my legs, trying to stop my scent from filling the cab of the van and smothering them all. Stupid floral stink. I stayed silent, focusing on anything else other than my travelling companions.

"Yes, *princess*, you're keeping it on," Kane said in a gruff tone. The princess felt a little sarcastic so I huffed.

"Trust me, I'm the farthest thing from an omega princess. If that's what you're after you really should have looked elsewhere. Then again, pretty, popular omegas usually have guards with them at all times," I grumbled. Talking was a distraction from the enclosed, highly scented space I was sitting in.

Kane only chuckled in response. The doors opened again and I felt movement as the other two got into the front set. I could already recognise their scents but I couldn't figure out who was driving and who was in the passenger seat.

"How long until we're there? I'm so tired. I don't know what you gave me but it's taking forever to leave my system."

Kane moved, I could hear the fabric of his clothes rustling. "Drink this. You need to be hydrated." He handed me the bottle and I easily navigated unscrewing the lid and taking a long drink, despite the blindfold. It wasn't until I had the rim against my lips I realised how thirsty I was, chugging until the water was empty. Moments ago he had been laughing at me, and now he was helping me? Grumpy was giving me whiplash.

"Thank you," I gasped. Holding the empty bottle in my lap, unsure of where to put it.

When Gage turned a corner particularly hard, I tilted over, and Archer had to hold out a hand to keep me steady. The lack of vision wasn't helping my stability.

CHAPTER THIRTEEN
Lavender

It felt like a decade later when we finally pulled up at the compound. My elbow ached from Kane holding it in a death grip, like he thought I was going to break free and take a leap out of a moving vehicle. Unfortunately I wasn't brave enough for that, otherwise I would have given it a shot. A deep feeling of unease was settling in my gut.

True Crime 101—don't let your captors take you to a second location, and what was I doing? Letting them take me to a second location. Was it actually their pack house they were taking me to, or somewhere discreet to chop me up into itty bitty bits?

Either way, I didn't have the strength or smarts to get out of this situation just yet, so my best bet was to go with the flow.

"Okay, Lavvy girl. We're here."

"Those roads are terrible," I groused. My ass hurt from bumping around in the seat so much on the way up. The jostling movement combined with being in a small space drenched in various alpha scents was getting my omega side all worked up. I was doing my best to control it, taking deep, slow breaths and praying I didn't perfume all over the place. I would rather avoid that humiliation.

"We're fairly out in the sticks. Here, take my hand, I'll help you out of the van." I felt Archer grab my hand gently, leading me out of the vehicle. Once I was at the edge he held me by the hips, and lifted me to the ground with an ease that, as much as I didn't want to admit it, impressed me and warmed me to the core.

"It's just a short walk to the house and then we can take the blindfold off," Archer assured me. After only one step I tripped over a rock. The ground was rough, made of dirt, and hard to navigate—more so without visibility.

Archer cursed and I could hear rustling before my legs were taken out from under me and I was airborne again as I was swung into Archer's arms. "It'll be easier this way."

He ignored my little squeak of surprise at the sudden movement.

I didn't want to like being in his arms. I wanted to hate it. He had betrayed me, and yet despite the blindfold, surrounded by his sweet scent I wanted to nestle my face into the crook of his neck.

Once we entered the building, Archer gently placed me on my feet, deftly removing the blindfold. Squinting in the sudden light, I took in the room around me. Minimal, clear, and striking. There were no scent blockers here—each facet of the pack's scent coated every surface in sight, drowning me in their presence. This had to be their pack home, they had clearly spent a lot of time here. At least they weren't lying about that. "It smells, uh, strongly in here," I choked out. There was another scent. Beta. Faint, feminine.

"I'll show you to your space," Archer said, his hand on my back to guide me. He went to turn down a corridor but Kane interrupted him.

"Put her in the south room. Not the downstairs suite." He gave Archer a firm look, and the two of them looked at each other for a moment, silently communicating before Archer nodded.

Footsteps alerted me to someone's presence behind me "The room you'll be in hasn't been touched in months, so there should be no residual scent there. We'll also get some scent cancelling air fresheners," Gage reassured me as he came in behind us, carrying a duffel bag. "Arch, go help Theo unload. I'll show Lavender her room." He threw his duffel into the corner, gesturing to the giant staircase, letting me go before him.

"Thanks," I muttered, then hesitated, why was I being polite to my kidnappers?

"I had a friend of ours drop off some women's clothing and toiletries for you, also some extra bedding. I don't know exactly what else an omega needs to be comfortable, but just tell us and we'll order whatever you need. I don't want you to suffer while you're here."

Sensing my hesitation, Gage gave me a nudge before leading the way, going up the stairs, through several corridors until we made it to the room they had assigned me.

My room did smell a lot cleaner than the rest of the house —no cloying alpha scents stuck to every surface. Ignoring the small part of me that lamented the loss of that delicious cacophony of scents I padded into the room, taking in the brand-new pillows and blankets, still in their plastic. I smiled to myself, happy to have some comfort items again.

The room was small, the walls painted a basic beige, but it

was clean and nice enough. For a prison cell, anyway.

"Kane is ordering some food, I'll bring some up when it arrives," Gage told me as he walked across the room, opening the small wooden door to the connecting bathroom so I could see. "You've got everything you should need here."

"A gun?" I asked, trying not to laugh.

Gage just glowered at me. "Anything within reason..." he reaffirmed.

"Yes sir!" I kept my tone serious as I saluted.

Gage rolled his eyes, his jaw tense. I didn't know why I was feeling so bold, but maybe if I was irritating enough they would get rid of me. Or kill me. It really wasn't a smart bet.

"I don't want you to be restricted to only your room here so we won't lock you in. You're free to explore the house, but there are locks on the doors and windows. Plus we are in the middle of nowhere surrounded by a lot of fences." He was making it very clear that I was still a prisoner, but with a little more freedom. "The door lock works both ways, so when your heat hits you can lock us out of the room."

"Okay, thank you." Being able to lock myself in did ease the tightness in my chest ever so slightly.

"I'll uh... let you settle in." He turned and strode out the room without a backwards glance, closing the door behind him. There was no locking sound. He was serious about me having more freedom.

I let out a sigh, relieved to be alone.

Left in the room, I wandered around for a moment, checking out the large ensuite bathroom and all possible exits. I knew running was unlikely. As Gage had warned, we were in the middle of nowhere and I couldn't drive. There had never been a need for me to learn and they didn't exactly offer lessons at the Haven. Omegas were to be protected, chauffeured around, and looked after. In theory, someone would always be around to drive them.

Opening the enormous wardrobe doors, I smiled to myself. This would be an ideal space to nest. Maybe I could drag the mattress in and make a pillow fort to keep me comfortable? I needed a space to help my jittering omega instincts feel more at ease. Omegas didn't do well with change, and I was no exception. Not being able to nest, and being away from Fawn and my fellow omegas was making me feel all out of sorts.

My skin itched with the need to make this space my own, to fill it with fluffy and plush things. Back home I had access to unlimited soft and squishy things, here there weren't many options. At least they had been thoughtful enough to give me pillows that were new.

Or would I rather have pillows covered in their scent?

All of the pack's actions until now had been with the purpose to protect me, even if the execution was a little questionable. They could have easily just gotten rid of me at the Haven to ensure I didn't speak. Instead, they had taken me and given me a room and kept me fed, even when I injured one of them.

Despite the severity of the situation, I didn't feel in danger. Unsettled? Sure. In grave danger? No. From day one at the Haven omegas are told to trust their instincts, that we know who is right for us, or if someone poses a threat. None of my instincts said that any member of Pack Rowe was a danger to me.

The bathroom was well stocked with toiletries and even hair ties and claw clips. All of them new judging by the scent. How had they managed to do that in such a short period of time? *Or did they know this was going to happen all along?* Shrugging off that thought and grabbing a claw clip, I twisted my hair up and out of my face. It only took me half an hour to make the bed, then bunch the pillows into a small, nest-like thing and explore before I was back sitting on it, staring at the walls once again. Spotting a remote control on the bedside table I pressed a few buttons, turning on the flatscreen TV on the far wall. I was shocked to find multiple TV shows and documentaries already downloaded. Archer knew my taste in entertainment, but there was a little bit of everything. Settling on a lighter true crime series, I snuggled into my pillows, curling up into a ball. It was less gore filled than I usually went for, but given I was in an unknown place and didn't feel fully safe, watching a true crime documentary on kidnapping serial killers would probably give me nightmares and stop me from getting any rest.

The protagonist's best friend was just about to be indoctrinated into a cult by the time Kane walked into my room, knocking, but waiting so little time for my response that he may as well have not bothered. He held a rice bowl in his hand. More Mexican food. I loved Mexican food but they didn't serve it often at the Havens, opting for fairly bland, but nice quality foods.

Without a word he placed the bowl on my bedside table along with a can of soda and a bag of candy. Sitting up I noticed it was a bag of gummy bears. The brand I liked. Archer remembered.

I glowered at the bag.

"Has the candy offended you?" he asked.

"I don't particularly want to eat candy that smells like that dumbass." I shrugged, my eyes never leaving the bag.

"I understand." Kane nodded, and picked up the bag.

"Thank you." I smiled at Kane as he retreated without a word, looking all too eager to get away.

CHAPTER FOURTEEN
Gage

I paced around the kitchen, my footsteps lulling me with their repetitiveness. Why had I let Kane of all people take her food? He probably would have scared her by now. He had been acting so harshly around her, I should have taken point on interactions. The last thing we needed was a scared omega acting out. Maybe I should have hidden the lamps before bringing her here. Theo could only take so many concussions, not sure she would get the drop on Kane though.

It had been my decision to give her some more freedom, so if this backfired, it was on me.

Kane had insisted that he take her food, just in case she had found any more potential weapons and was laying in wait. He had a thick head, he could take the assault if she managed to surprise him.

"She seems to have calmed down a bit," Archer commented as he dished up rice bowls for us. We were all surrounding the kitchen island, grabbing utensils and bowls.

Part of me was happy to be home, but all I could think about was the giant potential complication sleeping down the hallway from me. Two days wasn't enough time to get a read on her. She seemed fairly logical, if a little odd—blabbering about serial killers and such—but nothing about her screamed malicious or vindictive.

Kane came back, carrying only the bag of candy Archer had told him to give to Lavender. His face was unreadable, no trace of emotion, which was Kane's usual face.

"How did she seem?" I asked.

"Relaxed almost. Curled up watching the TV. She tensed up the moment I appeared, but I think she's happy to be left to her own devices."

"She's that way at the Haven as well—she socialises but nowhere near as much as the other omegas. Several times we had video calls during social events she opted to skip. Fawn, her roommate, was a social butterfly." Archer smiled when talking about their old video chats.

An uneasy feeling in my stomach bloomed at his wistful smile, and it took a moment for it to click. I was jealous. Archer had that connection, a friendly banter, with a woman. We had never had that. Maybe at one time we could have explored it, but our criminal records made that harder now.

"Well if we all keep our distance we can get through this with little suffering," I said. "Return her home and move on with our lives."

"It feels right in a way, doesn't it, having an omega in our home? The whole place smells heavenly, and horny alpha instincts aside, it's so calming," Theo spoke. "If only there was a way for her to stay, I wouldn't mind that." Theo shrugged.

"You already have an omega," Kane snarled. I gave him a firm look.

". I think Theo's just enjoying the pheromones, and who can blame him?"

The truth was we *didn't* have an omega, not in name or with us. Juniper would have likely *become* our omega, but she went missing before we had even considered starting the courting process and developed feelings for her. I had only ever seen her as a sister.

Kane glared at me. It was understandable that he had such strong feelings regarding this, she was his little sister, but he needed to make sure he didn't upset the omega living under our roof too much.

"She's been handling herself pretty well," Theo commented.

I nodded absentmindedly.

Kane growled, "Remember who this is for. Lavender has a home to go to after this, others don't. I don't like her being here, she's throwing you all off your game."

"We can still be nice to her," Archer implored. "The growly, barking act you've been using can't help anymore now she's in our home. Kind and keep our distance. The last thing I want is the scent of her fear wafting through the house. We'll never be able to sleep."

I had nearly choked on the sour, burnt smell when we had grabbed Lavender—she had only a brief second of fear before she was out cold, but that had been enough to make my eyes water and my instincts hum in pain.

"All her favourite candy is here, I ordered it in bulk a while ago," Archer admitted. "I liked sending her stuff she couldn't find."

Theo snorted. "I bet you did, the dopamine hit of caring for an omega is addictive, or so I've heard. I'm sure it also has nothing to do with how you smell very similar to said candy?"

"Well, she doesn't want it anymore. She gave the bag a death glare and told me to remove it," Kane said, grabbing a bowl and fork, digging in while leaning over the counter, his hulking frame taking up so much space.

Archer looked crestfallen, dejectedly staring at his rice bowl.

"I want to talk to her, but she's so mad at me."

"Be nice, but from a distance," I reminded him.

CHAPTER FIFTEEN
Lavender

The room wasn't terrible. They had provided just enough bedding to create a suitable level of squishy comfort, and the TV had plenty of entertainment. There was a twelve part series on a falsely convicted murderer I had been wanting to watch, so I threw myself into viewing it. The familiar content of gore and murder was comforting.

When I was alone in the room, I was almost at peace. It wasn't exactly luxury or the way I liked things done, but when I didn't have any alphas breathing down my neck, I could almost enjoy my time laying in bed, just lazing about and resting.

I hadn't been brave enough to try the door yet, I knew it was unlocked, and that I could explore, but *they* were out there. The solitude of my room just felt like the safer option.

Someone had left a whole pallet of water bottles in the corner of my room, and Kane brought me food pretty regularly, so I wasn't starving.

Three days passed with surprising ease. Occasionally a small cramp fluttered in my stomach, a nasty reminder that my heat was due soon, but I did my best to ignore it for now.

A knock on my door woke me from my nap, I had been doing that a lot lately, taking naps. There wasn't that much to do, so naps and TV shows it was.

"Come in," I called out, sitting up and running my hand over my hair, neatening it, even though there was no need to give a damn about my appearance here.

Archer looked in nervously. I sighed. He was the last person I wanted to see. I would rather have *any* of the others.

"Lavvy?" He said his nickname for me questioningly when he saw my disgruntled face.

"What do you want, Archer?" I snapped.

He walked into the room, right up the edge of the bed. I had to admit, he looked like crap. His skin was sallow, his eyes bloodshot, his hair was messy, and his scent strong, like he hadn't been showering all that often. He was a far cry from the clean cut computer guy I had gotten to know several months ago.

In his hand he had a bag of brown sugar gummy bears which he placed gently on my bed just inches away from me.

"We need to talk. I can't take this silence between us," he admitted.

"What do you want me to say, Archer?" I glowered at him. "You're not the person I knew."

"I *am*."

"No, I met a computer tech analyst who lived with his small town pack. You are a freaking criminal or maybe a stalker, involved in god knows how many depraved and disgusting things, like kidnapping omegas."

"Lavender, it's not like that."

"Were you ever legally part of the Haven? Or was it bullshit all along? Something tells me that there is no way in hell your pack would be approved to court an omega."

Archer's face fell and he sighed.

"We needed to look into some Haven records, so one evening I hacked into their servers. What I was looking for wasn't there, but I could see a lot of the active omegas. You had just been rejected by a pack for offending them, and I was curious, especially when right after they filed paperwork rejecting you they were blacklisted from the Haven."

Immediately I knew what pack he meant. They were a heavily religious pack, and they had reminded me too much of my family, so I had been rather blunt in my thoughts. They didn't like that and tried to file a complaint against me. It had backfired on them spectacularly. The Haven had actually given them an official warning and told them if they continued to insult their omegas they could take a hike, and they wouldn't be getting their fees back.

"Okay, but that still doesn't change the fact that I don't know you at all, Archer. Any friendship we had was built on a lie."

"I kept as close to the truth as I could. I'm still the Archer who loves watching murder documentaries with you, and who has an unhealthy obsession with orange soda." He chuckled at my cringe. "Please, trust me on this," he implored.

"It doesn't matter Archer, I won't be here long. I'll go back home, and you'll go back to doing whatever criminal antics you guys do, and we won't speak again."

"You wouldn't want our calls anymore?" he asked, shuffling from foot to foot. "They were the fucking highlight of my week."

"Our calls got me kidnapped, I think it's best we stay the hell away from each other. And take those gummy bears back, I don't want them." The smell of them only angered me now, reminding me of the betrayal from someone I had thought was my best friend. "Our calls were once the highlight of my week as well, but things have changed, don't you think? Also would your pack really be okay with you talking to me? Just make this easier on the both of us and leave, Archer," I ordered.

Archer looked like I had kicked his puppy, but he left, gummy bears in hand. With a groan I dived back into the blankets, my mind swirling. I missed Archer, but I was pissed at him and didn't want him near me. He was also the most familiar thing here, so part of me wanted to cling to him. Though another part of me wanted to thump him for this whole mess of a situation.

I knew my thought process was far from logical, my feelings on Archer were running hot and cold, and at this point I was giving myself whiplash.

Distance. We just needed distance.

I felt terrible. For the last four hours I had done my best to focus on the latest documentary I had lined up, but all I could focus on was the horrific pressure headache radiating through my temples.

Something felt off, maybe I was coming down with the flu? It wasn't heat related, I had been through enough heats to know the difference. Then again, it had only been a little over a week since I was drugged, so this could very likely be a residual effect of that.

As the hours progressed, the feeling only got worse, something just felt *wrong*. Like a gnawing pain eating me from the inside out.

I was too exposed. This bed wasn't a nest. That was what I needed, a small, comfortable and secluded nest. Sitting up I looked blearily around the room, my eyes landing on the walk in wardrobe. *Perfect.* I had noted the wardrobe before, but I couldn't bring myself to build a nest until it was completely necessary. It wasn't *my* nest and my omega was highly aware of that and extremely unhappy.

Stumbling out the bed I grabbed a handful of sheets and pillows, waddling over to the wardrobe, my steps clumsy due to the mountain of bedding in my arms. The wardrobe was sparse, there were just a few items of clothing and that was it, so setting up a small, enclosed nest was easy. It took several trips, I kept having to stop because the world was spinning on its axis and I felt lightheaded, but I got everything in the wardrobe. Then I had to organise it.

The darkness of the wardrobe wrapped around me like a hug. I would have liked some fairy lights, but I was hardly in a position to be picky. As it was, the more confined space coupled with the lack of light and mountain of blankets helped me feel a bit more secure and the pounding in my head eased somewhat.

I wasn't producing slick, and I wasn't dreaming about knots, so this clearly wasn't my heat. In the brief moments of clarity I ran through the potential causes. Flu? This felt like a pretty nasty flu. Food poisoning? None of the guys had mentioned being sick, but I hadn't seen them in a while and I wasn't vomiting.

My instincts were screaming for comfort. If something like this had happened back home Fawn probably would have taken it upon herself to crawl into my nest and keep me company. Her rose scent was always comforting, and she always gave the best hugs. Probably because the fancy pyjamas she wore were like some rare, uber thread count beauties that probably cost as much as a car. She always got the best gifts, and often she shared them with us.

She had gifted me an incredibly soft cashmere throw a few months ago, and I had slept with it every night since.

A pitiful whine that was pure omega distress slipped out at the thought of that throw. Shit, did I need more comfort items? I couldn't exactly ask for more, could I?

What about something with the guys scent on it? I stilled. Their dark, rich scents were just what I needed. The whisky and leather of Gage and Kane, the sweet brown sugar of Archer, and the crisp clean pine of Theo. All their scents together, wrapping me up in safety and warmth.

I needed it. My body screamed with the desire for those items, my heart rate skyrocketing as my temperature went haywire.

I needed it like I needed air.

But there was no way in hell I was going to ask for it.

CHAPTER SIXTEEN
Archer

She hadn't left her room in *days*. I was trying to give her space to process and come to terms with her situation, but it had been almost three days since I had last seen her when she threw yet *another* pack of candy at me. She was avoiding me, it was obvious. Hell, she was closer to Kane than me at this point, and it was eating me up inside. I wanted to crawl to her on hand and knees, for her forgiveness.

There was only so much waiting I could do. With Gage grounding me and telling me to avoid her I had been pacing my office constantly instead of getting any actual work done. We had found another seller, and we would be meeting them in two weeks. Apparently Julius had been 'waylaid'—a fancy term for 'likely murdered' because of his line of work. Now we were just waiting to hear from the new seller to arrange a sale date.

Slamming my laptop closed just a touch too hard, I rose, determined to deal with the issue. She couldn't avoid me forever, and Gage would just have to deal with it if she got cranky.

Three days of silence was unbearable. Heading for the kitchen I nuked some leftovers from the night before and plated them up. She hadn't left her room for food—I had been watching. Even Kane had mentioned it at dinner the previous night as we ate our noodles.

Food in hand I made my way up the stairs, her familiar floral scent filling my nose. As exciting as the scent was, it also soothed me, I could feel my shoulder muscles relaxing as I made my way to her door.

"Lavender?" I knocked on the door with one hand, leaning in to listen for any reply. "I have food. You've not been out in a while." I leaned closer, but there was no reply. "C'mon, Lavvy. Let me know you're okay." Still no reply. "I'll come in if you don't at least reply."

Concerned now, I knocked once more. Turning the door handle, I called out another warning before entering the room.

Lavender had closed all the curtains and windows, making it dark. The room was stuffy, and up close to her the smell of singed lavender thick in the air. *Burnt.* She wasn't happy. The smell was like a blow to my stomach, physically painful. Resisting the urge to whine, I followed my nose to the walk-in wardrobe. When had she done that? A wardrobe wasn't good enough for her, she deserved better. Kane had refused to let us give her the omega room with a nest, and this was what it resulted in. She had acquired even more bedding since I had last been there. My bet would have been Kane had been sneaking it in, I had seen him picking up several packages recently and I doubted that Lavender was brave enough to ask for them herself. Even though he hardly spoke to the omega, and disliked her presence here, he must have been ordering things and leaving them for her. Kane didn't see himself as part of our pack, he would go his own way once we found Juniper no matter how attached to the moody bastard we were. When he went his own way like he seemed determined to do, would he consider finding an omega for himself? He could join a pack that could afford the fees. Perhaps having Lavender around was good for him in a way. Or painful, possibly both.

Walking over to the nest I knocked on the wardrobe, waiting a second before poking my head in. It felt like I was invading her space. I hadn't been invited here. The scent alone was cloying, it was so potent, so sweet, but twisted. It hurt my stomach and made me feel sick. In the back of my mind I reminded myself that this was Lavender, *my* Lavender who traded true crime recommendations with me and debated the merits of each gummy bear flavour.

Shit. She was pale, sweaty, and curled up in a ball in the far corner of the nest. She hardly seemed lucid, like she was feverish. Her eyes were glazed over, looking at the wall blankly as she panted like she couldn't quite catch her breath. Cursing I put the food down on the first surface I could find and clambered over the mountain of pillows and blankets to her. Placing a hand on her neck gently, I was dismayed to find her boiling hot and coated in a thin sheen of sweat.

She groaned and closed her eyes at the contact.

"Hey hey hey, Lav, look at me." I gently lifted her across my lap, trying to get her to open her eyes, but she was limp.

"Arch?" she whined quietly.

"Yeah, it's me. What's wrong?"

She groaned, "Feel wrong."

"It's not your heat, is it? This doesn't smell like a heat." Not that I really knew what a heat smelt like, but from the little I understood of our biology I knew the scent of an omega's heat should be a mind boggling aphrodisiac. Lavender's floral smell had a slightly sour undertone, and it wasn't making me horny, it was making me panic. Everything told my instincts this scent was *wrong*.

Omega needs help.

I must provide help.

Grabbing my phone from my pocket with one hand while I held Lavender to my chest, I dialed Kane's number. My first thought was to call Gage, but he and Theo were out working on the trucks and probably wouldn't answer if they were distracted, so Kane it was.

"Yeah," he answered in his usual, gruff tone.

"Somethings wrong with Lavender—get Gage. Maybe the doc." I didn't wait for a reply, hanging up and throwing the phone onto a random pile of pillows and turning my attention back to Lavender, who was nestling into my chest. Her eyes were hazy, unable to focus on anything. I could see she wasn't fully lucid, her hair stuck to her face, and I gently brushed it away.

The thundering of footfalls alerted me to Kane's arrival. He burst into the room, a look of panic on his face. Wearing nothing but a pair of gym shorts, his abs on prominent display, it was clear he had just stopped in the middle of a workout to rush up here. I had joked many times that Kane must love steroids, because that was the only way he could have gained *that* much muscle mass and that many abs. He spotted the pair of us and his eyes honed in on Lavender's pale face.

"I called Gage on the way up here, what on earth happened?" he said as he kneeled at the entrance taking in the wardrobe nest with a frown. It really wasn't an ideal nest at all.

"I don't know, she's feverish. Help me get her out of here." I gestured to the pillow mountain we were currently buried in.

It would be easier to help her if she was extracted from the mountain of pillows.

"Do you think it's a smart idea to remove her from her nest?" Kane asked.

"I don't know, but I doubt that if the Doc comes, he'll be able to get in here," I said.

Nodding, Kane made his way over to us, kicking a few pillows as he went, ducking his head to avoid the coat hangers. Once he was within a few feet of me he held out his arms to take the limp omega off me. Hesitating, I handed her over, both of us able to lift her easily.

"Put her on the bed," I told him. There was a thin mattress and a sheet on it, but everything else was now in the nest.

Kane remained tense as he took Lavender off me. She whimpered at the contact, her clammy skin against his bare chest. Instinctively, she nestled into him, purring at the smell of Kane. Blindly, she nuzzled her face into his pec, humming in happiness as the scent relaxed every muscle in her body. Her breathing started to deepen.

I wanted her to be nestling into *me*. Not Kane. I was the one who knew her and cared about her.

Kane gently laid her down on the thin mattress, and Lavender's face contorted in pain as she gripped onto him desperately, her fingernails leaving little half-moon indentations.

"No," she mumbled in a desperate voice. "Stay." Her eyes flitted open and she looked at him, wide lilac eyes mesmerising.

Kane looked pleadingly at me, as I grabbed a few of the pillows from the nest for her. My head was spinning from the scent. Were it not for Lavender's ill state and the burnt tinge I doubted I would have been able to control myself with a scent so strong. I did find a second to be amused at the stoic Kane looking panicked at the small omega clinging to him.

"Oh." Lavender looked around hazily, noticing the alphas in the room. "I-I'm sorry, you should go."

"No way, Lavvy girl. What's happening?"

"I dunno," she mumbled. "Probably shitty omega stuff, just let me sleep it off." She moaned, running a hand through her hair, but it got tangled in the waves. Grunting she tried pulling her hand out but it just got even more entwined.

Kane bent forward, helping her untangle her hand, sweeping her matted hair behind her back. "Do you have a hair tie?" he asked, gently.

"Bathroom," Lavender groaned.

"I'll get the hair tie," I offered, as Kane was currently still being clutched by Lavender. A sweet, almost slick-like smell hit my nostrils in the bathroom. Had Lavender been doing some self-pleasuring in there? Unable to dwell on it, hair tie in hand, I made my way back to the bed where Lavender was still sitting up. Kane was before her, holding onto her forearms to keep her up. Her head was lolling slightly as he tried to get her to concentrate on him.

Kane gently combed his fingers through her hair, manipulating it into a loose braid to keep it off her face. I raised my eyebrows at him, wondering where he had developed this new skill. Kane's only reply was a glare.

The bedroom door swung open and Gage strode in, looking around frantically. "What the fuck happened here?" he asked, taking in the scene before him.

"Feverish, not entirely lucid, maybe a little feral. Did you call the Doc?" I asked.

"I will in a moment, I wanted to check on her first."

"I don't need a doctor," Lavender groaned. "Stupid omega shit," she mumbled the last part to herself.

Kane took the opportunity of Gage getting closer to back away, wincing at Lavender's whine of pain as he did so.

Gage walked over to the bed, taking in the sight of Lavender, pale and sweaty, the strap of her camisole pyjamas slipping over her shoulder. "What stupid omega shit are you talking about Lavender?"

"It's nothing—we get sick if our needs aren't met. Just leave me to get over it," Lavender grumbled, batting my hand away as I tried to feel her forehead.

"What have you been missing?" Gage asked. Hadn't he provided everything she possibly needed? Kane had taken pleasure in providing everything she could ever need, judging by the mountain of pillows dotted around the room.

"It's nothing. I thought I would be fine without it."

"Lavender." Gage made his tone forceful, putting a hint of a bark behind it. Not enough to force her to do as he wished, just enough to make her take notice. Her eyes widened at the tone, focusing on him for a moment.

"Human contact," she moaned, pushing away from us, reality still a little fuzzy. "That's one of the reasons omegas need packs."

"That makes sense," I said. "In a mated pack an omega would always have prolonged contact with their alphas. Their needs would be met without even realising it."

"But what about when they don't have a pack, at the Haven?" Gage asked.

"They're close to each other. Juniper was always taking cat naps with others, family, friends, anyone. She thrived off it," I confirmed.

Gage nodded at my words. "So... Do we need to call the Doc?"

"No," Lavender reiterated. "I'll be fine, just leave me alone."

"She needs contact. This space shit we are doing isn't working, Gage." I didn't pull my eyes away from her while I spoke.

"Can you control yourself?" Gage asked.

"You know I can, I'm not a monster."

"I'm right here," Lavender growled. Gage just smiled down at her, clearly amused by her little growl.

"We know you are, sweetheart, but you're clearly not a hundred percent here. I'll stay with you tonight, but then once you improve we will need to start rotating, making sure you're okay."

Lavender snorted. "You're not exactly my ideal snuggle partners."

"Yeah, yeah, Darling." Gage laughed ruefully. "Do you need to nest?" he looked over to the wardrobe and the makeshift attempt at a nest with a frown.

Lavender perked up instantly.

"Put her in the actual nest," Kane said. I looked over at him, jaw hanging open. *Did he just say what I think he did?* "That pitiful excuse of one in the wardrobe is a health hazard, she can't stay in there. Grab the pillows."

We didn't say a word. Gage nodded and gently picked up Lavender bridal style. She nuzzled her head into his neck.

"C'mon, let's get you to bed."

Lavender snorted. "Sexy."

"None of that. One condition of this mess is that we do not think about sex—we can control ourselves but let's not test that control," Gage said.

"If I didn't know better I would think you were saying I was pretty," Lavender smiled loopily at him.

"No comment."

"Nest?" Lavender asked again, a slight whine to her tone. I lowered Lavender a touch so she could grab some pillows to take with her. Between the omega in my arms and the squishy items my vision was obscured, but I knew the way around this house blind.

Despite the brunt edge to her smell, with her so close I could smell every facet of her lavender and vanilla. I ignored how right it felt having her in my arms, chalking it up to my daft alpha instincts.

The bedroom was large, with a nest where a bed would usually be; only this mattress was three times the size of a normal king. I gently put her down on the nest and she sat up, looking around with wild eyes taking in the space around her and the various soft items.

Lavender squeaked in happiness, diving headfirst into the pillows, making Gage smile. "C'mon, Boozy."

"Boozy?!" Gage choked out a laugh.

"You smell like alcohol... Whisky. Kinda smoky. It's nice." Lavender shrugged from her pillows. The nest was simple, with just a few large pillows and comforters in it but she would arrange them as she liked as soon as she felt up to it. Sighing, Gage crawled after her. I wanted to be the one in there with her, but she was mad at me, and I knew she was hardly in a position to make any informed decisions right then.

This space was much bigger—the other room was still relatively small and connected to the normal bedroom—but the nest had large windows, almost the size of two of the walls, both with specialist blackout blinds, so at the touch of a button the room could be either light and airy or dark and cosy. Whatever the omega felt like they needed they could have.

Laying back on some of the pillows next to Lavender, Gage frowned as he watched her shimmy away slightly.

"Not happening, Darling," he said, leaning over to slide an arm around her waist and dragging her to him. She didn't fight him, melting into his chest without a word. The TV that pointed to the nest was now playing a documentary.

"Seriously, Arch? Serial killer documentaries?"

"They relax her, this is one of her favourites." I laughed at Gage's look of confusion.

"I told you she was an interesting one."

"You did," Gage agreed.

CHAPTER SEVENTEEN
Lavender

Consciousness started to tug at my mind. I was blissfully warm, the perfect temperature, relaxing on top of a comfortable surface. I felt so well rested, I didn't want to open my eyes. The soft rocking of my dreams was euphorically relaxing, like soft waves lulling me into further oblivion.

Only it wasn't rocking, I realised with a start. It was *breathing*. Breathing from the freaking alpha chest I was sprawled on!

I sat up with a start. I vaguely remembered Kane putting me in a new nest, and for the first time I was able to see how it actually looked. Beautiful. The nest was illuminated by fairy lights, and daylight filtered in from the closed curtains from outside the room. Gage was in the nest with me, and I had been sleeping on him. He looked peaceful in his sleep. Calm. He had stubble growing on his face and was sprawled out on his back. I doubted he had been able to move all night with my gargantuan ass sprawled all over him.

My head felt clearer today. The chemical imbalance that occurred when omegas were touch deprived could be serious, but easily rectified. Some omegas were worse than others. I cringed at the realisation that I was an omega who needed a lot of attention. I had always imagined myself to be a little more independent. I had assumed I could get through it alone, and had been embarrassed to tell the men what was happening.

I felt grimy, my teeth almost felt fuzzy. I was wearing a pair of sleep shorts and one of Gage's shirts. When did I end up in his shirt? I couldn't tell you honestly. The last few days were a sickening blur. An oversized cardigan completed my ensemble, and my hair probably had a mind of its own at this point.

I looked around the nest. It was beautiful. I had no idea they had such a beautiful room in this house. Two of the walls were taken up with giant windows so I could see the woodland outside. A small remote controlled the electric black out blinds so I could get rid of the daylight in mere seconds and nestle down in the darkness.

The room was decorated in light neutrals. Aesthetic white bedding covered several large, overstuffed pillows and comforters. The nest was sparse—clearly intended to be decorated by an omega in the future. But fresh air, the instant darkness, and the stunningly soft mattress made it a pretty phenomenal nest, despite its sparse nature.

Clambering off Gage I stumbled over to the bathroom, doing my business. Looking in the mirror I noted my hair was in a loose, side braid. I hadn't done that. At least, I didn't *remember* doing that. *Did one of the guys do it?* The thought that they might've made me wistful. Taking it out felt wrong, even though I wanted to brush my hair so I opted to leave it in, padding back towards the bedroom.

Gage was standing when I came out, looking deliciously rumpled. He held a bottle of water out to me. "You need to drink," he insisted.

Gently, I took the bottle from him, he had already cracked it open for me, and took a sip. A sip quickly turned into me chugging half the bottle before taking a small break. I hadn't realised how parched I was.

"Thank you," I said softly, clutching the bottle gently to my chest. Gage looked me over. I already looked better than yesterday. The colour had returned to my face somewhat and I was less shaky.

"You need to eat, too," he told me, holding out his hand. The sight confused me. "And you need to be around us more, you were really unwell."

"But distance," I reminded him. I still had a heat creeping up on me.

"Distance can get fucked if it's gonna make you sick. We can handle ourselves. Sure we'll be walking around with permanent boners thanks to your scent, but we're big boys, we can handle ourselves."

Boners. Big Boys. Gage's words flamed a response in me, but my cheeks heated, and I was praying that my treacherous scent wouldn't show how much his words affected me.

I was not that lucky, though. Gage could smell my reaction the moment it happened. His nostrils flared and eyes widened ever so slightly, but he kept still, saying nothing. After a deep breath he took a step forward, gently grabbing me by the elbow and tugging me towards the door.

I didn't question him as he pulled me down the corridor

and fell into step next to him. He kept his hand placed on my lower back. The touch was electrifying, but I did my best to hide any reaction. I hadn't been out of my room much at all, so I needed the guidance. The pack house was so large and airy, I could easily get lost in it.

The kitchen looked like a food filled bomb had detonated. Pancakes, waffles, bacon, eggs, any breakfast food I could possibly want filled every side.

If I had an ounce of energy left, I would have been concerned about my appearance.

"Morning," Theo grinned at me from where he stood, stirring what looked like more scrambled eggs in a frying pan. "What can I get for you?"

"Food?" I asked, smiling sheepishly.

"Well there's a little of everything," Theo gestured to the counter. "Take whatever you want." I took an empty plate that was already out on the counter and perused the dishes, grabbing a waffle followed by some bacon and eggs.

"I don't know where Theo found these cooking skills, you've never cooked for us like that!" Archer laughed from his spot at the table, breakfast burrito in hand.

"I did!" Theo exclaimed, dishing up the latest batch of eggs.

"You would cook one thing, usually with a weird, unknown ingredient you were experimenting with. I remember the avocado and turmeric waffles!"

"They were nice. This sort of food feast is reserved for Lavender." He batted his eyes at me, and I snorted.

Archer winced dramatically, "Those waffles were toxic, Theo."

Theo put the dish down and glared and made his way over

to the fridge, passing me and letting his hand gently brush my hip. The innocent touch felt indecent, I did my best not to dwell on the sharp lemon and pine invading my senses. It was oddly invigorating.

"They don't sound the best," I admitted with a scrunch of my nose. Theo just smirked at me in response. I turned and headed towards the door, intending to go back up to my room and eat in the new nest, but was stopped by Gage in my way, leaning against the doorframe.

"No more eating in your room."

"Huh?" I was tired, cranky, and didn't want to be confused.

"You need to be around us more, we all discussed it. From now on you'll hang out with us at all times, either in our spaces or we can join you in your space, at least until..."

"Until my heat comes?"

"Yeah," Gage looked away, awkward. I did *not* want to be thinking about heats right now. The idea of me, desperate with need and slick... It was a recipe for disaster. These men were the farthest thing from ideal heat partners—I wanted someone I can trust and these men weren't exactly honest. I would be riding out my heat alone in an unfamiliar place. The thought saddened me. The new nest was beautiful though, and the room had clearly been designed with love and care.

A pang of worry lanced through me, was I borrowing someone else's nest? There were no scents present in the nest, no omega or alphas. It had just smelled clean.

"Okay..." I trailed off.

"Come sit with me, Lavvy girl," Archer called from the table, "I promise, Cereal killer, remember?" He held up his bowl of brightly coloured cereal with a smile. When did he get cereal? He was *just* eating a breakfast burrito.

Alphas apparently had never ending stomachs.

Archer's dark hair was damp and falling into his face, he must have freshly showered. Nodding at him with a small smile I wandered over, plate in hand and popped into the seat next to him. I could smell the pleasure radiating off him at the gesture.

I didn't have the energy to be mad at him anymore. It wasn't going to achieve anything. I could be friendly until I got home, then cut off contact. It would sting like a bitch, but I would get over it eventually. Exhaustion was weighing heavy on me and fighting wasn't worth it.

Gage, satisfied I wasn't going anywhere, wandered over to the pile of food adorning the counter, picking up a plate for himself and going straight for the breakfast sausage. "We should all probably talk about what we're going to do going forward about Lavender."

I stilled, a strip of bacon halfway to my mouth. We were going to talk about this now?

"She seems much better. Do you feel better?" Archer directed his question at me.

"Much. Still groggy and tired, but overall better." I took a bite of bacon, humming at the delectable salty sweet taste. "Has this got sugar on it?" I asked, furrowing my brows.

"I cook the bacon low and slow in maple syrup," Theo told me, proudly.

"It's amazing." I told him, another piece already halfway to my mouth. Omegas were known for their love of sweets, but salty sweet was its own, special category of delicious.

Gage cleared his throat before speaking. "I've been thinking. From here on out, one of us needs to be with Lavender at all times, and not just in the house at the same time, like we've been doing up until now. We need to be in the same room as her at the very least. If she's sick we have to actually touch her."

His tone left no room for discussion, and I just kept eating, happily munching on a chocolate chip pancake. It didn't feel like I was really part of this conversation, so I focused on the food. I hadn't eaten for days before my impromptu snuggle session so I was feeling the hunger.

"Darling?" Gage asked, getting my attention.

"Oh, am I part of this conversation now?" I snarked. I had completely missed the last thing he said while leaning back against the counter, watching over his pack as they ate.

"I asked if there is anything else we ought to know so we aren't surprised again?"

"I don't think so. This situation was a surprise to me. Omegas all differ in their needs,"

"How so?" Archer asked.

"Some require a lot of physical affection, some don't. I honestly believed I didn't need it. Our immune system can get funky if we're isolated, especially if we are getting close to a heat."

Archer leaned over, resting his hand gently on my forehead. "Your fever has gone down a lot, and you seem to be eating okay now." The sweet smell of him so near and his soft touch was hypnotic.

"Yeah, I feel loads better, thank you for looking after me, by the way," I looked over at Gage. He nodded, face expressionless.

While Gage was still sleepy, his packmates were clearly revelling in the urge to care for me. Kane, without saying a word had sliced some apples and strawberries, placed them in a small bowl and put them in front of me before walking away. I gave him a shy, appreciative look, picking up a strawberry and popping it into my mouth with a smile.

"Archer is going to be with you today," Gage informed me around a mouthful of sausage. I resisted making a sausage joke. He was being friendly enough but he was clearly still tired—how much did he actually sleep?

"A new documentary dropped yesterday, the one about the guy that murdered couples hooking up in their cars in abandoned car parks. I'm thinking gummy bears and a marathon?"

"Sounds good," I nodded. I wasn't lying, that sounded like a perfect day to me.

Archer and I got along well, we would often have virtual movie nights watching these documentaries back when I was at the Haven.

I sighed. I wanted to resist Archer, to fight and scream at him but I would be punishing myself as well as him.

"Though, I now think you had ulterior motives for those damn gummy bears," I grumbled.

"Whatever do you mean, Lavvy girl?" he asked his eyes wide in an overly exaggerated, fake innocent expression.

I just snorted. The fucker knew *exactly* what he had done... and I wasn't too angry about it anymore.

Lazy. I felt like a lazy, lethargic lump. Curled up in the nest, Archer on the armchair next to me we had spent all day watching true crime documentaries. Archer was always close, and every few minutes he would find an excuse to touch me, checking my temperature, passing me a snack, or even moving a blanket for me.

We had just finished an episode and were waiting for a new one to load when he spoke.

"Do you really hate me?"

Such a simple question for such a complex answer.

"Ultimately I don't, and I think you know that," I said, fiddling with the duvet cover, unable to meet his eyes. I didn't have it in me to hash out all the details at that point.

His only answer was to grin and turn back to the TV.

CHAPTER EIGHTEEN

Kane

I was pissed. I knew it was irrational, and I did my best to hide it from the others, but I could hardly restrain the urge to throttle Gage.

All three of those fuckers had been by Lavender's side the last few days while her temperature subsided. Yes, I was also there, but it was different. *I* wasn't spoken for. Fuck it, if I wanted to pursue Lavender, I could. There was nothing stopping me, unlike the others who were meant for my sister.

The last time I had seen Lavender she had been sitting up in the nest, bowl of soup in hand. The nest that was *meant* to belong to my sister. I didn't know what the fuck possessed me, telling the others to put her in here, I just couldn't watch her suffer. She looked a lot better. The colour had returned to her face, and she looked a lot more alert. I was shocked that I didn't mind the sight of her in the room that was meant to be Juniper's and somehow that only fueled my rage further. Lavender had been sick, and I know Juniper would have had my nuts for tennis balls if she knew I let an omega suffer needlessly.

I would be lying to myself if I told myself the only reason I did it was because I knew my sister would judge me. The sight of Lavender so sick hurt me so intensely. I was only human, and an alpha at that. I was raised with omegas, and I hated that I didn't realise that there was something that she needed. When she joined us all for breakfast a few days prior my body had moved on auto pilot, cutting up a bowl of fruit and handing it to her before I could even think about it.

She was getting familiar with the others though, and it was irritating me. It was obvious and I couldn't hide it, so when it was my turn to bring her some food, she called me out on it.

I put the food on her bedside table, not meeting her eye. She had just showered, and was sitting on the bed having stopped sleeping in the nest a day or two ago, wearing fresh pyjamas. Her damp hair was making the pyjama top ever so slightly damp.

"You're pissed." she observed. "Why are you pissed?"

"I'm not," I said as I collected the empty plate from the other side of the bed. The movement was a little too forceful and the plate clattered loudly.

"Kane, you've been stomping around the last twenty-four hours like someone tinkled in your cereal. And you won't look me in the eye."

I turned to leave, not bothering to reply when I heard her rustling behind me, her feet slapping on the floor as she came up to me with a surprising speed. Her small hand grabbed my bicep and my skin felt electrified where she touched it.

"Don't." I growled.

"Tell me," she frowned. "What have I done to upset you?"

"Why can't you just leave things be?" I asked.

"I have been told I'm rather stubborn," she said, looking up at me. This close she seemed so small, her head hardly reached the top of my chest and she had to really crane her neck to get a good look at me this close.

I took a deep breath. Wasn't Gage always telling me I should talk about my feelings more, let people know what I think?

"You need to stop mooning over the others," I growled. "They're not yours."

Lavender pulled back, her forehead wrinkling in confusion. "I know they're not mine," she said. "*You* kidnapped *me*, remember? It's not like I'm a willing participant in this," she waved her hand vaguely around the room, "mess of a situation."

I huffed in frustration, looking away. "You're having cuddles with a pack of alphas that aren't yours. They belong to someone else."

"What do you mean?" Her expression faltered, unease spreading across her face. "And if you think I wanted to play snuggle bug with them then you are even denser than I thought. You saw how sick I was. My hands were kind of tied, buddy."

"They already have an omega," I snarled.

"What?" Lavender's jaw dropped and her eyes searched my face. "Who?" she asked, her mouth opening and closing several times, like she wanted to say more, but couldn't find the words. The air filled with a slightly burnt scent, like caramel that had been cooked too long. She was either upset or pissed, but I didn't know her well enough to tell which.

"Is it important?" I growled. "Stop charming alphas that don't belong to you."

"I-I'm sorry," she stuttered. "I didn't mean to, I was just

being friendly given the less than ideal situation we were in—none of you ever mentioned another omega. I want to go home, I'm not looking to stay here."

"I also want that, but until this nightmare is over, don't get too close to them. Physically you don't have a choice but you don't have to be so goddamn friendly with them," I said, turning to storm out of the room while Lavender tried to find her words again.

I hadn't taken three steps before something soft hit the back of my head and a tiny, pissed off omega was stomping up to me.

"Hold up—you giant dick. You're going to have to explain that a little more, because if you assholes have *another* omega stashed around here somewhere, I should know!" She glared at me.

It seemed she found her words.

"I don't have to explain anything to you," I growled. "You're a captive here, learn your fucking place!" I said, taking several long strides so I was towering over her.

She didn't even flinch. She was *pissed*. It would have been cute if I wasn't so mad myself. Up close my nose was assaulted with her sweet vanilla and lavender scent. *Why did she have to smell so good? Why couldn't we have been stuck with an omega who smelled like onions, or motor oil?*

"Oh trust me, I know my place, and it's nowhere near this shit show. You keep talking about the others like you're not part of the pack, what's your damage?"

"I'm *not* part of their pack. My sister is their omega." I snarled. Why was she so fucking inquisitive? I was tempted to throw her into the closet and lock it to stop her following me, but that would be a twat move.

"Your sister?" she asked, running her hand through her hair, unease filling her voice.

I couldn't take it: the burnt sugar, her questioning face. I didn't have it in me to explain how I failed Juniper, how I kept fucking up at every turn.

So I just turned and left the dumbstruck omega standing in the middle of the room that was meant for my sister.

This time she didn't follow me.

CHAPTER NINETEEN
Lavender

The fucking nerve of that man. He had the audacity to kidnap me, then complain I was being too friendly with my kidnappers? The stupid jerk needed a reality check. Growling with anger I threw a pillow across the room in the general direction of the door, ignoring the fact he was long gone.

They had an omega? Where on earth was she? This nest was clearly intended for an omega, I was obviously the first one in it—there wasn't even a trace of another omega.

I needed answers, and not the answers a grumpy, overly stoic Kane would give me. That man's panties were so far up his butt crack he was forever pissed at the world. I knew who my best shot at getting answers was, so poking my head out of my door to ensure the grump was gone, I padded down the hallway, following my nose.

Archer's room was the same as I had seen in all his video calls: the cool, muted greys and minimal furniture covered by several computers in various states of repair. The curtains were open and the room well lit, so it didn't seem overwhelming. The scent of sweet sugar and gummy bears was thick in the air. A few weeks ago, I would have been obsessed with such a scent. Now it was a reminder of all the hurt feelings and pain he had caused.

The alpha I was looking for was sitting at his desk, a screwdriver in hand as he took some poor lump of technology apart. I hadn't bothered to knock when I entered the room, opting to simply storm in.

"Do you have an omega?" I spoke before he even had a chance to open his mouth.

He gaped at me, clearly confused. "W-what?"

"Kane just got really pissy at me and called me a terrible person for letting all you guys touch me when you already have an omega! Oh my word, I know you're not exactly morally perfect—hell *kidnapping*—but if you have another poor omega around here and didn't think to tell me, I will throttle you Archer!"

Archer stood up, his project forgotten as he moved toward where I stood in the middle of the room, hands on my hips. "No, we don't have an omega. It's—I don't know how to explain it, but trust me, we are in no way committed to an omega."

"Start from the beginning, buddy," I growled.

"I, uh. Let me call Gage. He's pack lead, if I'm going to talk about this, I gotta at least do it with his approval."

Why did he need to call him? Gage would likely get pissed at me. Archer was my best bet to get answers because he was still feeling sad over me being rightfully pissed at him. I just stood there, quietly seething as Archer practically ran back over to his desk, grabbing his phone and shooting off a message.

The phone pinged with a response mere moments later. "Gage is on his way... uh, why don't you sit down?"

There weren't many choices, the best chair or his neatly made bed. I opted to sit on the edge of the bed. It looked fairly comfortable, but I wasn't about to go and ask for a snuggle session, at least not until I had answers.

Footsteps in the hallway alerted me to someone's presence. Gage strode right in, not bothering to knock. His usual leathery smell was muted by motor oil, which made sense as he was covered in the stuff. Had he been working on a car? His shirt had several dark, greasy stains and even his face and hands had smaller marks on them.

If I wasn't so pissed, I probably would have swooned at the big dirty man.

"Arch, what on earth is goin—" Gage cut off when he noticed me sitting on the edge of Archer's bed, arms crossed.

"Kane's been running his mouth," Archer said simply, looking between me and Gage.

Gage sighed. "What did he say?" he directed the question at me. He looked...defeated? Like all the wind had been taken out of his sails. The alpha was clearly exhausted.

"He told me that you already have an omega, that I was wrong for letting you near me. Like I wanted to have these stupid omega needs that meant I had to get cuddly with my captors!" I snarled, but there was no heat in it.

"We need to explain, Gage. We can't just let her be confused over this. It's not fair, especially if she's going to be here for a few weeks."

"Fine." Gage strode over to the desk, leaning against it with his arms crossed. "What do you want to know?"

"Everything? Do you have another omega stashed around

here somewhere, and if not, why does Kane have a stick up his ass?"

"Kane is... it's hard to explain but—"

"He's living in a lala land of his own creation but we care for him and don't want to completely destroy what's left of his fragile emotions?" Archer helpfully finished Gage's sentence, smirking at his leader.

"I—yeah, that works," Gage sighed. "Kane lost his sister several years ago to trafficking."

Omega trafficking was a brutal and nasty industry. I instantly felt sympathy for Kane, but I still considered him a massive butthead.

"Something like what happened to Sage," Archer commented.

"Sage?" Gage asked, looking between us.

"A friend of mine. She was courting a pack when she was kidnapped by some folks. Kept in a cell and almost hurt pretty badly. She escaped and sought sanctuary at my Haven. I stayed with her and showed her around until her pack came for her."

"I think I heard about that, it was pretty big news. If memory serves, Lex Bove was responsible for that mess."

I nodded, that name sounded familiar.

Gage took another deep breath. "But to answer your question, no, we do not have an omega. We aren't committed to anyone, but Kane imagines that had things not gone wrong, we would have ended up with Juniper."

"She had a crush on Gage, and Kane knew it," Archer admitted.

Gage snorted. "I think it was Theo actually, no one could resist someone who nurses sick kittens back to health."

There *was* something stupidly hot about a man who cared about animals.

"But you have a nest in your house, why would you have that if you didn't have an omega?"

"We hoped that one day we would have an omega, and in the meantime it was a comfort to Kane," Gage admitted.

"But please, Lavender, just ignore Kane getting his panties in a twist," Archer said. "He'll get over it. How are you feeling?"

"Not great, but a lot less shitty than a few days ago... uh, thank you for that, by the way."

Why was it so awkward to thank someone for cuddling you?

"If you need anything, please talk to us," Gage said.

"I need Kane to take a long walk off a short pier, do you feel like helping with that?" I asked with a smirk. Archer laughed loudly and Gage just rolled his eyes.

"I miss peace and quiet," he grumbled.

"Not my fault you kidnapped me!" I laughed, getting up with a stretch. Exhaustion was creeping up on me, and I needed to sleep or I would be impossibly cranky.

CHAPTER TWENTY
Lavender

I was about to get up and go retrieve my comfy projectile when an intense cramp rippled through my midsection, making me bend at the waist. Clutching my stomach, I groaned in pain.

Shit. It's happening.

I had noticed the warning cramps, but I had pointedly ignored them, as if pretending they didn't exist would stop my heat from ever coming in the first place. The idea of a heat without my nest or familiar toys to get me through wasn't pleasant at all.

It's not like I could go wandering up to any of these alphas and ask them to procure me sex toys, they would look at me like I had grown three heads. Well Theo might cackle like a madman then get me some…

I shook that idea out of my head. I would have to make do by myself. It wasn't going to be fun, and my heart could literally give out, but there wasn't much more I could do.

Well, you could always go the old fashioned way and use some alpha dick. A small voice in the back of my head invaded my thoughts. I quickly shoved that down. I wasn't that desperate. Yet.

Everything ached. My bones felt sore, my joints stiff and I could not, for the life of me, stop sweating. One second I felt boiling hot, I threw off my blankets and starfished on the bed. Then the next I was freezing, and nesting down in the blankets turning myself into a toasty burrito.

I didn't know how much time had passed. I couldn't focus on anything to do with my surroundings. For all I knew, an army of people could have trampled their way through my room and I wouldn't have known.

Deep, gut wrenching cramps came and went, increasing in intensity every time. My eyelids were heavy. I was so goddamned exhausted. Every time I started to drift into the peaceful oblivion sleep offered, another cramp ripped through my body, and sleep would be long forgotten.

It could have been hours, or it could have been days. All I knew was pain and misery. My skin felt electrified, but not in a sexy way. It itched and ached at the same time.

Large, powerful hands gripped my forearms and hauled me up in a gentle manoeuvre. I felt my body moving, but didn't bother opening my eyes.

"Come on, little nuisance, you need to eat," the soft voice muttered. The rim of a water bottle touched my lips and I whined. I didn't want water, I wanted knots! The buttery leather smell filling the air could only be an alpha, so why were they trying to give me water? I didn't need water.

"Omega!" The voice growled, commanding. Powerless to deny an alpha I opened my mouth and drank, but I wasn't fucking happy about it. Somewhere in the recesses of my mind I realised that it was Kane holding me. I chalked it up to my brain being messed up thanks to the heat. There was no way he was the one handling me gently.

"Good girl," he rumbled, taking the water away and bringing a sandwich up to my lips. I tried to turn and face him. I could convince him to knot me. I'm sure I could, if I tried hard enough. What alpha could resist an omega in heat?

Kane. That's who. With one arm banded around my waist keeping me in place with my back against my chest he slowly fed me bites of sandwich, ignoring me whenever I grumbled.

Halfway through the sandwich I was sick of it. I hurt and he was doing nothing to help.

"Just knot me, goddamnit!" I growled.

Kane's only response was to chuckle. Chuckle! Even that low vibrating sound in my ear made another rush of slick leak between my legs.

"Sorry, nuisance. No knots for you today, now eat your sandwich."

"You're my least favourite, you know." I growled, batting his hand away and the offending food.

"Too bad. Now are you going to eat or do I need to restrain your hands and force you?"

"You wouldn't dare."

"I kidnapped you."

"I'll gouge your eyes out with a rusty nail," I snarled.

That elicited a large belly laugh from Kane. "Oh, I would, but let's save the gouging for when you're feeling better."

"I won't forget," I grumbled, taking a bite of the sandwich with a frown.

"It's a date."

I finished the sandwich. Even in my hazy state I knew the asshole would restrain me further. After the last bite he leaned over to the bedside, grabbing something. The nest was dark so I couldn't see what. The shifting movement made me slide back even closer to him. I could feel his cock, hard as steel against my ass.

Yes please.

"*Kane,*" I whined, rubbing my ass against him. He growled in response, pulling me closer to him to stop my movements.

I needed friction, some relief. My hand flew to my sleep shorts, sliding in easily, diving straight for my clit. *Fuck I'm slick, I need a knot.*

If he wasn't going to help me I would just have to take matters into my own hands.

Circling my clit, I groaned—I needed more, but this would have to do.

"Lavender!" Kane growled, yanking my wrist away and ignoring my pained whine at the loss. *Stupid butthead asshole.*

"No!" I cried.

"Take these painkillers," he growled. He was growling a lot. I liked it. Maybe he could growl while stretching me on his knot...

I tried tugging my hand back, but Kane grumbled. "Stop trying to touch yourself, let me take care of you *then* you can do that alone or I'll have to restrain you," he warned with a pained sigh.

Restraints? That could be fun!

Opening my mouth to beg again. He popped the tablet in and brought the bottle back to my mouth before I could say a word, shocking me into swallowing before my brain could catch up. Asshole.

"What was that?" I asked, my speech slurred.

"The doc recommended it. It'll help you sleep and won't hurt your kidneys," Kane spoke gently.

I didn't want to sleep! What I wanted was a knot. Scratching at his arm holding me, I tossed and turned in his grip, but his arm remained immovably in place.

"No," I whimpered pathetically. "Please."

"Sorry, no can do." I closed my eyes. Despite the darkness, my eyes stung from trying to keep them open so I gave into the urge to close them and slumped back against the hard chest of Kane. "That's better," he praised. His hand reaching up and gently running through my hair.

I wanted to be knotted repeatedly in every position, but I would accept head scratches. The effect was immediate. I relaxed even further, to the point I was almost boneless. A slight rumble on my back lulled me into a peaceful state.

Kane was purring. For me.

"I thought you hated me?" My words were slurred.

"Not you, little nuisance. Just the situation." His hand never let up the scratching of my scalp. That combined with the purr and the medication had a potent and sedating effect.

"You're not terrible," I admitted, sleepily. "Maybe I won't attack you with a rusty spoon."

"I thought you were planning to use a rusty nail?"

"Spoons are better for eye gouging," I informed him.

"Good to know." There was a smile in his voice. I wanted to open my mouth to speak, but my body had other ideas. Heavy and exhausted, I finally drifted into sleep.

When I woke up, Kane was long gone. Only the faint smell of leather remained on my sheets. I had a killer headache and I needed a shower, but the desperate need for a knot had ebbed. The nest stank of arousal and slick. Washing the bedding would be a priority, as soon as I showered and ate.

Turning on the shower, I looked around the bathroom for a moment before deciding I didn't have the energy to stand in the water, opting for a bath instead. Filling it to the brim with bubbles and salts I sank into the water, moaning in delight at the warm sensation on my tired, crampy muscles.

Leaning back I took a deep breath and relaxed, trying my best to let my racing mind rest. I got through the heat with no knots. Thank god. The guys had kept their distance from me. All except Kane.

I sat up, remembering that Kane of all people had been in my nest. While I was in heat. And didn't touch me in that way once. Was he a eunuch? No alpha in their right mind could resist the smell of an omega in heat. It was basic alpha and omega biology. Yet... he had fed me, given me painkillers.

The rest of the heat was a little fuzzy after that. I didn't remember being in too much pain. He must have given me some damn good drugs.

My hand absentmindedly went to my forehead, to my hairline. He had given me head scratches and purred. What sort of alternate reality was I living in? The way he had handled me was downright caring.

"Lavender?" a concerned voice called out from my room.

"In the bath!" I called back.

"Your heat broke then?" The voice got closer to the door. Kane.

"Yeah, I just needed to get clean. I felt icky," I said, talking before I thought.

Kane chuckled. "I imagine. There's a chicken Caesar wrap on the bedside table for you, some fresh water and more painkillers if you want them."

He had really thought of everything. Why was he taking care of me so much? He didn't have to.

"Thank you."

He didn't respond but I heard footsteps as he retreated.

After the water had gone cold, I pulled the plug and wrapped myself in one of the new fluffy towels that had appeared in my room.

Padding back into my room I stilled for a moment when I noticed something was different with my nest.

It was bare. Someone had stripped all the sheets and blankets off, like I had been planning to. The windows were opened, letting the fresh air in.

Kane. He must have taken them to launder.

This kindness was making my head spin.

CHAPTER TWENTY-ONE
Lavender

Archer's eyes had lingered on me when he came into my new room, bottle of water in hand for me. "Are you okay?" He had seen the aftermath of solo heats before. They were brutal, but as I stretched lazily, even I had to admit, those drugs Kane had given me did wonders and I was feeling semi human already. I would have to ask where he got them.

Currently I was occupied with rummaging through the mountain of pillows and comforters that had appeared just before my heat started, courtesy of the guys and deciding which items would be included in my new nest. Once I had placed several comforters, I had clambered in with the curtains open so Archer could pass me pillows to see if I wanted them inside. Some of them were rougher in texture, so I quickly discarded them. Some were velvety soft, or soft *and* fluffy, those were the ones I picked to line it, making it an amazing, comfortable cloud.

"This is looking mighty fine Lavvy girl, I'm sorry we didn't have time to do this before your heat hit." Archer complimented me as I single mindedly focused on my bed. Every alpha knew that omegas loved to build nests, for comfort, for heats, for family. They were our safe space. Our sanctuary. I was pleased with this one. I stacked the pillows up to make several little walls, wrapped blankets into various shapes, creating a U shape dent inside. The perfect size for a small omega to sink into. Once the pillows were plumped just so I sank into them, making a little squeak of happiness.

Archer moved the TV so it was at the end of the bed, and pulled an armchair next to the it. This way he was close to me, but wasn't directly invading my space. He flicked on the TV, finding the documentary he'd mentioned earlier and starting it. We fell into a comfortable silence, enjoying the show. Archer lent back on the armchair, placing his sock covered feet on the corner of the nest, looking over to me to see if I reacted negatively. There was zero change. My eyes remained trained on the screen so he laid back, feet up and let himself enjoy the show.

We were three episodes deep when he felt his phone vibrate. Picking it up he rolled his eyes at the message before turning to me.

"Food time, Lavvy girl. You coming with?"

"I suppose I should move," I agreed, sitting up and smiling lazily at Archer.

Standing, I extracted myself from the nest. I was sad to be leaving it, I wanted to remain cuddled up in the blankets.

"Lead the way," I mumbled sleepily.

Archer procured a small feast consisting of fresh fruit he found already cut up and prepped for him, some cheeses, cookies and chocolate, piling them into various bowls on a tray. I sat on a stool at the counter, picking bites to eat while he dished and reheated the pasta Theo had made.

"I never did ask how you met your pack members," I said between bites of fruit. "I was too nervous to ask when we were video chatting."

"We all grew up together. Gage, Theo and I were inseparable from a young age, even though Theo is a few years younger than us. Kane is a few years older but our families all run in the same circles, so he had always been in our lives as well." He didn't look at me as he spoke, I didn't know if I could pry without causing issues. We were at a nice level of amiability and I didn't want to do anything that would rock the boat.

Cracking open a soda, I chugged half the can without taking a breath. Archer, noticing my thirst, went back to the fridge, returning with a bottle of water and handing it to me. I warmed at the gesture. Despite being an omega I wasn't used to someone being so attuned to my needs, anticipating them. I could feel myself starting to enjoy it. Thrive off it. I would be home soon, but part of me wanted to enjoy the experience while it lasted. This was part of the allure of packs, they protected and provided—the Haven would help me find that —eventually. Part of me kept forgetting that I was technically there as a captive. The last few days had felt so relaxed and easy. I could see myself falling into a routine with these men, and that was dangerous.

"I'm so full," I groaned, stretching.

"C'mon, we've got another six episodes to get through today."

"You think we can handle another six episodes today?"

"Ye of little faith."

"You have a binge watching problem," I laughed.

"A binge watching problem you gave me. It all started with that documentary with the cops trying to frame that guy for murder. I was meant to watch one episode. One. We have a huge job right now, and I needed to get some sleep. I started watching and next thing I know, the sun is coming up and I have to work on zero hours sleep." I laughed, shaking my head. Archer grinned back at me, his eyes lighting up as he looked me over.

My eyes travelled over his torso, roaming over his well-defined arms and strong jawline. I crossed my legs to hide any errant perfume leaking out. If Archer could sense my reaction, he didn't show it.

"Worth it though, am I right?" I asked as I nibbled on a slice of apple. Archer nodded, grinning as he grabbed a few snacks and jerked his head in the direction of the exit.

"Let's take these for the road. We are wasting valuable watching time!" he declared, piling all his goodies into one hand, grabbing my hand with the other and dragging me upstairs.

CHAPTER TWENTY-TWO
Theo

Gage had been so grumpy lately. He clearly needed to get laid, but when I offered he brushed me off with some nonsense about how we all need to keep our minds off our dicks while we had an omega in the house.

Personally, I thought this was the perfect time to be playing with our dicks. But Gage was the boss. So I had been putting up with him being surly, Kane being Kane, and Archer hogging Lavender. It wasn't fair.

Lucky for me, fate intervened.

Minding my own business, I was laying in the den on one of the tacky leather couches. I hated leather couches, they just felt wrong on my skin, Archer had bought these couches so I put up with them. Controller in my hand, I was playing a mindless zombie shooter game. My personal mission was differing somewhat from what the game developers probably intended. I didn't give a fuck about protecting the people from the zombies—let them get their brains chomped on—but the random German shepherd I'd found? He needed protecting at all costs. The people could get fucked.

There was a film I had watched ages ago with Kane one evening where the main character was an agent badass or some shit, and the bad guys killed his dog, so he went and basically nuked their asses in many magnificent, glorious ways. That shit was the most relatable for me. I could get behind that a hundred percent.

Dogs weren't even my favourite. I was a cat guy through and through, and Gage said we could get pets once we settled down, but fuck knows when that would be. I wanted something big, like a Maine coon. I loved those big fluffy bastards.

My mind drifted to the omega upstairs, currently hanging out with Archer. What kind of pet would she want? I could picture her with a rabbit, a cute little floppy eared bunny, carrying him around or just relaxing in the garden with him. Did the Haven even allow pets?

Kane lumbered into the room. He looked like shit, god knows when he last slept. Our lives were stuck in a weird holding pattern, just waiting for new information.

"Stop playing, we have a lead."

"I'll get my gear!" I grinned, throwing the controller across the sofa. Lightly bullying someone for information would definitely liven up my day.

"We need Archer to hack a cell phone on the move, so you're here with Lavender."

Even better!

"Yes!" I exclaimed gleefully. Standing from the sofa with a stretch. "You need anything from me?"

"No, just Archer."

"I'll send him your way!"

Bounding from the room, I took the steps two at a time,

almost gleeful at the prospect that my day had just become so much more exciting.

I didn't bother to knock, if Archer was doing something with the omega that he shouldn't be, I wanted a front row seat...for totally innocent reasons of course.

Unfortunately, nothing indecent was happening. Archer was slouched in the armchair, eyes on the screen. Lavender was curled up in a ball in her little nest. She had piled her hair haphazardly atop her head in a bun, and it was falling out in every direction. She was clutching a pillow to her in a sleepy manner. It looked fucking comfortable, perfect for snuggles and fucking.

Then again, every time I saw her nest I had been overcome with the thought of how it would feel to be in that warm, soft, cuddly space.

At my entrance they both turned to me, Lavender sitting up. I couldn't help but grin at the pyjama set she was wearing. The lilac T-shirt and short set was covered in little coffee mugs and said *thank a latte* over the breast pocket. It was adorable.

"Everything okay?" Archer asked with a frown.

"Yep, I'm just here to take over. Daddy needs you." Archer didn't answer, looking at me like he was trying to process.

Has he had any sleep of late?

He was acting like he was the one who was recently concussed, even though I was the one who had that esteemed honour. I sighed dramatically. "Work calls, you're needed to either track a cell phone or break into a database on the go. I honestly forget which. Either way you're going out with the others, which leaves *me*," I turned with a smirk to Lavender who was giving me a soft, sleepy smile, "with our little Lavender."

"Are you sure?" Archer's brow was raised.

"We won't get into too much trouble, I promise! Now chop chop, you know our bossy man doesn't like waiting."

Instead of waiting for a reply from Archer, I just strode over to the bed and flung myself onto it. Fuck laying in that uncomfortable looking armchair. I much preferred the bed/nest hybrid and a sweet, floral smelling omega nearby.

It was like I had jumped onto a freaking cloud. No bed had the right to be this squishy and soft. It was pure luxury and I didn't want to leave. Every inch of the nest was heavily coated in sweet lavender and vanilla.

Lavender let out a cute little yip of surprise and scuttled backwards a little to make room for my invasion. If she wasn't so adorable and cute I would be calling her a spoilsport.

"You'll be fine with me, won't you?" I asked her, batting my eyelashes. I probably looked daft, but I didn't care, because it made her giggle.

"I can talk to Gage about staying," Archer told her, the crease between his eyebrows was going to become permanent if he didn't stop frowning so much.

"We'll be okay," Lavender assured him in a soft voice. Even her voice was pretty and delicate. I considered asking her to give me head scratches and just talk to me in that melodic and calm voice until I fell asleep. But I didn't want to scare her away. Yet.

I hadn't slept on my own in a long time. Not since the accident that killed a considerable amount of my brain cells. The nightmares were just too vicious. Gage was usually by my side at night, but I would happily take a sleepy floral little omega.

"I'll be back before you know it," Archer reassured her. Did he think she wasn't safe with me? Or did he assume he was her favourite and she would just wait for his return. Fuck that. *I* wanted to be the favourite. The cogs in my brain started turning, but I kept quiet until Archer was gone.

"How's your day going, sweet Lavender?" I asked with a smile. She looked down at me with a soft gaze, I liked it.

"I'm having an okay day, lots of good TV about serial killers and cults."

"I'm down to watch something about cults!" I said enthusiastically. "I could totally see myself liking cults."

"As the topic of a documentary, or as an actual entity?"

I scratched my chin, pretending to be deep in thought. "I think I would make a good cult leader. Heck, even a good cult follower. I'm easy to win over."

She gave an adorable little snort. "I could see it, but you would suck at leading a cult if you had to interact with people too much. Cult members aren't always the sharpest tools in the shed, do you really think you could put up with that day in and day out?"

"Oh god no, I would be wanting to throw people off a cliff far too fast."

"I agree, even though I don't have that much tolerance. Also I'm sure there's already a cult with death by cliff. You would be terribly unoriginal."

"Well that's just not acceptable, I'll have to go back to the drawing board."

"I'm sure you'll come up with something," Lavender chuckled, leaning over to grab her water bottle. The movement made her shirt ride up, exposing the smooth expanse of her stomach. Just an inch more and I would have been blessed with some delectable under-boob.

"So..." I started, my voice sing-song. "How would you like to do something a little more fun?"

She turned to me, a quizzical look on her face. "I'm not opposed to it, but I feel like this may be a slippery slope. What do you consider fun?"

"That would be telling!" I jumped off the bed, striding over to the wardrobe. I grabbed jeans and a large oversized hoodie belonging to Gage. There were so many items of our clothing in her wardrobe, and it gave my alpha a sense of joy. "Put these on! We are going outside."

Lavender sat up straighter, far more alert than she had been second ago. "Outside?" she asked.

Now that I thought about it, she hadn't actually left the house once since we'd brought her here.

"Yep, outside. I need to change into something more suitable. Meet me in the kitchen in ten." she nodded. Her face was brighter than before. She was excited. Her scent was sweeter, a surefire sign she was happy.

I was easily going to be the favourite.

She was downstairs before me, sitting at the kitchen island with a soda in hand. As soon as I entered the kitchen she beamed at me.

"You seem excited," I observed playfully.

"It's been a while since I've been outside." She admitted.

"Nature lover?"

"Not usually, but I do like to go out occasionally, touch some grass. Be one with the trees. It's good for balance, or something like that," she smirked at me.

Oh, sweet girl. What I had planned was far from balanced. "That's all good, but sometimes, you gotta get that rage out!"

"Rage?" Her eyebrow quirked up. "I suppose so, everyone needs an outlet."

"What's yours?" I asked, plucking the soda out of her hand and taking a large sip. She glared at me, but there was no heat in it. She rarely finished a full can—so I was actually helping her.

"Usually some kind of exercise class."

I grimaced. That wasn't anywhere near good enough!

I nodded at her to follow me out the back door. She did without a word, and we made our way down the gravel path for five minutes to the large grey, unassuming garage that served as my fun room.

"So...what are we doing?" she asked, her voice wavering a little as she looked around. The area did look a little creepy, like I was taking her to my lair, which I kind of was—but in a good way?

"I'm showing you how I relieve stress."

"That sounds...dirty." Her nose scrunched as she spoke and I couldn't help but smile.

"If only! Nah, this is a whole other kind of physical." I opened the garage door and Lavender gaped at the room in front of her.

"Uh... What is this?"

The room probably looked insane to those who didn't know what it was. Gage had the idea to build me a rage room last year when my mood swings got out of hand and lifting weights and running just wasn't enough of an outlet. There were smashed plates, several kitchen appliances in various states of destruction and even a few bits of household furniture.

Lavender took a few tentative steps into the space, passing me with a waft of sweet vanilla and lavender that made my mouth water. Fuck, I bet she tasted amazing.

"Wait, is this a rage room?" She spun around to look at me, unbridled glee in her voice. "I've heard about these! A few of the girls wanted one at the Haven!"

Was the idea of a little violence exciting her? Instant boner. Where the fuck had this dream omega come from?

I sauntered into the room, grabbing a sledgehammer off the floor and holding it out to her, that was confirmation enough that her assumption about the room was correct.

"You're giving me a weapon?" she asked, incredulously looking between the sledgehammer and me.

"I won't let you get the drop on me again, beautiful." I moved so I was mere inches away from her. "Even if that little stunt was the hottest thing I've ever experienced."

"I still feel bad about that." Her nose crinkled as she spoke.

"Don't you dare." My voice was firm, and I ensured there wasn't even a hint of playfulness. "Now, let's put your goggles on, and what do you want to smash up first?" I held out the sledgehammer, nodding at her to take it.

"The microwave?" she asked tentatively, reaching out and grasping the wooden handle. Her teeth worried her bottom lip, and I wanted to release it with my own teeth.

"Perfect."

She passed the sledgehammer between her hands, acclimating to the weight of it, looking around she took in all the potential smashing targets before settling on the microwave.

Walking over to the side table, I picked up two pairs of goggles, sliding a pair on myself and walking over to Lavender. She held out her hand to take them off me, but I ignored her, wanting a moment to get close and take a sweet lungful of her scent. So I walked up close to her and placed them gently on her face while she looked at me with that same small smile.

Her large sweatshirt covered her torso perfectly and she was wearing heavy boots, so with the goggles she was good to go. I wanted her to have a good way to vent her frustration, but not if she got hurt. I couldn't jeopardise my status as up-and-coming favourite by risking her getting hurt.

"You look good," I chuckled lightly. The blush that rose in her cheeks pleased me.

"Thank you...so do I just...hit things?"

"Yep." I gently turned her around so she was facing the microwave she had her eyes on. "Just go smash. Imagine it's Kane's face."

Lavender's snort was adorable. "Okay."

Her hands tightened around her weapon as she assessed her soon to be victim. The bright red microwave had been in our kitchen until one day the screen stopped working. Any appliances with even minor faults ended up in this room.

With a grunt Lavender lifted the sledgehammer. It was a weighty tool, and just swinging it would have taken her a good amount of strength. Watching her, I tried not to laugh. She closed her eyes and scrunched her nose as she swung the hammer down, like she didn't want to see the result. It landed on the top of the microwave with a deep thudding noise, but it hardly made a dent in the metal body of the appliance.

Lavender opened her eyes. Her posture relaxing, shoulders sagging as she took in the lack of destruction.

"Is that all?" she asked with a little frown, her bottom lip protruding in a pout. I wanted to bite it.

"Again. Harder," I commanded.

"Bossy," Lavender laughed.

I wanted *her* to boss *me* around. She could command me to do anything she wanted as long as she made me cum my fucking brains out as she did. Lifting the sledgehammer again, she squared her shoulders, her face set in a look of determination.

This time the impact was much harder, and the glass of the microwave door shattered.

"Did you see that!" Lavender cried out, looking between me and her destruction as she jumped up and down a few times with excitement. I grinned at her.

"Fun, isn't it?" I leaned back against the far wall, and made a gesture for her to carry on before crossing my arms and settling in to watch the show. "Have fun."

Lavender's eyes lit up and she looked around the room. "Is everything fair game?" she asked, her gaze hungry.

"Yes. Anything you want." Including me, but I didn't say that.

With permission, she threw herself into the fun of the carnage. Several quick, violent hits to the microwave was followed by the quick and brutal destruction of an old bedside table, shards of wood flying everywhere. I would have to check her for splinters later, not that I was complaining in the slightest.

Lavender was fucking stunning. She panted deeply as she whipped around the room, grunting with each blow she delivered. Her wild hair was falling from its bun, framing her cheeks. Her face was hungry with the feeling—one I knew well. Destruction was heady and addictive. I revelled in it, and seeing Lavender throw herself into it was downright pornographic.

It didn't matter that she was covered head to toe in baggy clothes, no female had ever made me this hard. The smallest actions from her lit me on fire. Soft and warm one moment, fire and heat the next. I wanted to pin her down and show her what I could do to her, but I also wanted her to take whatever she wanted from me. For her, I would be a good boy.

I rarely even behaved for Gage. That was the power she had on me. She had my balls and my brain in a vise-grip, and she didn't even realise it. Lavender was a sweet little flower that needed both protecting and ruining.

If it was only up to me, she would be ours.

Her little smashing rampage must have only lasted three minutes but when she had eviscerated the bedside table she stood in the middle of the room, leaving her weapon discarded on the floor, looking at me with wide eyes full of amazement as she panted deeply.

Vanilla and lavender bloomed in the air, more saccharine than usual. Resisting the urge to groan I took a deep breath. Fucking delicious.

"That is so fun!" She strode over to me and wrapped her arms around my waist. Pulling me into her so her head was just under my chin, every sweet curve of her body pressed up against mine.

The last thing I was expecting was a hug, but I wasn't going to complain. I quite liked having her in my arms.

She stiffened for a second, no doubt realising that I was supporting a monster boner, which was entirely her fault, but she relaxed only a fraction of a second later. Interesting.

"I needed this," she admitted, looking up at me with a grin. "How much time do you spend in here?"

Weaving an arm around her shoulder I pulled her closer, refusing to let her break the hug. "It depends on the day. If I've been struggling, then a fair bit. I'm pretty sure I've destroyed half of the appliances thrown away in this town. A washing machine is good fun to smash as well, I'll have to get you one."

Her eyes lit up and her scent intensified at the prospect of doing this again. Fuck, she really was perfect for me.

"If any of the pack members are pissing you off or you just want to come here for fun, just ask. I'll make it happen."

"Thank you," she said softly, finally breaking the intense

eye contact. I wanted to whine at the loss as she gently pulled away, stepping back a few inches. She had felt so right in my arms, and I wanted her back.

"They seem like good packmates... when they're not kidnapping omegas."

"They are, they felt so bad after everything happened they built this place for me."

"What exactly happened? If you don't mind me asking," she rushed the last part, her voice wobbling.

I hardly spoke about it with the others, but with Lavender it felt easier, almost natural.

"I almost drowned. Fuck, I guess you could say I *did* drown."

Lavender gasped, a frown marring her features. "What do you mean?"

"My heart stopped, I wasn't breathing, so pretty dead. We were on a job, and it went belly up. The guy we were trying to find had some information we needed. I met them as a potential drug dealer, it was an easy in. They realised I wasn't who I said I was so they knocked me out with a brick and threw me in a lake. By the time Kane got to me and pulled me out of the water, it had been five minutes."

I let out a shaky breath. "Things... weren't the same for a while after that. Everything felt so unbalanced. Before I had been so relaxed and easy going. Now I'm always on edge, quick to anger. I got into loads of fights with my pack. If it hadn't been for the accident they would have thrown me on my ass for how I behaved, but because of how it happened they feel guilty, like they should have gotten to me sooner and helped me before there was any damage."

"Is there permanent damage?"

"We couldn't exactly go to a hospital to find out for sure,

but the doc checked me out. I can manage, but my brain has probably taken one blow too many."

Lavender let out a noise of horror. "And I hit you with a lamp, over your head! Oh no, I am so sorry Theo." Her hand raised to her mouth in shock. I couldn't help but laugh at her concern.

"I think your reaction was more than fair considering we kidnapped you, I just didn't expect that level of fire from you, but I must say I wasn't disappointed. The omegas I've known were a lot more... calm in nature."

"Are you saying I'm not calm?" Lavender chuckled.

"Oh, on the contrary, I feel rather balanced around you *but* I wouldn't call someone who clubs people over the head with lamps and throws things at Kane a calm person in general."

Lavender pursed her lips in thought. "Okay, I accept that. I can sometimes behave like a feral racoon, but to be fair, you guys seem to bring out the worst in me!"

"The worst? Or the best?" I asked.

"I'm not sure, honestly," she admitted with a small shrug. Her expression sobered. "I'm sorry that happened to you."

"Don't apologise, it wasn't your fault I got damaged."

"You're not damaged!" Her voice was sharp and her eyes narrowed at me. "Who the hell has been giving you that idea?"

I raised my hands in a surrendering gesture. "I have brain damage, in the literal sense."

"I don't care. I like you as you are."

I stilled, my hands still raised as I appraised her with raised eyebrows. "You like me, do you?" A grin spread across my face. I couldn't help it. I'd known she didn't hate me but her admitting she liked me felt glorious, and I wanted to hear her say it again and again.

Lavender sighed with a roll of her eyes. "Yes, Theo. I like

you. You're fun, you don't take things too seriously, yet you clearly love your pack and will do whatever it takes to protect them. Even if it's things that aren't exactly ethical or legal. Pack should come before all else, so in my eyes that makes you a good man. Don't let that inflate your ego too much, though," she grumbled.

My hands reached out of their own volition, grabbing her hips and pulling her to me again, making sure she could feel every inch of how hard I was as I gently pressed her forehead to mine. Her scent bloomed, it was so thick I was almost choking on it. She *liked* what she felt. I wanted to yell in excitement.

"You've been here just a few weeks, but you're worming your way past all the walls," I mumbled in a low voice.

Why was Kane so set on Juniper being our omega? I knew we needed to find her, there was no question about that, but when it came to love? None of us had loved her, not in the sense of real, all consuming love. Juniper was a soft and fragile beauty, she wouldn't be able to handle me as I was now. And with what she'd probably gone through after she was taken, I was doubtful she'd even want to try. I couldn't imagine being with her anyway. None of my packmates had even held her freaking hand.

While I had been warring with myself mentally, Lavender had started to pull away. Decision made, I pulled her that much tighter against me. Grinning as her breathing hitched at the sensation and her scent turned somehow even sweeter. Slick. She was turned on. Good to know I wasn't the only one.

Letting go, I took a step back. I wanted to reach out as Lavender stumbled slightly, a dazed look in her eyes.

Here, standing in front of me was a stunning woman who could go toe to toe with us, smelled like sin and heaven all wrapped up in one and I kept being told she was wrong for us.

How could she be wrong? Every one of my instincts was screaming that I needed this omega.

And I was sick of fighting it.

"I'm giving you one chance to go back inside and walk away from me, because if you don't, I'm going to kiss you." I warned her, my voice rough. All I wanted was to grab her, but I had to let her leave. If that's what she wanted. I wasn't a monster. At least, I wouldn't be a monster to *her*. I couldn't be.

I expected her to turn on her heel and scamper away, to flee back to the safety of her temporary nest and forget about the last hour.

What I didn't expect was to feel her delicate hand reaching up and twisting in the hair at the nape of my neck as her gaze hardened, the corner of her mouth tilting up in a small smile as she looked me dead in the eye as she spoke.

"I'm not going anywhere."

Those words made me snap. I grabbed her by the hips, turned, and pressed her against the wall. There was no fear, her scent didn't char, instead it only sweetened. Oh, she wanted this.

The painful tug of her hand in my hair was a drug, and I wanted more. Lavender made me feel more alive than I had in months and I hadn't even tasted her yet.

Despite the bruising grip I had her in I was gentle, taking my time lowering my lips to hers.

She was so soft, so pliant. Her lips were just as pillowy as I had imagined and as I brushed my lips against them I marvelled at how well I was keeping my composure.

Her lips tasted sweet. So freaking sweet. Vanilla and lavender, a floral baked treat, and I wanted to devour her. I set a slow, leisurely pace, taking my time exploring every inch of her mouth. Her little whimpers of need only spurred me on.

Pushing my body into hers even harder, the friction on my rock hard cock was mind blowing.

If I was this hard from a little kissing and grinding, what would happen if I let this go further?

The picture of her on her knees, feeding her my cock as I stood in the room of carnage and damage we had created. Fuck. I would instruct her to play with herself as she sucked, making her moan and gag around my cock.

I let my hand wander, trailing up her stomach to cup her breast, lightly flicking at her nipple. Did she have dusky brown nipples or rosy ones? I needed to know. The moan she let out was downright pornographic, and I mentally made it my mission in that moment to see just how many noises I could pull out of her.

A vibration in my back pocket yanked me back to reality. Pulling my lips away for a second as I did my best to catch my breath, looking down at the bleary eyed omega who was looking at me like she wanted to jump me.

"W-What's that?" she stuttered, of course she could feel the vibration. It wasn't like a phone ringing, it was more melodic. It was an alert that Archer had set up on all our phones ages ago, I was surprised she didn't recognise it.

"The pack's home from work." I grinned down at her. "We'd best straighten up."

She looked mussed up and fucking beautiful. Her hair was downright feral between the violence and the foreplay, and she smelled like pure sex. All she needed was the smell of my cum on her and she would be a goddess.

"Oh!" Her hand flew to her hair as her face turned beet red. "I must look like a mess. They'll be annoyed with me for ambushing you," she started to mumble. I tutted and pulled her hand away, moving my face so close to hers our noses touched.

"You look fucking perfect. I'm only warning you because I know you wouldn't want them seeing you like this." Yet.

If I had my way we would all be enjoying our time with her. The idea of watching as Gage made her fall apart on his cock? That was the shit wet dreams were made of and the mental image I would be playing with in the shower that evening.

"And don't, for a moment, think that this is over." I leaned down, giving her another quick, bruising kiss before pulling away and taking a step back. She stood in front of me, panting and gazing at me with pure hunger in her eyes. "I fully intend to do that again."

"O-okay." She nodded, looking dazed. I had done that. I wanted to haul her in front of my packmates and show them just how much of an effect I had on Lavender, but I knew they wouldn't approve. Assholes. I felt more alive than I had in years, and I refused to let them take that away from me.

Lavender was mine. She just didn't know it yet.

CHAPTER TWENTY-THREE
Lavender

Holy hell. Theo could *kiss*.

What was it with this pack? I had been kissed by two of the pack members and both times had made me see stars and seriously consider just ripping my shirt off and begging them to make me orgasm.

Theo was completely unashamed of what had happened. He had simply grabbed my hand and led me out of the rage room, talking about how we should go kick up our feet and watch some TV after that. The last thing I needed was for the entire pack to take one whiff of me and know what we'd been up to.

What would have happened if they hadn't come home? Would Theo and I have taken things even further?

Theo was acting so relaxed, like nothing had happened. Did that mean it was nothing to him and he wasn't phased, or was he just that good at hiding his emotions? He was humming to himself lightly as he flicked on the TV, settling us on the sofa. He was constantly touching me, a hand on my lower back, taking my hand in his as we walked down the hallway. He hadn't stopped since the kiss and I wasn't complaining.

Clattering sounds from the hallway alerted me that the pack was on the move. I hadn't seen them yet, but I could hear the slamming of cupboard doors from the entryway and the heavy footfalls as they made their way to the kitchen.

Archer appeared in the entryway den. "Hey," he interrupted us.

One look at Archer's face and it was clear that something wasn't right. His eyes were clouded and he looked exhausted. His clothes were rumpled. Jumping up, Theo frowned and asked "Everyone okay?"

"Okay, but Kane's got a nasty cut to the head and Gage is gonna be feeling his bruises for a while. Kane's gonna need stitches but the doc won't be able to come here anytime soon."

I stared at Gage with wide eyes, what the hell had happened for them to need stitches?

"I'll get the first aid kit," Theo nodded, striding out of the room, me hot on his heels. I was anxious—which was bizarre given what I was to them, but I couldn't help it.

Gage and Kane were both in the kitchen. Gage had his shirt off, displaying a dizzying array of darkening bruises across his torso as he sat at the breakfast bar. Kane held a towel to his forehead dotted with blood.

"What on earth happened?" I asked, going to Gage first. I gently brushed my fingers against the bruises on his ribcage, forgetting how close I was or how my mouth was now mere inches away from his.

"Nothing to worry about," Gage assured me in a gruff voice.

I frowned. "Nothing to worry about? Gage, you look like a

patchwork quilt!" I prodded his ribs to prove a point and he winced in pain. I gave him a knowing look.

"Okay, I'll admit it's a little sore, but I'll be fine with a few days of rest."

"I don't like this," I muttered, walking over to Kane and taking the towel from him to look over the cut on his forehead. It was deep, but not deep enough for stitches, a few butterfly bandages would do the trick.

"Don't like what?" Gage asked, hissing in pain as he stood up straight.

"You putting yourself in dangerous situations!"

"We don't have much of a choice, just because we're nice to you doesn't mean we're good people in general, Lavender."

"I don't believe that." There was always a choice. The sight of them injured made my heart heavy. I didn't like it in the slightest.

"Well you should. I'm going to grab another shirt." Gage growled, storming out of the room.

With a sigh, I dabbed at Kane's wound. He sat, silently letting me fuss over him. "Do you have that first aid kit?" I asked Theo, who handed me the box he had pulled out of the cabinet.

Rummaging through, I was happy to find it quite well stocked. I grabbed some rubbing alcohol, doused a cotton ball, and dabbed the wound clean. Kane didn't even flinch even though it must have stung. The last time I'd done the same to a scraped knee it had hurt so badly I had teared up.

Once it was clean and the bleeding significantly less, I located some butterfly bandages and gently placed them, keeping the gash closed so it could heal a bit easier. Happy the wound was cared for, I then turned my cotton ball of rubbing alcohol to the blood stain running down Kane's face, taking my time to clean it away gently, ensuring there were no more traces of blood. It took several cotton balls to clean it, but I worked slowly and methodically.

I didn't mind cleaning up blood and I was practical and precise with it—I would have made an excellent serial killer.

"All better." I gave him a small smile, stepping back. Kane's hand snaked around my hip, keeping me close. I leaned into the touch, relishing in the leathery smell for a second. Who knew when Kane would be this nice to me again? I enjoyed it, probably a little too much.

Not the time to get horny, Lavender.

"Thank you," he said, looking up at me.

"You're welcome," I replied softly, heat rising in my face.

"So why did you guys get beaten up today?"

"We were found trying to track something down we shouldn't know about," Kane answered, exhaustion heavy in every word.

"Are you safe now?"

"Yeah, no one's left who knows what happened."

I was confused for a moment, then realised he probably meant that those who found them were now *dead* and no longer an issue.

"I'm not judging, I'm just curious. You guys have so much to lose. I don't like seeing you hurt."

"You're too kind, you know that?" Kane asked.

"I clubbed Theo with a lamp the day I met him," I reminded him.

Theo laughed from the counter where he was cleaning first aid supplies. "I still have the scars to prove it."

"It wasn't hard enough to scar!" I gasped. "Was it?"

Theo's joyful laugh told me that he was just joking with me.

"Asshole," I mumbled under my breath, making Kane smile up at me. It was a beautiful sight, one I wasn't used to seeing. Despite the scratches and bruises he was beautiful. His green eyes were bloodshot and he had bruising clearly visible under his buzzed hair.

"I may be an asshole, but you like me anyway!" Theo smirked. "Would you go take some of these ice packs up to Gage while I start dinner? He always forgets to ice his injuries and gets stiff the next day. I would take them, but he'll just shout at me. I doubt he'll be anywhere near as grumpy with you."

"Sure," I nodded, holding my hand out for the ice packs. Theo wrapped them in a tea towel before handing them over.

"Good luck," Kane chuckled as I headed towards the stairs.

CHAPTER TWENTY-FOUR
Gage

Everything had gone to shit. We went to buy an omega, and yet somehow we were jumped and had a lot of the shit on us stolen. My ribs screamed in pain from the kicks, but we had all got out intact, and that's what mattered.

A soft knock on my door disturbed me from inspecting my bruised knuckles while sitting on the edge of my bed.

"What?" I answered gruffly, thinking it was Theo coming to mother hen me. Taking that as an invitation to enter, Lavender let herself in. Her brow furrowed when she looked over my injuries again. Was she worried? She had no reason to worry about us, yet it was clear as day she was worming her way deeper into our lives.

But her worry warmed me. Part of me wanted her concern, her care. Someone to confide in, to care for me like I had to care for the pack as its leader. Lavender was both soft and comforting and strong, she could handle a pack like ours who had rougher edges.

"Theo asked me to bring you some ice packs, he says you always forget to ice your injuries."

I barked a humourless laugh. "He's right, I usually just grin and bear it."

Lavender padded over to the bed until she was inches away from me, standing between my knees so she could get better access to my injuries. Her hair was down, falling in her face. I resisted the urge to move it so I could see her better. Handing me the ice packs she looked me over. Up close, her scent hit me like a tidal wave. I stupidly hadn't noticed downstairs, but she smelled sweet, like *slick* sweet, and Theo's distinct lemon and pine scent was mingled with hers—like they had been close... very close.

"I must look scary," I grunted, noticing her watching. Not liking that my appearance could be making her unhappy.

"Not that scary. I'm not even intimidated." She laughed lightly, her hand lifting to my hairline and gently checking the side I was pretty sure had a nasty bruise forming. "You are losing weight though. You need to rest."

I'd admit my focus had been on my pack and looking after myself had often fallen to the wayside in all the excitement, but none of my pack had noticed, yet she had?

"I can't rest."

"I know you're on this mission, and I'm pretty sure it's something to do with Juniper, but tell me this, how would she feel if she saw the state of you right now?"

Lavender's words hit hard. It would have fucking gutted Juniper to see us like this.

"She would hate it." I admitted, my voice thick with emotion.

I hated it. Every day I woke and was faced with the reality that I wasn't helping my pack thrive. We were hardly surviving.

I was meant to help them thrive, instead we are chasing a ghost, my pack is getting injured and we aren't happy."

My feelings weren't important. I kept them bottled up for a reason. "Juniper would hate that we are putting ourselves in dangerous situations, I know that. I'm constantly failing my pack," I admitted with a whisper.

"Gage." Lavender's hand reached for my shoulder. "It's clear as day you love and care about your pack. I don't know everything that's happened, but if you're talking about what happened to Theo, it's obvious he doesn't blame you at all."

My head shot up so fast the room spun violently, and I pushed down the rising nausea. "How do you know about that?" I asked.

"Theo told me." She offered a soft warm smile. "He took me to his rage room and we smashed up a microwave."

That sounded like something Theo would do.

But he had trusted her, told her about his darkest moment, and yet she was still standing here, looking at me with warmth. She knew how I had failed him, how I hadn't pulled him out of the water until his brain was so starved of oxygen he may never be the same.

Lavender was coated in Theo's scent... had they done that *after* he had told her about his past? My head felt fuzzy. Theo struggled to trust anyone outside our pack, yet this omega had wormed her way into his head easily. I wasn't totally oblivious, even an idiot could see that Theo had been so much happier the last two weeks, humming to himself, far less anxiety attacks, and I was starting to think that was due to the woman in front of me.

What was I doing? We were going to find Juniper, there was no question about that, but... was she really the one for us? Was I causing more hurt and damage by allowing Kane to keep hold of his delusion? If Theo was developing real feelings for Lavender, then would I be a terrible pack leader to stop him? He had sacrificed for this pack, fuck—he had nearly died for this pack He deserved to be happy.

Did she reciprocate those feelings? We'd kidnapped her, she could just be being polite and friendly, or trying to endear herself to us so we're better.

Then again, her scent was far from distressed. From the smell of it she enjoyed whatever it was those two were doing.

I felt stuck.

Warm hands gripped my shoulders, and I was pulled against Lavender. My head resting on her chest as she stood in front of me, her arms wrapping around my head in an off balanced hug.

A hum started in her chest as her scent became more floral and relaxing as it grew in intensity. She was *purring* for me. The vibrations worked their way through my body, forcing every muscle to relax.

"Fucking hell, you're amazing," I mumbled. "I've heard a purr or two in my time but this shit is potent." I stretched lazily in her arms. The bruises on my side didn't even bother me. I felt so at ease. Her legs were bare in those tiny, hardly there sleep shorts. The urge to wrap my arms around her and touch the expanse of smooth skin in front of me was powerful.

I didn't know how long we stayed there, her hugging my face, purring as I just...floated.

I smiled at her, marvelling. I tucked a strand of her hair behind her ear, letting my hand linger as it ran down her neck. Her skin was so damn soft. I wanted to taste it.

"You shouldn't be so nice to us, we've been monsters to you," I frowned.

"Even monsters need love, Gage. You've fed me, kept me

safe and provided a nest—I'm really not difficult to please. In fact I kind of like it here now, it's a nice break from the repetition of the Haven."

"I guess we got lucky it was you Archer stumbled across." My hand rested on her hip as I looked up at her. She should be nervous, being this close to an alpha but everything about her body language suggested she was completely comfortable.

We had been chasing a ghost for so long. Would it be so wrong to put ourselves first, just this once? It could be temporary.

"Gage..." Lavender's voice was breathy.

We were only inches apart. I knew what was happening, but it felt as though we were powerless to stop it. Lavender's entire body jolted with the shock of our lips meeting. Soft, warm, and delectable. My hand snaked up to the back of her neck, tangling in the hair at the nape, holding her in place.

The faint sweet slick smell that had been clinging to her ever since I'd come home intensified. Her taste was delicious, but there was a citrus edge to her that hadn't been there before.

Theo.

With that realisation, all my blood rushed south and I was consumed with thoughts of her sweet slick pussy impaled on my cock, bent over the bed, whimpering and whining as I made her mine. Ours. Fuck, Theo and I could take her together. His taste on her tongue was the best kind of drug, and I was running headfirst into addiction.

I pulled away, hating the loss of her warmth and her taste, drawing Lavender down onto my lap so our foreheads pressed together. My hand gripped the smooth expanse of her thigh I had been admiring earlier as her legs draped across my thighs. "I shouldn't have done that, but for some reason I can't find it in me to care."

Her weight on top of me was heady. Her hands ran along my chest gently up to my neck, leaving an electric sensation in its wake. I readjusted my sitting position and winced, reminding her of my current state, going still for a brief second before attempting to jump off. Only I refused to let her, wrapping an arm around her waist to keep her in place. The action ground her against my erection and my eyes rolled back at the sweet friction.

"Am I hurting you?" she asked, softly chewing on her bottom lip.

"Not at all, in fact this is helping," I smirked at her.

"Well in that case, I guess we should continue?" Lavender laughed, pulling away "But you need to ice your bruises, or you'll never hear the end of it from Theo."

The short distance between us helped me gather my wits. Lavender's perfume was like an aphrodisiac. The closer I was to the source the more I felt my mind becoming addled. She moved backwards, standing. I wanted to whine at the loss of her.

She leaned forward, placing the wrapped ice pack on my ribs, making me hiss at the cold contact. Lavender's eyes were flitting around the room and a touch of anxiety was creeping into her scent.

"Uh, we probably shouldn't have done that, I'm sorry," she mumbled. "I accosted you. Stupid pheromones. Let's just blame those."

I snorted. "Hey," I tugged at her until she looked me in the face. "It was a mistake because you'll be gone soon. I didn't kiss you just because you are an omega, I kissed you because you're Lavender."

"Huh?"

I laughed, and pulled her down gently for a soft kiss. "You

need to understand that while this was a mistake, I'm under no false impressions of who you are. You're the woman who watches enough true crime to give grumpy old bastards like Kane the creeps. You're intelligent and quick, and you mesh so well with everyone in my pack—even the aforementioned grumpy bastard. You aren't terrified of weapons, and I'm pretty sure if given the chance you would become a better shot than any of us. In another world, you would be pretty fucking perfect, you know that?"

Lavender blushed at the praise. "I wish other packs saw me that way."

"I'm sure they do."

"The last pack I spoke to for longer than three hours told me I was rather inconsiderate racking up debt on my education when I would just be a mother one day. They made it clear they would pay all my debt though because they knew I held at least that much value in my reproductive abilities. I decided to look into a second degree that day."

Of course she decided to get a second degree, she was too smart for her own good at times.

"Didn't any work out?" I asked, brows furrowed.

"There were plenty who were nice, offered me shiny things, gifts, and money, but none of them really wanted *me*; they wanted an omega. Any omega would have done. Not a single pack recognised me for me, unless it was traits they deemed to be negative that could reflect badly on their pack one day. None of them wanted to be known as the pack with the quirky omega."

"That's not fair. You're amazing."

Lavender rolled her eyes. "I'm not sure how to take flattery from the man who kidnapped me."

"Well, if Theo's right, in the sort of books you read, kidnapping is considered foreplay."

Lavender snorted at that reply. "Keep icing your bruises, I'm going to go check on Kane."

I nodded. "But first." I wrapped a hand round her waist again and pulled her close in another bruising kiss. "I'm sick and tired of resisting this, even if it's a mistake."

"It probably *is* a mistake, but I don't mind." Lavender shrugged.

Would it really hurt to explore this for a week or so until Lavender left? I doubted I had the strength to stay away from her.

I needed to talk to my packmates.

CHAPTER TWENTY-FIVE
Lavender

Everyone had been in their own rooms by the time I had left Gage's, so I made my way back to the nest, deep in thought.

I kissed two members of the pack today—and I enjoyed it. A lot. What was holding me back? I didn't feel unsafe. I believed that these alphas were doing nefarious things to help others. They were practically Robin Hood, only sexier, smelling like sin and with far more abs.

Every time I kissed one of them it felt like I was coming to life, electric and invigorating. Would it feel the same way with a different pack? I had no idea, but I had never been able to fall into such easy conversation with a pack before. That alone made me want to explore this. Even if it was just for another week or so until I went home.

I padded over to the bathroom, intending to shower. I hated the idea of losing the smell of Theo and Gage on me but my slick was out of control. Between the two of them I had soaked clean through my panties and was starting to feel a little nasty.

Stripping and throwing my clothes haphazardly in the hamper, I turned on the shower to extra hot, letting the steam fill the bathroom. Testing the temperature with my hand first I stepped into the spacious cubicle. The hot water felt glorious, soothing my sore extremities from the rage room. So much had happened today that the rage room felt like so long ago. It had been late when I went to check on Gage, and it was easily past midnight at this point. I was exhausted.

I had just started soaping up my arms when a gust of cool air from the shower door opening grabbed my attention, spinning around with a squeak of surprise. Theo stood in the doorway, hungrily looking over me, totally unabashed.

"Err, hello?" I squeaked. I was naked! What on earth was he doing?

After a moment of confusion a new panic set in—what if he didn't like what he saw? Under the harsh fluorescent bathroom lights everything was on stark display. I wasn't the most well-endowed, and my hips were several inches wider than I would have liked. His gaze was pure heat and hunger though, and my body reacted in turn. An embarrassing rush of slick leaked down my thighs making my face heat. Theo's nostrils flared as the scent hit him. The small space and warmth only amplified the scent and his eyes were dark, pupils wide.

He only wore a pair of dark coloured boxers. He must have rid himself of his clothing earlier. His chest was smooth and defined and I wanted to reach out and touch it.

"I said we would continue this later." He smirked, stepping into the stall. I automatically stepped back until I was pressed against the cool tile, the sensation making me shiver.

"You shouldn't be in here." My voice was weak even to my own ears.

"I think I'm exactly where I need to be." His hand came to rest next to my head as he looked down at me. His chin length blond hair was falling loose, almost touching his shoulders, wet from the downpour. "Do you want me to leave?" he asked softly.

I didn't have to think long before answering. "No. Stay."

Despite my nerves I desperately wanted him.

My words unleashed something in him. He went from hovering near me to pressing me up against the tile, lips crashing against mine. Tart citrus. He was making me an addict, and frankly I didn't give a fuck.

"You're beautiful," he said as he looked down at me, shameless in his perusal of my body. His hand reached out, running a finger over a nipple and smirking when it puckered from the attention. "Oh, this is going to be fun," he murmured, lightly pinching the nipple, gently rolling it between his fingers. I whined at the attention. My entire body felt coiled tight, like it was ready to burst. "These are perfect, just as I imagined."

"Theo," I whimpered.

"Feeling a little needy, are we?" he asked with a chuckle, his hand trailing down and brushing against my folds, making me mewl with need.

What were we doing? I was beyond caring. I needed him. The fighting, the resisting, I was sick of it.

He was far too overdressed. I was completely exposed and all I could see was the considerable bulge in the front of his now drenched boxers.

"Why are you still dressed?" I asked, voice weak and breathless.

Theo tilted his head to the side, a smirk spreading across his lips. "Good question, maybe you should take them off?"

My hands shook as I reached out—not from nerves, from *need*. He reached for my neck, pressure gentle as his thumb brushed my pulse. It made me whine. I was a puddle of want. Stuff everything else, I wanted to feel good.

My hand found purchase, sliding into his damp boxers and pulling him out. *Holy fuck, that is not fair. That's bigger than some of my toys!*

"You're looking at it like it's going to eat you," Theo chuckled, his lips dancing across my neck.

"I get that the whole thing about being an omega is that we can stretch and take a lot, but this feels…" I trailed off, my hand grasping around his length and moving experimentally.

Theo's rough groan in my ear let me know he liked that. Slightly emboldened, I gave him a few experimental pumps and was rewarded with another moan. Toys I was familiar with, but I had never actually been with an alpha, I hadn't been with anyone. The Haven kept them at a safe distance so I was somewhat sheltered. I had never had an alpha moaning in my ear before, but damn it, it was glorious and made my inner omega quiver in happiness.

What other sounds could I pull out of him?

"Sure, it'll be tight, but just think about how good it'll feel to be stretched out over your alpha's cock," he hummed, nipping at my neck. The whisper of a bite called to every one of my baser instincts and my slick flowed at an embarrassing rate.

His hand started moving in time with mine, gliding through my folds and finding the most sensitive area. Gently circling my clit and sending me wild as he teased me.

"More," I growled as I leaned forward and nipped at his

shoulder. He stilled, his lips leaving my neck, rearing back to stare at me, his gaze pure heat.

"Don't do that, little omega," I shivered in pleasure at the nickname, "unless you're ready to deal with the consequences."

"And what are those?" I asked softly, my voice turning to a strangled moan as his fingers slid deep, finding that sweet spot inside that made me see stars. Fuck toys—Theo's fingers would get the job done faster. It was like his fingers had a homing beacon for my G-spot.

"My cock," he rumbled, "buried to the hilt in this sweet, perfect slick coated pussy." He punctuated each word with a thrust of his fingers, making me squirm. I whimpered. *Holy fuck I'm already getting close.* I usually took my sweet time when I played solo, but Theo was getting me there and getting me there *fast*.

I looked directly into those smouldering green eyes with a smirk before leaning forward and nipping once again at his throat.

The whine I let out at the loss of his fingers was almost painful, but it turned into a scream of pleasure when strong hands grabbed my thighs, lifting me against the shower wall, and lining his cock up with my slick coated entrance. My hands flew to his neck to balance myself as my eyes locked on his.

"Last chance to back out before I fuck you full of my cum." Theo's words were guttural, like he was struggling to maintain control.

"I'm not going anywhere," I whispered, my forehead resting against his as I clutched his neck. I was there for the duration. I wanted to know how it felt. I *craved* it. "Fuck me, alpha."

He didn't hesitate, thrusting forward. The stretch was painful, but so damn good. It felt like I was being split in half.

The shower stall was clouded with thick steam, the scent of lavender, lemon and pine was so thick it clouded my every sense. I loved it. Our scents blended together so well. Combined with my slick and Theo's obvious arousal made my tentative grip in reality shakey. *Fuck. Claim. Own. Let alpha fuck me.*

"Fuck, you're like a vise," Theo ground out. "I'm not even halfway in yet."

Not even halfway? I whined. I wanted all of it. Why was he holding back on me?

"Give me all of it," I whimpered, my voice pathetically needy. Thankfully he didn't reply. Instead pulling back and thrusting forwards so quickly I didn't have time to agonise over how empty I felt without him.

"So fucking perfect, such a good little omega." Theo cooed, slowly filling me inch by inch. "You're strangling my cock, princess. Are you hungry for my cum? Because you're going to get every. Last. drop." He punctuated the last three words with thrusts, each time he filled me to the hilt, making my body radiate with electricity.

It wasn't loving, but somehow I still felt worshipped. His hungry gaze was obsessed, and I revelled in it. His thrusts were far from gentle, but I wasn't complaining. I had already been so close just from his fingers. Each time his tip scraped against that sensitive spot inside me I hurtled closer and closer to the edge.

"Theo..." I whined.

"I can feel you tightening around me, are we getting close?" he purred. I nodded, losing the ability to form words.

"*Please!*" My voice was strangled.

Theo pulled back, putting my shaky feet on the ground with a dark grin. I whined. I was so empty. Only I didn't have to wait long. Strong hands gripped my hips, spinning me around.

"Hands on the wall, omega," he instructed me.

I complied with his command, powerless to deny him. With my hips in his bruising grip he lined himself back up, filling me in a single, powerful thrust. *Fuck. He feels even bigger this way.*

He didn't wait for me to adjust, he pounded at the pace of a man possessed. One hand slid from my hip to my clit, roughly rubbing. It was too much, I couldn't take it.

Lips found my neck. "Cum on my cock. Do it now, and then I'll fill you up." His words were guttural, punctuated by the rough sensation of his fingers on my clit. He wasn't gentle. He was powerful, dominating.

The bite threw me over. Theo's teeth found the juncture between my neck and shoulder and bit down lightly before sucking the skin, not hard enough to break the skin. Falling off the edge, I opened my mouth to scream as my legs trembled violently. All the while, Theo spoke in my ear, pausing every few words to nip at my neck.

"Such a good omega. You feel so good coming on my cock, I'm getting close. I'm going to fill you up. Do you want that?"

I was blissed out and only just coming back down to earth, but I wanted that. His pace slowed to almost a leisurely one as he groaned in my ear, chasing his release. I didn't have to wait long before he followed me off the edge.

We stood there, wrapped up together, panting under the water.

"Fuck, I'm keeping you," Theo groaned with a laugh.

If only.

CHAPTER TWENTY-SIX
Lavender

We spent the next twenty minutes lazily cleaning each other. Theo wanted to ensure there wasn't a single inch of my skin left unwashed. It felt so natural and comfortable. When I had imagined how it would be with alphas, I had imagined it would be a touch more awkward. Theo made everything *easy*.

That was how we found ourselves downstairs getting a late night snack, me wearing only Theo's T-shirt, and Theo only wearing a new pair of grey sweatpants. Between the deep clean and the body spray I had lathered on no one could tell what we had just been up to.

I had to resist the urge to blush at Theo every time he glanced my way, but I wasn't ready to discuss everything that happened with anyone else.

"Grab me the bacon out of the fridge, Lavender," Theo asked, his eyes never leaving the pile of celery he was cutting. He had decided he was going to make us a salad to go with the frozen pizza cooking. Theo was skilled with knives. Every movement was precise and even, his hands never wavering. He didn't let me near the knives for food prep.

I nodded even though he couldn't see with his back to me, pushing myself off the counter and going over to the large two door fridge. With every step the soreness between my legs made my face heat with memories.

Most of the food once opened was stored in glass tubs, making the fridge look sleek and aesthetic inside. Archer had told me about it, and when I'd asked why he'd said they "didn't want to be a dick to the environment".

Reaching up on my tiptoes I grabbed the bacon from its spot on the top shelf. I had to strain to reach, I wasn't as tall as the permanent occupants of the house. As I turned towards Theo, bacon in hand, my vision tilted and I was momentarily unsteady on my feet. The glass tub slipped from my fingers and shattered on the floor. *Crap!* The dizziness had only lasted a brief second, I was already feeling far more steady. I cursed myself. Freezing I looked around, opening my mouth to apologise and leaned down to start grabbing the larger shards.

"Don't move!" Kane's aggressive bark from behind me made my spine turn to steel and I froze in place. His voice had held so much power. I could feel it deep in my spine—a sensation I had never felt before. He had barked at me... no one had ever barked at me.

I couldn't move.

I *physically* couldn't move.

My muscles refused to respond.

Kane came up behind me, grabbing me roughly by the waist and lifting me from my crouch on the floor, depositing me on the nearby kitchen island.

"You've got bare feet," he muttered in a way of explanation.

He didn't even give me a second glance before bending down and gathering the broken glass.

My stomach felt cold and I didn't know what to say... I started to shake. *Why does my stupid body let me shake but not move?*

"Kane!" Theo growled, making me shrink back further. Well, hunch away slightly as that's all I could do. My body was screaming at me to leave. Get out. Escape. Get away from the angry alphas. Go to the nest. Nest was *safe*. Only my body wouldn't listen, it was firmly stuck on the counter, unable to move.

"What?" Kane growled as he discarded some glass.

"Don't fucking bark at Lavender!"

Kane's head shot up, taking me in. He muttered a curse, standing up and coming over to me. His normal leathery smell was dirty. Like he had been running around a busy city in his absence.

"I'm so sorry." He sounded upset, not at me, but at himself as his face twisted in displeasure. "I would never force you to do something. I was worried you would hurt yourself..." He trailed off. Looking around the kitchen at the last piece or two of glass.

"That doesn't fucking matter, Kane. You can't talk to her like that!" Theo growled, grabbing a broom and helping clean away the glass.

"I'm sorry, all right!" Kane yelled.

"The fuck is happening here?!" Gage asked from the doorway, taking in the scene in front of him, confused and obviously annoyed at the shouting. He looked exhausted. He really should have been resting with his bruises. His nostrils flared. Crap. Could he tell what Theo and I had been up to?

"Kane fucking barked at Lavender!" Theo shouted, and Gage's face turned thunderous.

"I didn't mean to! I just told her to stay still so she didn't step on glass!" Kane reasoned.

Gage made a beeline for me. " Are you okay, Lavender?" he asked, eyes trailing over me sitting on the counter, his voice soft. I was shaking and there were unshed tears in my eyes.

I tried to move, but it was like there was an invisible force keeping me on the counter, I *physically* couldn't move myself from that spot. Tears overflowed and I stuttered. "I can't move."

Theo frowned, "The glass is gone, it's safe to move."

"No. I can't. Kane told me not to move... and now I can't move at all." More tears spilled over and I berated myself. I felt so weak, literally glued to a goddamn counter simply because I had been told not to move.

Every alpha's face in the room dropped at my words, and Kane let out an uncharacteristic, strangled sound.

"Release her," Gage thundered. He sounded livid. I wanted to melt into the countertop. Theo was also snarling, but I couldn't make out the words. Were I not physically unable to move I would be fleeing from the room as fast as possible.

"Do whatever you want?" Kane said, looking confused. "Does that work?" He looked completely lost. "You can move?"

That did the trick. I could feel the heavy weight on my shoulders eased. I slid off the counter, stumbling slightly as my feet hit the ground. Sheer exhaustion weighed me down. Kane was giving me a pained look, but I didn't dare meet his eyes. I went to take a step toward the door and stumbled, my legs shaky.

Gage cupped my elbow to keep me steady while doing his best to avoid being too close into my personal space.

"Let's get you upstairs," he whispered gently. I only nodded in reply. I went to take another step but my jelly legs made me stumble once again. Gage swept me off my feet, holding me close to his chest as he carried me out of the kitchen. As we got to the bottom of the stairs I could make out the sounds of Kane and Theo arguing once again in the kitchen.

"I didn't mean to make them fight," I whispered, tears still flowing.

"Hush, none of this is your fault. It was an accident. Kane didn't mean it."

"I know he didn't, but it's still not a nice experience."

Gage kicked the door to my room open with his foot, taking me straight over to the nest. Placing me down, he cupped my cheeks, looking me in the eyes. The concern in those eyes was too much for me and the floodgates opened.

"I'm sorry, I'm over reacting," I mumbled between sobs.

"No. This is a totally normal reaction," he reassured me. "An alpha's bark can have a horrible impact on an omega, especially if it's not one of their bonded alphas. We were always told to watch our words growing up just in case."

"Bonded?"

"Yeah, apparently if you're bonded, like truly bonded, the bark is nowhere near as effective."

"Oh."

"Yeah, you shouldn't feel bad. If anyone should, it's Kane. He's been around omegas plenty. He understands," Gage soothed, sitting on the edge of the bed and pulling me in for a hug. I didn't fight it, sinking into him and embracing his warm, whisky scent.

"Juniper?"

"Yeah," he confirmed, gently rubbing his hand up and down my back. "He's just seen some omegas get hurt in the past, and he's a touch overprotective. I bet he barked before thinking. He'll be feeling horrible for this, but he was completely in the wrong."

"I'm okay though." I wiped my eyes. "It just freaked me out not being able to move from the counter."

"You've never experienced bark compulsion?"

"Never, it was insane, I physically couldn't move. Apparently, that was commonly used centuries ago? Fuck I feel bad for the old omegas."

"I'm sorry it happened this way."

"Your injuries," I said sleepily. "You shouldn't have been carrying me."

"Hush, I can handle it." As he spoke, his hand brushed over my hair, lulling me into a restful sleep, the physical exhaustion finally getting to me.

CHAPTER TWENTY-SEVEN
Kane

I looked at the CCTV for the hundredth time. Someone had been near or even on the property of the pack house, and I would not stand for it. Ever since I'd done my walk around the day before, I'd just known something wasn't right. The air had felt wrong, but I'd continued on, doing my best to brush it off as paranoia.

This was different. One of the silent alarms had been tripped. The moment the notification had come through on my phone I'd dropped what I was doing, leaving my half-eaten sandwich in the kitchen. I rushed to my laptop hoping to catch a glimpse of the intruder.

It could be a deer. When we had first moved in the alarms had been activated several times by the wildlife in the woodland area surrounding the pack house, but Archer had made several adjustments and there had been no alarms since.

Sure enough, Detective Rouche had parked his shitty little beater of a car just on the outskirts of the property lines and appeared to be nosing around. What the fuck was he doing here? We hadn't seen him in years. He was one of the officers who'd investigated Juniper going missing. He was a few sandwiches short of a picnic, as Theo would say, and he'd been hellbent on this idea that Gage, Archer and Theo were responsible for Juniper's disappearance.

Lavender hadn't been outside in several days so her scent wasn't prevalent out there, and since Detective Rouche was a beta, his sense of smell was nowhere near as good as our alpha noses. I still didn't trust him in the slightest.

Without taking my eyes off the screen I pulled out my phone and speed dialled Gage.

"Yeah?" He answered after a single ring.

"Detective Rouche of all fucking people is outside."

"Shit. Where's Lavender?"

"Not with me, maybe Archer?" Of course she wasn't with me. She had been avoiding me ever since I'd accidentally barked at her, and while I didn't blame her, it still stung.

"Find her, I'm going to go outside and deal with him. Don't come out if you've been near Lavender—I don't want to risk him smelling her on you. I just showered so I should smell pretty neutral," Gage ordered.

Throwing my phone down without even a goodbye I strode out of the room, on a mission to find the pesky little omega.

Archer was in his office, and had been most of the day so I knew Lavender wasn't with him. I headed for the kitchen, I could hear the faint sounds of cupboards banging and pots scraping.

Theo was standing next to the microwave, a sleepy, happy look on his face.

"Is Lavender here?" I asked. Theo looked confused.

"No, I think she's in the sun room. Our feral beastie wanted some space to rest and read. Why?"

I cursed under my breath. The sun room was made entirely out of windows. *Of course* she would be in the most open room of the entire compound right when Detective Rouche was snooping. Couldn't we catch a fucking break?

"Detective Rouche is on the property, gotta make sure she's hidden," I growled as I stalked out of the room. I ignored Theo shouting something behind me and the clatter of his dishes.

Lavender was indeed in the sun room, curled up in a ball on the green sofa, a soft sherpa blanket thrown over her legs. She looked cosy and content, focused on the screen of her e-reader, basking in the sunlight of the fall afternoon.

At my not at all quiet entrance, she turned her head to me.

"Oh! Kane, how—"

I didn't slow my approach, and instead of greeting her, I simply leaned down, grabbed her and tossed her over my shoulder. She was tiny and it was easy enough to do. She let out a small yelp of shock before shouting my name as I strode out of the room. I had just entered the hallway when we passed a startled looking Theo.

I didn't care if she was mad. I needed to get her to safety. We couldn't have another omega in danger under my roof. I refused.

Even though I still felt like shit for barking at her, her safety came first.

"Are we playing kidnappers? That could be hot!" Theo followed us with a lazy grin.

"What's happening?" Lavender asked in an exasperated voice from over my shoulder. There was no fear in the air, despite me having grabbed her.

"We have company," I growled, turning to Theo. "Basement," I ordered.

"You have a basement?" Lavender asked in astonishment. We had never shown her the cavernous space that served as a giant panic room. It was well hidden. "Why are we going there? Answer me!" A sharp smack landed on my ass. I suppose Lavender was face to face with it, but her hands were tiny, and made little impact.

Theo laughed from somewhere behind me. "Oh Lavender, you don't want to do that. Kane does the spanking around here!" He paused a second, his footsteps still following me before saying, "I've texted Archer to let him know what's going on."

A loud metallic door clanged and the hardwood floors gave way to stone and metal. "Where on earth are we going?" Lavender asked, still confused.

"The basement is kind of a fortress," Theo admitted, following us down the stairs. Lavender didn't have a chance to reply before I hauled her off my shoulder, placing her on her feet in the middle of the room. She stumbled slightly as I released her, but Theo was by her side in a heartbeat, keeping her steady. Despite the fact I'd just been touching her, I was jealous of Theo for how he handled her with such ease.

She looked around curiously. Grey walls were adorned with CCTV screens and several guns on a wall rack, with a table and a set of chairs filling up the rest of the space.

"A detective that's been a pain in our asses for a while has probably got wind that we were near the Haven the night you went missing. He's been nosey, but now he's on our property." Theo did his best to explain to Lavender.

"He's gone too far, this is private property. I'll kill the bastard," I growled.

Theo frowned at me. Was he shocked at the lengths I was willing to go to? "He came right onto the grounds—and Lavender was in a room made of windows," I explained.

"But he didn't see me, right? There's no actual evidence linking you to me being missing?" Lavender asked, her eyes wide and full of worry. Part of me wanted to laugh, she was concerned for us. Two months ago she would have fed us to the wolves in a heartbeat, and she would have been right to do so.

"Nothing concrete," I admitted, begrudgingly. "But this fucker is relentless. He's been trying to pin something on us for months. He knows if he caught us with Lavender it would be game over for us."

"I don't want that," Lavender admitted with a frown.

"Gage is scaring him off, he had showered so he wasn't covered in your scent. It's still private property, Archer owns this land outright so he shouldn't be here without a warrant."

"Archer owns this place?" She asked, distracted.

"He made a load of money a few years ago on an app or something computer related and he bought this land and the main house. It was run down at the time and when we decided to make this our base, we spent almost a year renovating to make it liveable." Theo smiled, likely remembering the days of painting, moving furniture, and knocking down walls.

"So what do we do now?" Lavender asked. "How do we keep you safe? I'm sorry about the sunroom." I frowned.

Theo sighed, pulling her in for a hug and kissing her on the forehead. "Don't apologise, you love it there. This place is supposed to be safe from outsiders."

He was right. This was our home, our sanctuary. Even if her stay here was only temporary, it was unacceptable that the fragile peace we had built was being threatened.

CHAPTER TWENTY-EIGHT
Gage

Of all the people to turn up at our pack house, Detective fucking Rouche? He hadn't darkened our doorstep in almost a year—I thought the asshole had finally forgotten about us and decided to chase other stupid, fanciful leads.

Usually we had nothing to hide, but we had learned the hard way that Rouche was the kind of asshole who would get a search warrant for the stupidest things. Only now we had a missing omega living on our property, and if he discovered her...

No. I refused to let that happen.

I rounded the corner, immediately noticing that beat up, piece of shit old car belonging to Detective Rouche who was nowhere in sight. His scent—burnt apple—was everywhere, so I followed my nose. While the car had been on the outskirts, the beta had trespassed *onto* our property. The thought enraged me. We had been hyper alert when it came to protecting Lavender, and after everything that had happened with Juniper, I would never allow an omega to be taken from me again—even if this omega was just a temporary acquisition.

The panic I felt at someone finding Lavender didn't feel like the worry over a temporary captive though. My every instinct flared, demanding I hunt down this intruder and tear him apart to keep *my* omega safe. I reminded myself that, as much as I wanted her, Lavender was not in fact my omega, no matter how many times we kissed, or how desperately I wanted to taste every inch of her skin.

Judging by the trampled plants it seemed that Rouche had wandered down the treeline, possibly trying to find the back gardens? This place was large, and sprawling. We had built the house with our future in mind. We had even built an omega suite for Juniper one day, before we realised we were a pack, and Kane wouldn't be going anywhere.

Sure enough, Detective Rouche was by one of the back windows, leaning against the glass, cupping his hands around his eyes to get a better chance of looking in.

"What the fuck are you doing on my property?" I growled. Detective Rouche jumped back, taking in the pissed off alpha towering over him. I didn't care if I scared him, the little shit deserved it, as he'd been a constant terror to my pack when Juniper had been taken. Luckily his... zealous actions had meant that he lost some of his good reputation.

He should have lost his badge.

"I-I have every right to be here!" he insisted. "I thought I heard someone in distress so I came to investigate."

He looked like crap. His hair was dishevelled, his suit creased and face sweaty. A far cry from the neat detective he had been the last time I'd seen him.

"Bullshit, you're snooping on my property and I have the

camera footage to prove it. You didn't hear anyone in distress, my pack are the only ones here."

"I don't think so," Rouche said, his hand going to his hip where his gun was holstered.

"I suggest you don't do that," I growled. "I have cameras *everywhere*."

"We both know that it's not just you and your packmates here—you know something about the missing omega who vanished two months ago. Omega's tend to disappear around you, don't they?" He said with a grin, the effect slightly dampened by the obvious fear in his eyes.

"I suggest you watch what you say. You have no legal grounds here and you've been harassing us ever since Juniper disappeared, I will remove you from these lands myself and press charges against you. You know, It's kind of creepy that you're still this obsessed with Juniper after she rejected you. you know she's not going to fall in your arms even if you find her. How will your superiors react when they learn you've been harassing us again?"

"You can't touch me, I'm an officer!" he gasped.

"I can, legally. You're on an Alpha's pack lands, without permission, harassing us. Didn't you learn that lesson last time? Now if you're not out of here in the next two minutes I will raise all sorts of hell and physically drag you out of here myself," I said. "And if I do that, you won't be well enough to come back for a good long while," I growled, approaching Detective Rouche, who'd started to back away.

"I'll leave for now," he replied. "But I'm not letting this go —I know your pack is mixed up in this and I wouldn't put it past you to kidnap an omega for your own perverted desires." He spat, walking past me and back to the boundary of the property. He was eager to escape now that he had been discovered. He had likely thought that none of us were home because our cars were all away in the garages, not out front like they normally were.

Did that mean he was watching us? Had he caught a glimpse of Lavender?

I followed Detective Rouche as he walked off the property, glaring at him as he got in his car and drove away. The fucking idiot thought it was okay to invade our home? Because he had a hunch? He was just looking for something to pin on us.

Once I was certain he had left, I stalked back inside checking my phone. Theo had messaged me saying they had taken Lavender to the basement so she was safely hidden.

The whole pack were all sitting around the table in the basement with Lavender when I arrived. She was absent mindedly chewing on her thumbnail.

"Is he gone?" Kane asked as he saw me enter, his voice low and dangerous.

"Yeah, he had no real reason to snoop, he claimed he heard someone in distress and it was his right as a police officer to investigate."

Archer snorted. "What a crock of shit, he clearly still has it out for us."

"Yeah," I agreed.

"She was in the sunroom," Kane said, tilting his head towards Lavender. "Did he get anywhere near there?"

"He was looking through windows in the back east, nowhere near the sunroom. If I hadn't grabbed him when I did he may have seen something." I sighed, relieved he had been nowhere near Lavender, but simply being on the property was far too close for my liking.

"So he didn't see me?" Lavender asked softly, getting up and padding over to me, gently wrapping her arm around my waist. Pulling her into me, I inhaled the sweet scent clinging to her hair, letting it relax and reassure me.

"No," I confirmed.

"He's a twat for even coming near us! Coming near her, that fucking beta should be strung up," Kane snarled, his face turning red with anger. Lavender jumped back at the vitriol in his voice. Kane was physically shaking with rage.

Then, to my shock she walked right up to Kane, hugging him round the middle, nestling her head into his chest. Kane looked down, surprised as a delicious, relaxing hum filled the air that made us all feel completely boneless. Lavender was purring to calm Kane down!

The effects of the hum quickly took effect, the tension visibly seeping out of Kane's body, and he gently hugged Lavender back.

"He didn't see me," Lavender insisted. "That's what matters." She smiled up at Kane. "I'll stay out of the sunroom from now on... just to be safe."

"But you love that room," Archer frowned.

"Yeah, but I also love my nest and at least when I'm there, you aren't at risk of getting in trouble by a federal peeping tom." Lavender started picking up various papers, poking around. "I don't want you guys getting in trouble," she mumbled in a low voice.

"You're too good to be around us," Kane whispered, kissing her on the forehead. My heart stuttered at the sight, Kane was getting very touchy with Lavender—was that a good thing?

"I know, I'm awesome," Lavender joked, pulling away from Kane with a smile. "So awesome, that Theo is going to get take out pizza tonight?" She smiled at Theo questioningly.

"I'll go place the order." Theo smiled at her warmly, and left to make the call.

"Oooh! I'll ask him to make more cinnamon buns for dessert!" Lavender decided, pulling away from Kane and scampering after Theo up the stairs, calling his name.

"She's got him wrapped around her finger, hasn't she?" Archer laughed.

"She's got all of us wrapped around her finger," Kane said, looking at the stairs where Lavender had been mere moments before, with a frown.

CHAPTER TWENTY-NINE
Theo

That night, once Lavender was curled up and I'd extracted myself, I made my way to Gage's office where the entire pack was assembled. I hated leaving her side, the moment I did everything just felt less relaxed, like I was that much closer to snapping.

I had given Lavender only the basics on who Detective Rouche was, then diverted her with my fingers—much to my pleasure—and soon enough she was one sleepy, blissed out omega.

I ensured I scrubbed my hands before leaving, because the others would have smelled Lavender's slick from a mile away and given this new threat, I didn't want to distract everyone.

"What's the plan?" I asked, striding into the room, plastering a fake grin on my face.

"I think we need to send Lavender home," Kane admitted, ignoring the sounds of protest from every other packmate. My grin dropped.

We couldn't send her home, I *needed* her. Despite her being a feral house cat, I hadn't felt more relaxed in years. Maybe all I needed was some omega loving, forget treatment for brain damage, Lavender was my remedy.

"Why?" Gage asked, frowning. I was sure he wouldn't even consider it. Lavender was one of us now, in a way and I couldn't picture her just leaving. Her absence would leave a gaping hole. To suggest sending her away seemed... abhorrent.

"We know she wouldn't say anything against us. She knows why we're doing what we're doing. Her being here just puts her in danger. If Detective Rouche can get onto the property so easily then the fuckers who took Juniper could do the same. Lavender would be safer behind the walls of the Haven."

"You really are a heartless bastard, you know that? You know full well we've become attached to her—you just want her out of the way," Archer spat, furious.

"Am I wrong?!" Kane growled, turning on Archer. The pain was clear on his face, he didn't want her to leave either. "I don't *want* to send her back, but it's the safest for her!"

I raised my brows. Did he actually want her here? Was *he* getting attached? The urge to prod and find out more was strong as fuck—but Kane was hard to talk to on a good day, let alone when he's stressed and grumpy.

"Stop it, the both of you," Gage commanded. "Kane is right, we know Lavender would be safer in a Haven—"

"You seem to forget that *we* kidnapped her from a Haven!" I interjected. "so some other fucker certainly can too, she's safer here, with us."

"True, but that was only because Archer stumbled across her. If that had never happened she wouldn't have ever been wrapped up in all of this. She would be mated to a good pack, and kept safe."

"That doesn't change the fact that we did kidnap her! We can keep her safer than any other pack," Archer said.

"We could," Gage agreed, "if we weren't wanted criminals. Our search for Juniper is going to get us in more trouble and danger, and we can't be dragging Lavender into that."

Archer cursed, turning to look at Kane. "Kane, I love you, you are my pack but we don't even know if Juniper is alive, we haven't seen or heard any evidence since she vanished four years ago! I refuse to avoid living my life to chase a ghost!"

"Juniper is alive!" Kane thundered, rounding on Archer and bringing a fist to his jaw, and sent him sprawling to the floor. Gage quickly stood between them, frowning while physically restraining Kane.

"This isn't helping," Gage said. "You know we hope Juniper is alive, Kane. We've spent years searching and even became criminals trying to find her! She is our family."

"I'm not letting Lavender go," I said simply, crossing my arms. Everyone looked at me, varying levels of surprise in their faces at my statement. Only Gage knew how far Lavender and I had gone, and he was clearly conflicted about it, because he hadn't told the others yet.

"Theo..." Gage started.

"No. After everything I've done for this pack..." I trailed off, it was a low blow, but I went with it because she was more important. "She makes me feel good, for the first time in a long time. We deserve to be happy, and I'm not letting her go."

"If we can't all come to an agreement, she stays." Gage sighed, running a hand through his hair. "I refuse to let us be divided on this." I turned to Kane, "can you look at upping security?"

"I guess I'll have to," he growled.

CHAPTER THIRTY
Lavender

Archer stretched lazily next to me. We hadn't left the nest in days, other than bathroom and snack breaks, and we had binged so much true crime that I felt like I could recite the cases of several mass murderers by heart. I had stuck to staying in my room with the curtains closed and only occasionally ventured into the kitchen, just to be safe. Occasionally Archer did some sort of work on his laptop, but I didn't pay close attention. He mentioned something about trading stocks and tried to explain the basics, but I was useless. Knowing me, I would pick something to invest in purely on its vibes and not its actual potential.

Who was I kidding? I could have done that *before* our binge watching sessions, it was just... reinforced now.

The whole pack had been tense, on edge. Detective Rouche's visit had shaken them, but I could tell they were trying to hide it. They were constantly looking around, as if an enemy was going to jump out around every corner. The darkness wasn't that bad, and they had the fancy cool light bulbs so it wasn't that noticeable.

"Pizza?" Archer asked, scratching at his stubble. He was usually so clean shaven. The change was kind of nice. "I think we have a few frozen pizzas left."

"Sounds good, but I think Theo may have demolished them," I admitted.

"Human garbage disposal, that one," Archer chuckled. "In that case I guess it'll have to be pasta."

"Oh no," I giggled, "what a hardship!"

"Brat," Archer said, launching a pillow at my face that I easily caught and cuddled. It was a really soft, squishy pillow, and I couldn't resist.

Theo was already in the kitchen, eating a frozen pizza of all things. I couldn't resist smiling at the sight. He was kind of predictable, but that wasn't a bad thing. I liked it.

"Hello there." He beamed at me, abandoning his pizza to wrap me in a hug and spin me around, despite my weak protests.

As soon as he put me down, my hand darted out to steal a slice of pizza, retreating back to Archer's side before Theo even realised.

"You deceptive trickster!" He pouted. My only response was to take a bite of the pizza with an exaggerated satisfied hum, even though the pizza was actually kind of stale.

I looked over to Archer with a grin, holding my pizza up in victory.

"Archer! Can you help Kane with the security upgrade this afternoon? I'll stay with Lavender," he grinned, eyes raking over me.

Don't get horny. That was the last thing I needed. This

thing with Theo was still pretty new, and I didn't think Archer knew yet.

"Sure, I guess I've been monopolising her the last few days. Good luck, Lavvy girl." He pulled me in for a quick hug, kissing the top of my head before letting me go so I could stay with Theo. "Shout if you need me."

Once we were alone, Theo pulled me in for a kiss, and I didn't fight it, sinking into his embrace.

"What do you want to do?" he asked, moving away with a cheeky grin. Judging by the prominent bulge in his sweatpants, I knew *exactly* what he wanted to do.

"Hmmm," I tapped my chin, trying to look thoughtful. "We could play chess?"

"Nope," he popped his lips on the *P*.

"No?" I raised my eyebrows.

"Not allowed. Chess is banned. Pick something else."

"Video games?" I smirked.

"While that is tempting, I'm not feeling it right now."

"I guess I may as well have a shower. I've been stuck in my bed all day, and I'm all sweaty so I could use a good clean."

"That is the best idea you've had all day!" Theo laughed. "Now, maybe I should come with, you know, for safety reasons."

"Oh, we take safety very seriously, don't we? I've seen your shower skills before."

"But a repeat never hurts, does it?" he asked.

"No, it does not."

Two hours later I was standing in Theo's room, legs feeling like jelly as I explored his space. My hair was still damp from the shower and I wore nothing but one of Theo's T-shirts.

His room was warm with a brown and green aesthetic. There were textbooks everywhere, mainly on animal anatomy and care.

"How long has it been?" I asked, picking up a textbook and turning it over in my hands. "Since you were a vet?"

"A few years," Theo admitted from where he was lounging in a pair of boxers on the futon in the corner of the room.

"Do you miss it?"

"I do. I used to love being around animals."

"Why don't you have any pets?" I put the book down and padded over to him. He opened his arms with a smile and I sat across his lap.

"I wanted to, but I was unsure, given everything that happened to me, my temper became somewhat…explosive. The last thing I wanted to do was lash out at a pet."

"You talk about being half crazy, about having this mad temper, but I've never seen it."

He smiled down at me indulgently. "You calm me. There's something about you."

"Lavender is a very calming smell," I grinned. "You deserve to have a pet. If you could have any animal, what would it be?"

"A cat. They were always my favourite to treat, even when they were being assholes and needed to be wrapped into a blanket." His face lit up when he spoke about it.

"What pets did you hate treating the most?"

"Tiny dogs, those things were often pissed at the world and wanted you to know it. I never got so much as a scratch, let alone a bite from a big dog. Those small fuckers must have given me hundreds in a few short years."

I snorted. "Is that how you got these?" I asked, my hand trailing along the faint thin scars on his forearm.

He nodded. "Yep, angry little fuckers. Did you ever have pets growing up?"

"I wish. My parents were more focused on what their kids could do for them, not what they could do for their kids. They saw pets as just another useless mouth to feed," I shrugged.

"They sound like cold hearted jackasses," Theo replied, his nose crinkled in disgust.

"That they are. I've been pretty much ignoring them since I joined the Haven."

"Surely they're concerned you're missing?"

"I doubt they know. I made it clear I wanted none of my personal information given to them. They were ready to sell me off as a teenager to the first pack of old church men who had money and zero moral compass. I want nothing to do with them. I'm happier doing my own thing."

"I get that, we haven't really spoken to our families in the last few years either." His hand gently clenched my bare thigh and I snuggled deeper into his chest.

After a moment's silence, I spoke. "What are we doing, Theo?"

"Whatever the hell we want."

I smiled into his chest. I liked that idea. There was no denying the pull I felt to this pack, and frankly I was sick of resisting it. It felt too good. Theo had made me see stars, smelled like delicious lemons *and* was a good cuddler, what more could I ask for?

His fingers trailed up my bare leg, sending shivers up my spine. As he inched closer and closer to my core I found myself wanting him again. Never mind the three orgasms he had just given me in the shower. This alpha was making me feral with need. There was no such thing as enough.

"Please?" I whispered, clutching his shoulder tightly.

"Well considering you asked so nicely," he smirked, wasting no time, sinking his fingers straight into me as his thumb found my clit and started circling it lazily.

I closed my eyes, humming in happiness as he took his time winding me up. Just as I approached the edge he stilled. Opening my eyes I looked up at him, he had a wicked glint in his eye.

"Why did you stop?" I whined.

"I'm taking my time," he smirked, making me frown. What was the fucker up to? My doubt was quickly forgotten when he started moving again. "How can I resist you when you're flooded with slick for me?"

"Beats me," I chuckled, approaching the edge once again.

Until he stopped. Again.

"Theo!" I snarled.

"Hush, let me have my fun."

"I'll hit you with another lamp," I threatened. He only laughed in response. Fucker.

I was so close to reaching that point again when the door opened.

Gage strode in, pausing at the sight of the two of us curled up on the armchair, Theo's fingers buried in me. I froze for a moment, panicking. Gage was the pack lead, he could easily order Theo to leave me alone, and he would have to. Shit.

"Hello Gagey!" Theo chirped happily. "Come to join the cuddles?" he asked innocently while increasing the pace of his fingers, and eliciting a strangled moan from me.

I was waiting for the anger, the shouting.

Imagine my shock when Gage started *laughing*.

"This room smells like sex," he chuckled. "And now I have a boner, so thanks for that."

"Not the first time I've given you a boner." I shrugged, biting my lip. Theo's chest shook with laughter.

"Same! I've given Gagey plenty of boners over the years, haven't I?"

Gage stood in the middle of the room, hands on his hips. Was he angry? He had said he was sick of resisting whatever was between us when I was icing his bruises, but did he still feel that way? Maybe he had slept since and regained his common sense.

I untangled myself from Theo, ignoring his little grunt of unhappiness at the loss of me. Gage's eyes raked over me as I walked over to him, resting on my bare legs. The T-shirt I had borrowed more than covered my butt, though my lack of underwear made my scent a lot more... potent.

"Are you mad?" I asked quietly. We hadn't really spoken since the last time he had kissed me, we had all been distracted by the detective.

Gage rolled his eyes, arm sneaking around my waist and pulling me into him.

"No," he replied simply, leaning down and taking my lips in a bruising kiss.

"Fuck yeah!" Theo crowed from behind me. "I knew you'd come around, Gagey!"

I pulled away, smiling as I turned to grin at Theo. "Actually, he kissed me long before you did."

His face dropped and he pouted. "No! Or was it just a kiss?"

Gage laughed. "Two kisses, actually."

"Well," Theo smirked, lounging back on the armchair, a

look of pride firmly on his face, "*I* was the first one to make her come, the only one in fact."

My face heated and I buried it in Gage's chest as he chuckled.

"Hmm, maybe we should change that?" Gage murmured.

My mouth opened and closed a few times as I tried to find the words. But before I could form a thought, my body reacted, the smell of slick so thick in the air I was surprised they could breathe.

"Uh..."

"What did Theo do to you?" Gage smirked at me.

"Today, or in general?" I asked in an innocent tone, biting my lip as I looked up at him.

Gage's eyebrows rose.

"He keeps accosting me in the shower," I shrugged, giggling nervously.

Gage groaned, closing his eyes. "That's a mental image that's going to stick with me."

Theo's hands clasped my waist, drawing me back to him. I had been so focused on Gage I hadn't heard him approach.

Lips descended on my neck, gently kissing a path up and down.

Next thing I knew, I was laying across Theo's bed with him on top of me while Gage watched excitedly.

Hands roaming over my body, hiking my leg over his hip, filling the room with the smell of my arousal.

Did Gage intend to stay? Or did he intend to join?

CHAPTER THIRTY-ONE
Theo

I was in heaven. I had Lavender under me, smelling like slick and myself, and Gage was watching us.

"You just going to watch or join in?" I asked Gage in a smug, gleeful tone, lips never leaving Lavender's neck.

Gage's eyebrows rose. "I'm going to do whichever Lavender prefers" he asked, directing his question to Lavender. Naturally he would be more concerned with her desires than mine at that moment. I distracted myself with my mission to leave my mark on her. If I thought too hard about Gage joining us, I would have finished in my pants like a hormonal teenager. The mental image of Gage behind Lavender, buried in her warmth, making her squirm and moan. Dominating her, making her his while I watched, had been haunting my dreams for weeks.

She held her hand out to Gage and motioned for him to join.

Holy shit.

Dreams do come true.

My boner was so hard it must have broken some sort of world record, but I was in no position to be testing that shit right now.

Leaning back I allowed Lavender to crawl out from under me, over to where Gage stood at the edge of the bed.

"Hello darling," he murmured happily.

"Hi," she grinned up at him, her eyes wide and wild. Her neck was littered with my bite marks and her lips were swollen from kissing.

Fucking perfect.

I fell back into the pillows, and settled in for the show.

Gage's hand reached out, gently placing his thumb on her chin, tilting her face up to look at him as he looked down at the sweet little omega on all fours in front of us on the bed.

"Theo's marked you up good and proper, darling," he smiled and his finger trailed down her throat. A wave of sweet slick filled the air. Gage turned to me, eyebrow raised.

"Oh, she loves marks." I grinned, and Gage's eyes filled with delight, I could practically see him mentally filing that information away for later use.

Sitting up on her knees, she reached out for Gage, gripping his sides as she leaned in for a kiss. They took their time, slowly relishing in each other, Lavender's hand slipping under Gage's shirt, exploring the expanse of skin underneath.

"What was Theo doing to you before I came in?" Gage asked, pulling back slightly.

"He wasn't letting me come," she pouted adorably.

I wanted to bite that protruding bottom lip. Gage beat me to it, making her whine with need.

"Well, that's just mean, isn't it?" Gage grinned.

Lavender nodded.

"She's just so fun to play with," I admitted, shrugging my shoulders.

Lavender pouted at Gage. "I'm considering clubbing him with a lamp again if he doesn't let me come soon."

Gage laughed before pulling her in for another quick kiss. "Well," he told her, pulling back "it's a good thing that I'm the boss of him then, isn't it?"

This was going to be good. Scratch that, this was going to be phenomenal.

Lavender's hand trailed down, stroking Gage through the fabric of his trousers. She smirked up at him, biting her bottom lip. She knew exactly what she was doing.

Gage's moan was music to my ears. "Take it out," he instructed.

Being a good little omega, she did as she was told, pulling his length out and giving it a few lingering pumps.

"Like that?" she asked, her tone teasing.

"Harder," Gage instructed, his fingers trailing over her throat gently, tightening for a moment.

Her lips were mere inches away from his glistening tip. The sight was too much. I pulled out my cock, gently working on myself while I watched Gage pull his shirt off, his focus never leaving her.

The moment she stuck her tongue out to taste him, I nearly came all over my own hand. Gage glanced over at me and all I could do was smirk, he was hardly holding it together himself if the way the vein in his neck was bulging was any indication.

Taking his moan as a good sign, Lavender threw herself into sucking him, taking him deep with no warning.

This was better than any porn I had ever seen.

Gage let out a strangled groan, his hand flying to the back

of her head, tangling in her hair as he gently guided her lips up and down his shaft, mesmerised at the sight. She looked rumpled and flushed, my T-shirt hanging off her shoulder. Her position on her knees at the edge of the bed, leaning forward ever so slightly gave me a stunning view of the slick covered folds my hands had been buried in moments earlier.

Taking control, he set the pace. The muscles in his arm flexed as he manoeuvred her head.

"So fucking good," he murmured, eyes never leaving Lavender. "Such a pretty little mouth, that's it, take every inch."

Despite the rapture on his face he didn't let her play for long, pulling out of her mouth with a pop, he crawled onto the bed with her underneath him, her legs winding around his waist.

"You want to know a secret?" I asked her.

Gage trailed his hand up her shirt, completely exposing her before him. "Gage here likes control, he's worse than me, he'll only let you come if you ask very, very nicely."

Her low whine in response was beautiful.

Gage pulled back, ignoring her whimpers of protest. "What do you want, darling?"

"Fuck me!" Her voice was an adorable growl.

"She's feeling a bit needy, I think."

Gage looked up, noticing me playing with my cock before lowering his lips to Lavender's ear. "I'll fill you up, but you've got to take care of Theo while I do, how does that sound?"

"Yes," she whimpered.

In seconds they had pulled apart and Gage flipped her over like she weighed nothing, back on her hands and knees, only this time she was facing me.

Warm, wet lips descended on my cock, and I wanted to cry

with relief. Her mouth was heaven. I needed to get her pent up more often. Granted I hadn't intended to do that, but I just didn't want to stop playing with her. Her frustration, and that fire in her eyes, was just a beautiful bonus.

My hand tangled in her hair, directing her to look at me as she swallowed my length. I wanted to watch her reaction. I wasn't an insecure alpha, I knew I could fuck, but Gage was bigger and I wanted to see the expression on her face as he filled her for the first time. "Eyes on me, princess," I commanded.

Gage looked down at her ass as he sunk into her with a look of pure bliss on his face. Lavender's eyes went wide and she moaned around my cock.

"Fuck, it feels so good when she moans around my cock, make her do it again," I panted.

"With pleasure," he said, his voice breathless as he pulled out and filled her with a single thrust. The vibration of her moan was heady, all coherent thought leaving my brain.

All I could focus on was the warmth of her mouth as she slowly took me deeper and deeper into her throat.

She was close, she had already been so near when I'd been torturing her, so it wouldn't take long. That was a relief, because I was already there. A few seconds of her mouth on me and I was ready to combust.

"How does she feel?" I asked Gage, who had his head thrown back in bliss as he fucked her.

"So. Damn. Good." He grunted, punctuating each word with a thrust. "I can feel her tightening."

"Are you getting close, princess?" I asked, looking down at her soft lips sliding up and down my shaft. She nodded around my cock, never stopping her ministrations. "I'm getting close, too," I warned her, because I doubted she wanted a mouth full of cum, as glorious as that sight would be.

Instead of backing off like I thought she would, she doubled down her efforts, hollowing out her cheeks and taking me somehow deeper.

She is going to suck my soul out through my cock, and I am fully okay with that.

"Looks like our girl has other ideas," Gage chuckled, breathless. "Come in her mouth."

The command tipped me over the edge, the electric tingling in the base of my spine bubbled over. Throwing my head back I moaned graphically as I finished. Lavender didn't miss a beat, swallowing around my length, milking me for every drop.

Once she had drained every last ounce of come from my cock she released me from her lips with a pop, and threw me a satisfied smirk.

Unable to resist, I leaned down, kissing her. She tasted like her usual sweet lavender and my own salty musk. I loved the combination of us.

Pulling back, I smiled at Gage before looking at Lavender. "Have you ever been knotted, princess? I haven't had the chance to knot that pretty pussy yet, have I? I thought Gage might like that honour."

"Oh really?" Gage asked.

Lavender bit her lip and shook her head.

"Do you want to be knotted?" I asked.

"Yes," she whined, looking up at me with pleading eyes.

Gage looked elated, leaning forward so he could mutter in Lavender's ear.

"Do you want me to knot you, darling? Do you think you can handle it?" he asked, nipping at her neck and making her moan. My mind wandered to how she would look with our marks littering her neck—and I was rock hard again.

"Show me."

Obliging her, Gage set a punishing pace and I leaned back to enjoy the show as her eyes widened and her mouth fell open. Had I not just come so hard my brain felt like mush, I would be taking that open mouth as an invitation.

Her little gasps of pleasure were coupled with Gage's harsh grunts in a way that made my already hard cock that much more desperate to get back into the action. Lavender's eyes drifted close, and I couldn't have that. I wanted to watch the moment she fell apart. Leaning forward I gently placed my hand on her throat, using my thumb to direct her to look at me.

"No closing your eyes, princess. Look at me while Gage fucks you. Does it feel good? Being shared?"

She nodded wordlessly. "You're making Gage feel so good, he can hardly form words while buried deep in your warmth. I know just how fucking wet and perfect you are."

"I'm not going to last. She's like a fucking vice on my cock," Gage panted.

"Knot her," I told him, then turned back to Lavender. "Ask him nicely to knot you, ask him to stretch that sweet pussy until it's full to the brim with his cum." Her eyes glazed over, rolling into the back of her head. She was stunning like this, I wanted to see it every day.

Gage's thrusts became downright feral, he was a man on a mission, chasing his own release. "Play with her clit," he instructed, his voice rough and uneven.

"With pleasure." I smirked, reaching forward with my hand that wasn't wrapped around Lavender's throat, finding her clit and pressing down gently. Her whimpers increased in speed, she was getting close.

"How does it feel?" I asked her.

"So good," she moaned. "So close. Please let me come on your knot. *Please*," she sounded desperate and I was fucking enthralled.

Gage leaned down, his lips inches from her ear. "Then come on my cock like a good girl. I want my knot buried deep in you when you finish."

She opened her mouth to say something else, but Gage roared loudly, thrusting into her, burying his knot deep in her walls, cursing as he did. She stilled, her eyes widening, the sensation throwing her over the edge, as she came with a long, keening whine.

Gage came with a groan, clenching Lavender's hips tightly as he pumped every last drop he could into her. He slumped forward, gently kissing the back of Lavender's neck with a hum of happiness.

"Fuck me you're perfect. I think you drained me dry."

"You're not half bad yourself," she chuckled weakly. "I can't feel my legs."

I guess I would have to carry her. *Oh no. How terrible.*

Her eyelids drooped as she flopped down on the bed, snuggling into me. I grinned at Gage, who was smiling happily as he hovered over her, still firmly locked inside her. Did he understand there was no letting her go now?

CHAPTER THIRTY-TWO
Lavender

My body was deliciously sore. How many times had I come that day alone? It was a new personal record for sure. I had played with myself many times during heats, but those orgasms paled in comparison to the things these men did to me.

Sharing... that was a new one for me, but I wouldn't say a single bad thing about it. Having two alphas focused on me, playing my body in expert ways, resulted in the most intense orgasms. How the heck did omegas with packs get anything done? I had only sampled two of the pack members, and my legs were jelly, I was exhausted yet still unbelievably horny.

When Gage had knotted me, I was surprised I didn't black out with the intensity of it. I only managed to stay awake for a few moments before dozing off.

It was several hours later I woke up, my limbs tangled with Theo's in his bed. It was so comfortable, I didn't want to move.

"Welcome back," Theo chuckled, kissing the top of my head.

"No, sleep more," I grumbled, nuzzling my face into his bare chest.

"I'm happy to stay right here," he soothed while running a hand lazily over my hair. "But, when did you last eat?"

My stomach chose that exact moment to gurgle loudly.

"I'm fine," I said, clutching him tighter.

"Hmm, I think your stomach is voicing its protests, princess."

"You're hearing things." I mumbled into his chest, which started moving with his laughter.

"How about we get some pasta? Or I could make waffles."

"Waffles?" I asked, my head popping up to look at him hopefully.

He nodded sagely. "I do them super sweet, with ice cream, berries, brown sugar and even—"

Placing both my hands on his chest I gently shoved him away, scrambling up. "Waffles. Now. Please."

Theo's eyebrows rose. "Waffles are the way to your heart then?"

"Sugar is the way to my heart, and you just described something glorious. Chop chop, waffle boy." I pointed toward the door as Theo extracted himself from the sheets laughing.

"You know I'm not the kidnapee here?"

"I'll handcuff you to the bed, then you can be the kidnapee, but first, waffles!" I ordered, ignoring the way his eyes darkened at the mention of handcuffs.

"We'll be revisiting the cuffs right after, princess," he promised.

"Do you even have cuffs?" I asked, looking around the

room for my leggings I'd discarded hours ago when he had first dragged me into the shower.

"Oh, I have handcuffs, and I'll gladly let you use them on me."

I stopped my search, straightening up to look at him.

"You'll let me use them on you?" I asked.

"Oh, I'll beg you to, princess," he smirked, grabbing my leggings, handing them to me. "But first, waffles."

Hopping into my leggings while he put a T-shirt on I pouted at the loss of his chest, it was a damn good pillow.

But waffles. I would behave for waffles.

"Have you got a hair tie?" I asked, suddenly feeling shy. For some reason, even though we had fucked several times in the last two days, I felt nervous asking him for a hair tie? I knew he had them because I had seen his chin length blonde hair thrown into a bun on occasion.

My hair probably looked wild, considering how many hands had been in it, so a messy bun was my best option.

"Here," he grabbed one off his bedside table and passed it to me. I thanked him and quickly wrestled my waves into a semi manageable style. It was going to be a bitch to brush out later, but that was future Lavender's problem. Current Lavender was focused on waffles.

Padding after Theo I resisted the urge to shove him in the back to make him get to the kitchen faster. I couldn't recall the last time I had an indulgent, sweet dessert. I gave into the thought and gently pushed him forward.

"Hurry up!" I grumbled.

Theo laughed loudly.

"You're feral for waffles, I need to remember this."

"I will do downright evil and criminal things *for* waffles, but I will do downright criminal things to *you* if you delay me getting said waffles—and not sexy criminal things, before you open your mouth!" I groused, pushing him forward.

"Okay, okay! Come on, feral beastie."

He turned, grabbing the arm I was pushing him with and pulling me into him. Keeping me close as we made our way to the kitchen.

Theo was mixing the batter while I cut up berries, the waffle iron heating up on the counter. Every other berry ended up in my mouth so it was taking me a fair amount of time to get enough for the waffles.

When Theo pinched one, I playfully pointed my knife at him. Raising his hands in surrender he said "Okay, don't fuck with the omegas sweets, noted," he said with a shit eating grin on his face.

"Part of me feels like you would enjoy getting stabbed a little too much," I grumbled, turning back to my work.

I had almost finished my pile, and was feeling rather proud of my work, when Kane walked in. He was covered in a light layer of sweat, wearing just a pair of gym shorts. I pointedly avoided looking at his chest—it really wasn't fair for a man to be *that* large and have so many abs. Nodding at us as he made his way to the fridge, he grabbed a glass of water and chugged half of it.

"Heya, want a waffle?" Theo asked with a smile, spooning some batter onto the iron. "Though I think Lavender ate most of the berries."

"There's a few left," I grumbled. Not a lot, but a few.

"Sure," he said, breathing deeply.

"I'll get the syrup," I smiled, walking over to the fridge, and passing Kane. As I walked by I did my best to ignore the thick leathery smell that was extra potent thanks to the added sweat he was now glistening in. Sweaty alphas should be disgusting, but my daft omega hormones *loved* it.

Grabbing the bottle, I turned back to Theo, but was distracted by Kane who had gone unnervingly still, staring at me with wide eyes, his nostrils flared.

The smell of burning filled the room, and a quick glance toward Theo let me know the smell wasn't coming from the waffle iron.

"Uh... Kane?" I asked, concerned.

"You smell like *him*." He thrust his head in Theo's direction.

"Of course she does, she smells like all of us," Theo said nonchalantly

"No, she smells like *sex*!" He snarled, looking at me with straight up hatred.

"Lavender, come here." Theo's voice was level and controlled.

I scampered over to him, thankful to have the counter between us.

Kane looked between us with disgust on his face, launching the bottle across the room so it smashed against the wall behind Theo.

I yelped, jumping out of my skin and shaking. Now the room was filled with the smell of burnt sugar, the scent of my own distress.

"Fucking traitor!" Kane snarled, looking between us for a moment before storming out of the room, slamming a door behind him loudly.

"H-he's really pissed," I stuttered. Theo pulled me in for a gentle hug, running his hand up and down my back.

"Don't mind him. Let me text Gage, then I'll get us those

waffles, okay? Gage will take care of Mr Crabby Pants," he said, pulling us apart to look me in the eyes. "You've done nothing wrong," he reassured me.

"It doesn't feel like it." I looked at the door Kane had stormed through. I knew he didn't like me, but I didn't expect him to be quite so... violent.

CHAPTER THIRTY-THREE
Gage

"We need to talk," I directed my words at Kane who was pummeling the punching bag like he had a vendetta to settle. I couldn't blame him for his anger, he had been so set in his plans for the future. Knowing about Theo and Lavender had clearly sent him into a tailspin.

Theo had texted me, saying Kane had smelled him on Lavender, and hadn't reacted well. I had assured him I would take care of it. He had told me Kane had scared her by throwing the bottle of syrup across the room, and now she was acting skittish. I hated that, and didn't want her to feel anxious. Now we were in it together, for as long as she was with us.

Archer, having noticed me entering, put his weights down and wandered over to us. His gaze was cautious, his steps slow, like Kane would turn on him if he said the wrong words. To be fair, that *was* a possibility. He was going at that punching bag with fury.

"So talk," Kane growled, eyes never leaving the punching bag.

"I get that you're pissed, but you can't take it out on the others, throwing shit at them is a dick move."

"He betrayed my sister, you should want to kill him as well."

"There was no betrayal, Kane. None of us are committed to Juniper, and you know that. I refuse to deny Theo some happiness after all he's been through."

"He had fucking sex with her!" he snarled, each punch landing with an impressive thud.

I knew the next words out of my mouth were going to get a reaction, and my face was probably going to be receiving some of those punches, but it needed to be said.

"I did as well," I admitted.

Kane stilled. *Shit. Maybe I should run? He's a big fucker, and while I'm not exactly small, he can kill me with his bare hands.*

I held my ground as he turned to stare at me, his eyes wide, lips pressed together tightly. He was almost vibrating with rage, and the entire room stank like something rotten and acidic. I resisted the urge to gag, he was *livid*.

"You... what?" he asked so quietly, I almost didn't hear. Archer was looking between us, his mouth opening and closing repeatedly. I probably should have given him a heads up, but I hadn't really thought this through, otherwise I would have waited until Kane was a bit calmer and feeling a little less punchy.

"I also slept with Lavender—and I don't regret it."

I was expecting the blow, but it still hurt like a bitch. My cheek throbbed, and I wouldn't have been surprised if he had fractured it. There was going to be an impressive bruise.

"Kane! What the hell!" Archer shoved Kane away from me, but I raised my hand to stop his advance. Kane needed to get his feelings out, and if my face was the casualty, then so be it. I was done tiptoeing around this topic.

"How could you!" Kane snarled.

"How could I?" I asked. "I like her, Kane, a lot. Now don't get me wrong, I love Juniper, but not in the same way. Juniper is a sister to me, to all of us."

"No." Kane shook his head vigorously. "You would have been perfect for her!"

"She will find the perfect pack for her when she comes home, Kane. I promise, but that pack isn't us." Kane shook his head and started pacing like a caged animal. "You know we consider you pack, Kane."

"I'm not, Juniper is."

"Juniper is family. She's the sister of a packmate," Archer spoke, looking Kane in the eye.

"After everything Juniper's undoubtedly been through, she deserves the sweetest, most pristine pack, and that isn't us. Could you really picture Theo with her now? He's not who he used to be. Would Juniper even recognise him?"

Kane's pacing faltered, my words had hit home. "I... I can't, Gage. She wanted you guys."

"She wanted who we were five years ago: a butcher's assistant, a computer tech and a veterinarian. We aren't those things anymore. We have blood on our hands—none of us regret it, especially if it brings her home, but she is such a sweet soul. She deserves more than what we've become. Lavender... she can go to bat with any of us, and I can't deny how attracted I am to her."

Kane sighed, deflating, dropping onto the bench, head in his hands. "I know! Okay, I know."

"You like her as well," Archer said, placing a hand on Kane's shoulder in a comforting gesture.

"Of course I do, but I'm not spoken for."

"Neither are we," I reiterated. "Though, the whole we kidnapped her thing might complicate this situation further."

"Lavender will want to go home," Kane said. "You can't keep her here. She'll move on, then maybe when Juniper is home... she would understand if you weren't able to wait the whole time she was gone."

He was reaching, clearly at the bargaining stage of his grief. "You wouldn't want that for her," I told him. "She deserves better. As does Lavender."

Kane couldn't look me in the eye, he just stared dejectedly at the ground by his feet. "I know. It's just hard to let go. She's all I have left."

"That's bullshit." Archer's voice was more aggressive than normal, making Kane's head snap up to look at him, confusion and anger on his face.

"What?"

"You have *us*. We are your pack, I don't give a fuck what you say. You're pack to us, and we aren't going anywhere—no matter how many times you punch us and throw tantrums."

"But..."

"Archer's right," I said. "We are all in agreement, you're part of this pack, come rain or shine. It's time you accepted that, I get that it's going to take some time for you to come to grips with it, and we can hardly file official papers considering we are currently up to our eyeballs in criminal shit—but you are my pack, Kane Evans."

He sat there, looking between us, a dumbfounded look on his face. "It feels like I'm betraying her if I accept," he admitted quietly.

"We know, which is why you take all the time you need, but let us be happy, even if it's for a short time."

"I won't stand in your way." He heaved himself up, running his hand over his buzzed hair. "I, uh, I'm going to shower." He didn't look at me as he spoke, striding out of the room without a backward glance.

"That didn't go terribly," Archer grinned. "You're going to have a nasty bruise though."

"I'll have Lavender kiss it better," I smirked.

"When the fuck did that happen, by the way?" Archer turned on me.

"You've been busy, though I thought you would have picked up her scent on us."

"I had no idea... does this mean I can, you know?"

"You're welcome to do whatever you want, but if she opts to taser you in the balls, that's on you."

"She doesn't have a taser... right?" He looked nervous.

"I wouldn't put it past Theo to give her one, honestly. He's obsessed with her."

"Shit, I'd better up my game."

CHAPTER THIRTY-FOUR
Lavender

I had insisted on going back to my own room after the waffles, telling Theo I wanted to shower alone. He had pouted, but eventually relented when I said I would come find him after. He knew I was shaken from Kane's anger, and while he made it clear he didn't want to leave me alone, he respected my wishes.

I wanted to crawl into the nest. The curtains were constantly closed, encasing the room in darkness. For all I knew Detective Rouche could be lurking on the grounds again, so blinds closed it was. Even though I was on the second floor two of the walls were made almost entirely of glass, looking out at the dense forest—I'd be visible from a mile away.

But I smelled like sex, and I was still a mess of sticky, dried cum. Until Kane had reacted so badly, I hadn't minded—in fact I'd liked it. Having the alpha's scent on my skin was comforting, but now I just wanted to be clean now.

I was finger combing my hair out, trying to make it a bit

easier to manage once dry, when the first cramp hit. On the scale of cramps, it wasn't bad, like a tight fluttering deep in my stomach, annoying, but not particularly painful. It wasn't a period cramp, no. It was a heat cramp.

How? I just finished a heat! I racked my brain, by my poor mental arithmetic, I had finished a heat only two weeks ago, I wasn't due for another one for months! I thought back to all the information that had been thrown at us back home.

I never really paid attention, assuming I wasn't going to match with a pack anytime soon, so I often daydreamed and did my own thing. Now, it was biting me in the ass.

Vaguely I remembered talking about how heats would increase in frequency once you had a pack. All those hormones flying around could really fuck with an omega.

Pack Rowe wasn't technically mine, there were no bite marks on my neck, just a varied assortment of hickeys—thank you Theo. But all the sex may have thrown my heat cycle into chaos.

Setting the shower too hot, I made quick work of washing away all other scents on me and lathering up my hair in conditioner to try and make it somewhat less tangled. Once I was sure I was clean and didn't have any lingering smells on my skin I dried, throwing on a clean sweater and sleeping shorts and padding over to the nest.

I was exhausted, mentally and physically. Collapsing into the nest I grabbed one of the more squishy pillows and hugged it to my chest, hoping that I was just crampy and tired, and that I didn't have a heat coming on.

If I were back home I would be relaxing with a cup of tea and talking to Fawn, or at the very least I would have been able to video call her. Here I had no one to talk to but the four alphas that had kidnapped me.

It had only been a few weeks, but my heat was coming, and it was coming *fast*. A lot of the pre heat cramps had hardly been noticeable thanks to the copious orgasms Theo and Gage had been giving me. I could have been feeling them for days, but chalked it up to the sensations those two had been stirring up in me.

There was only so long I could hide it for, though. I left it too long to speak to the others last time. When I realised my heat was truly upon me, I was too pissed at Kane to talk to anyone, I wanted to avoid that mistake—especially if I wanted some of them to join me.

I didn't want to do it alone this time, Theo wouldn't have *let* me go through it alone, the sight of me in pain would be too much for him. He had been sticking to my side of late, and I wasn't complaining. Cuddles and orgasms were a potent drug, and I was addicted.

They were honourable guys though, and if I didn't make it crystal clear to them that I wanted company before my heat hit, Gage probably wouldn't let anyone near me because he would never trust me in the midst of a heat. Omegas got needy in heat.

But I had tried a real knot. Toys would never match up again, and the thought of a heat without a knot was depressing. With a groan of frustration I threw the pillow across the nest, clambering out of the bed.

Kane could go suck a dick—I didn't care if he was pissed. I needed to talk to Gage... and possibly Archer. While he had been busy the last few days, there had been... moments between us, and with a start, I realised I wasn't opposed to him joining for my heat. I trusted him, which was a very odd realisation considering he was the reason I'd been kidnapped. He had never purposely hurt me though, and I trusted that he wouldn't.

Padding out of the room I dithered for a moment. Where was safest to go? I didn't want to go to the den or the kitchen, in case Kane was stalking around.

Theo's room was my first idea, but he would just drag me to bed and keep me there blissed out on orgasms. It would be lovely, but I was on a mission. I needed to talk to Gage.

I had been in his room before, the last time had been when I was icing his bruises and he had kissed me. Heat pooled in my stomach at the memory.

Knocking on the door, I waited a moment, but there was no answer. Could I just walk right in? Yes his cock had been buried in me mere hours ago, but just walking into his room felt like a violation of his privacy, but standing out in the hallway felt exposed, so I twisted the handle, surprised to find the door unlocked.

The room was the same as it had been the last time I was there, minimal, coated in a warm whisky scent. Without thinking I made a beeline to the bed. It was snug and smelled like alpha. I needed it.

Gage could be mad if he wanted, but my omeganess was riding my ass—hard. Preheat was a bitch and I wanted to be comfy, and surrounded by the smell of alphas, so I crawled in, wrapping myself up in the comforter like a little omega burrito. For having such minimal bedding, it was surprisingly comfortable.

Lulled by the scent and comfort, I let the exhaustion take over, ignoring the weak, annoying cramps.

CHAPTER THIRTY-FIVE
Gage

After our conversation with Kane I had expected to find Theo and Lavender curled up together, so I had gone to his room first. He informed me with a pout that she had gone back to her own room to shower and rest, saying she wanted to be alone.

I couldn't blame her. My head would have been spinning if I were in her position. Heading to my own room I resisted the urge to turn around and head to Lavender. She was addictive, and now that I'd had a taste, I wanted nothing more than to have her with me constantly.

Once I was in my own room the smell of vanilla and lavender hit me like a tonne of bricks. There was a bundle of blankets on my bed with wavy locks of brown and purple spilling out. *What is she doing in my room?*

Not one to complain about an omega being in my bed, I sat on the edge, gently moving the blankets. Her soft snore let me know she was sleeping. I couldn't deny the rush of pride at finding her here though. She had chosen to come to my space, to *me*, over my packmates. While we didn't play favourites, I could still revel in the fact that she came to me first, that I had managed to make her comfortable enough to do that in spite of everything we had been through.

"Lavender?" I called her name quietly. She moaned and turned to look at me, her eyes half lidded with sleep, her lips soft and pouty, and her hair wild. I wanted to wake up to that sight every day.

"Gage?"

"What are you doing here? Not that I'm complaining at all —you're more than welcome."

She sat up, looking at me with hazy eyes. She was clearly exhausted, I probably shouldn't have woken her.

"I'm going into heat." She bit her lip, swaying slightly. My heart stuttered. Did she just say *heat*? Hadn't she just been through one alone? And if she was going into heat, why had she come here?

Unless she wanted me to be part of it?

My heart started beating erratically. I was pack lead, I was meant to be cool, composed, but I suddenly felt like a teenage boy who was about to ask a girl out for the first time.

"And you came here?"

"Because I don't want to do this one alone. You and Theo totally caused it, with all those mind blowing orgasms." Her eyes widened as she saw my own startled expression. "But, uh, I can do it alone, if you want. Sorry, I probably shouldn't have come," she started babbling, trying to extract herself from the blankets and failing miserably.

"Woah, woah, woah," I rushed to say, grabbing her by her upper arms so she couldn't escape. "I most definitely don't want you to do it alone, I was just surprised. We caused this?"

"Omega get's knots and orgasms, omega's body thinks it's heat time. Well not normally, but because I've never really satisfied a heat, now I'm getting knots my body is freaking out." she explained. "It may be another day or so before it really kicks in, at the moment I'm just tired. I needed to talk to you first, to know where we all stood." She shrugged.

"I would be happy to help you when it hits," I told her with a smile, gently brushing a wayward curl out of her face. "I'm also pretty sure that Theo would try and stab me if I stood in his way as well."

She laughed lightly and I pulled her into me. "What do you want to do right now?" I asked.

"Rest, maybe we can tell the others later?"

"Sounds good. Do you want me to stay?" She nodded into my chest, so I kicked off my shoes and joined her in my bed, digging my way through the various blankets she was still entangled in.

We laid there, her snoring lightly for several hours. I took the time to memorise every inch of her face, from the slant of her nose, to the curve of her full, pouty lips. The way her chest rose and fell under the blankets her small hands clenched close to her.

I was falling for her, there was no denying it.

Lavender didn't so much as flinch when Archer knocked on the door, poking his head in. Taking in the sight of Lavender asleep next to me, he smiled softly.

"I went to check on her and she wasn't in the nest," he explained. "Is she okay?"

"Yeah, just exhausted," I whispered as she stirred in my arms, her eyes opening blearily.

"Archer?" she asked gently, her voice cracking with sleep.

"Just me Lavvy girl," he replied, walking over to us as she sat up and I followed suit. The action of removing the blanket from around, her scent a waft of concentrated lavender and vanilla through the room, making Archer still as his eyes widened.

"She's in preheat," I explained.

He swallowed, and nodded. Archer clambered into the bed, laying on the other side of him and pulling her in gently.

Lavender sat on the counter, looking sleepy and rumpled, stealing bits of the vegetables that Archer was cutting up. Judging by the shit eating grin he kept shooting her, he wasn't mad about the extra work. Theo had even grabbed a pot of hummus out of the fridge so she could dip her pilfered snacks.

She had them wrapped around her finger, and she didn't even realise it. Wearing the same men's shirt and tiny sleep shorts, she looked like she was ready to crawl back into bed at a moment's notice.

I had been doing my research. Omega's needed a lot of rest before their heats, and could become extra sleepy in the days leading up to it to help prepare them for the fuckfest that was to come. The thought of what we would be doing soon made my pants tighten. The fact she actually wanted us there for her during her heat was mind blowing, and I was struggling to contain my excitement.

Heavy footfalls reached my ears before Kane meandered into the room. "Hey," he murmured, never meeting Lavender's eye or even looking her way.

He needed time, and I had reassured Lavender that it

wasn't her fault. Still, her face fell as he slumped into a chair at the table.

Opening my mouth to attempt to engage Kane in some sort of conversation, I was cut off by a knocking sound from the front door.

All the alphas in the room stilled, but Lavender was momentarily oblivious, munching on a bit of carrot and swinging her legs absentmindedly. Who the hell was at our front door? And why hadn't our extensive security measures alerted us to someone being in the grounds?

While Lavender hadn't heard the knocking, she noticed our reaction, looking around the room with confusion.

"Make sure she's out of sight," I ordered, looking at Archer who was closest to Lavender. With a nod, he put down the knife he was using and gently grabbed Lavender by the hips, lifting her off the counter and ushering her out of the room, ignoring her protests.

"Are you armed?" Kane asked in a low voice.

I wasn't, but I had a gun hidden in the kitchen. With a shake of my head I strode over to the cupboards, hopping onto the counter to pull out my stashed gun kept at a safe height.

"You?" I asked simply as I checked the gun to ensure it was both loaded and clean—the tops of the cupboard got nasty and dusty very easily. Luckily this gun looked entirely usable.

"Yep. Let's go." He strode out of the room, his body tense, and ready to pounce. Stashing the gun in my waistband, I followed. Hopefully Archer had enough time to get Lavender squared away, if this was Detective Rouche, the last thing I wanted was for him to smell Lavender, her scent coated every surface of the house and he was like a demented hyena with a bone.

We glanced at each other with a nod as I reached out for

the door handle. We needed to look natural, just two regular alphas opening their front door. I didn't want to give that fucker any reason to arrest us, because he would. I was honestly surprised when he didn't try to arrest me for kicking him off our grounds.

Sure enough, the fucker was there—Detective Rouch, a smug look on his face.

"Hello, Mr Rowe." He grinned.

"What the hell are you doing on my property," I growled.

A condescending smirk overtook his features. "Now, Gage. Don't take that tone with me, I'm here on official business. There's been reports of noises of a concerning nature coming from this property, and I was sent to come check it out."

"I can assure you, nothing untoward is happening here," I said, doing my best to keep my voice even. I doubted there was actually a call. Rouche was looking to find his way in and was faking something more legitimate—it was obvious.

"Either way, can I come in and take a look?"

If I denied him entrance it would likely only anger him further, but every surface was coated in Lavender's scent.

"I'm sorry, we have a lot of confidential client information out in the open," I shrugged apologetically. "I can't let you in without a warrant, I'm so sorry." I did my best to look sincere.

"Are you sure? I can always get the warrant and come back, but I doubt you want something like that on your record, Kane, come on, be reasonable. I just need to make sure nothing criminal is going on, then I can go on my way."

"Sorry," Kane shrugged. "Client information, as Gage said. We would be in shit if you saw something without a warrant—surely you understand, being a man of the law."

Rouche's condescending smirk faltered. "You're not going to cooperate at all?"

"I'm sorry, our hands are tied."

Rouche stilled, clearly running through the options in his head. The fucking nerve of this beta. He was acting like he hadn't just broken onto our property only a few days prior. And using the excuse that someone else had heard noises? It was such an obvious fabrication—he had used the same excuse a few days ago.

Taking a deep breath, Rouche opened his mouth to speak, but stopped, taking a deep breath. "Your place smells amazing by the way, I wonder what cleaning products you use?" He scratched his chin thoughtfully.

"Kane sometimes works with omegas, for security jobs. He comes home smelling like a sweet shop," I said casually, despite the fact my heart was starting to beat a million miles a minute. My scent was giving some of my stress away, but I hoped the beta wouldn't be able to pick it up. Was Lavender's smell that obvious?

"Oh well, in any case. I'm sure there won't be any need for a warrant, but I'll be popping in and checking on you guys again soon. You're so isolated out here, maybe the noise complaint was a wild animal, in that case you could be in danger—so it's best I keep an eye out."

"Thank you," I smiled. The asshole was telling us he was watching like it was a comforting gesture, but I knew it for exactly what it was—a threat.

Rouche turned to leave, before sticking his finger in the air like he had just thought of something. "Lavender!" he exclaimed, turning in the entryway, and smiling at me. My body froze, heart rate so fast I was shocked I didn't go into cardiac arrest. "That's what I can smell—delicious. Anyway, I'll stop by and see you guys soon!"

Rouche sauntered down the path, looking around as he

went, taking in our property. I looked at Kane, too stunned to speak.

"He fucking *smelled* her," Kane snarled as soon as the door was closed.

"He had no way to know it was an omega," I soothed, though my nerves were fucking rattled.

"He's like a dog with a bone. We need to put him down."

"He's harmless usually, but I would be lying if I said I wasn't concerned," I admitted, running my hand through my hair. "He was so convinced that we hurt Juniper."

Rouche had a crush on Juniper, many, many years ago, but given he was only a beta, she had zero interest in him.

"I don't know. I don't trust him," Kane growled. "I'm going to go check on Lavender," he said, storming out of the room. I followed, my inner alpha hounding me, telling me I needed to keep my omega safe.

She and Theo were in her room, curled up in the nest watching TV quietly, she was fast asleep.

"She conked right out," Theo laughed, noticing my confused look at her. "She was all stressed out, then the moment we laid down, out like a light."

"It's the preheat," I said.

"Yep. Who was that? Are they gone? Why didn't our security kick in?"

"Rouche again, he's getting stubborn. As for the security I don't know what happened but we better figure it out."

"He didn't get wind that Lavender was here, did he?"

"I don't think so."

"What was his excuse for being here?"

"Noise complaint, total bullshit excuse," Kane growled. "He came in like a goddamned alpha and wanted to enter our home. We said no, of course." Kane said as he wandered over to the side of the nest, eyeing Lavender intently, checking to see if she was okay. I guessed his alpha was also riding him hard about her safety, but he didn't want to admit it.

"So you didn't let him in?" Theo asked, his hand running through Lavender's hair as he spoke.

"Yep. She's safe, he doesn't know Lavender's here." I sighed, sitting on the edge of the bed, looking around at my pack. "I say we put some fences up around the property. Big ones. We've had too many unwanted visitors on our land in the last few days and I don't like it. This place was always meant to be remote and almost unreachable."

"To be fair, until this week I don't think we had a single guest here that we didn't invite," Theo muttered.

"No, something seems to have lit a fire under his ass, and I want to know what it is," I said.

"I'm safe, aren't I?" a small voice asked. Lavender, opened her eyes and was looking intently at me over Theo's chest. He pulled her tighter into him, almost crushing her with the intensity of his hug.

"We will keep you safe," I vowed.

CHAPTER THIRTY-SIX
Lavender

Kane and Gage were outside doing something with the security system. I knew why they needed to do it, Detective Rouche was like a dark storm cloud that was hovering over the pack house. I was sticking indoors, keeping the curtains closed and avoiding anything that could make me more visible.

So I couldn't go outside and annoy Kane and Gage, because I needed to stay inside, but I was still craving attention. My heat was approaching fast. Maybe a day away at most. Theo wasn't in his room, and frankly I knew that if I went and pestered him it would probably end up in more mind blowing sex, and my poor bits could use a break.

So I stomped down the hallway, not even bothering to knock as I made my way into the room. I knew who I wanted to see—I had important things to hash out before I became completely mind messy from heat.

"Hey Lavvy girl, you're stinking up the place," Archer

smirked over the screen of his laptop. Sat at his desk with his feet resting on the surface, and laptop in his lap he looked like the epitome of laid back. He wore a slightly thicker set of glasses today—they had lenses to help with screen glare. He had told me about them during our calls.

"I know, this stupid preheat is driving me insane!" I snarled, throwing myself down onto Archer's bed. "I never used to have preheats like this," I whined. "It's from being around all you idiots," I grumbled with no real anger in my voice. "My body has never been around alphas, and now my body is freaking out over all the dick in my general vicinity."

Chucking, Archer stood up, placing his laptop on the desk. He strode over to the bed and crawled in next to me.

"Someone a little grumpy?" he asked.

"Yep," I said, popping the P.

"Come here." Archer gently guided me into his arms, my head resting on his chest. The sweet, gummy brown sugar smell that coated the room increased tenfold when I moved closer to him.

"Of all the candies for me to become obsessed with, goddamned gummy bears," I chuckled weakly.

"My scent is irresistible, I know it," Archer said in a smug tone.

"You sure about that?" I asked.

"Well, you hurling bags of gummy bears at my head did give me pause, but look, you came around!"

I weakly slapped Archer's chest next to my head. Archer's only response was to laugh.

We laid there for a moment, enjoying just being there. Despite the turbulent nature of my body I felt calm curled up against Archer, his arm around me.

"Are you happy with... ugh," Archer stumbled over his words. "What you and... uh... Theo and—"

"Fucking your packmates?" I said as casually as possible, though casual was the last thing I felt. My entire body was tense, dreading Archer's response.

"I see we're not beating about the bush," Archer laughed. Looking down at me. I sat up so I could see his face better, we probably needed to be eye to eye for this.

"If... you know... well..." I stumbled over my words. Taking a deep breath I steeled myself. "If. *When* I go into heat again they'll probably join me. Would you..." I trailed off. Nerves battered my chest.

Archer sat up straighter as a smile spread across his face. "Are you asking if I want to join you?" he asked.

"Yes?" I squeaked. It came out as a question, instead of an answer. When Archer just stared at me wide eyed for a moment I started hastily backtracking.

"You don't have to! Theo and Gage will be amazing, and I don't want you to feel pressured. Or if you don't feel comfortable with me doing that with your pack I—"

Archer was above me, a smirk spreading across his face. Before I could say another word his face descended, capturing my lips in his.

He tasted like gummy bears. Goddamned *gummy bears*. All the times I had sat in my nest at the Haven dreaming about what this alpha tasted like—and now I finally knew. It was better than anything I could have ever imagined. I never wanted to stop kissing him.

My hands flew to his shoulders clutching at his T-shirt as one of his arms circled around my waist, pulling me closer. His stubble scraped against my cheek, and instead of irritating me like I had imagined it would—it only served to heighten every sensation; the heat where our bodies touched, the cold air on my legs, the sweet aroma clouding my senses, the slick flooding my panties. I was hyper aware of every part of his body, including the very prominent erection grinding into my hip.

Part of me wanted to open my legs and beg for that sweet friction, but if we started that I doubted either of us would be able to stop. Perfume filled the room and my stupid preheat made it nearly impossible to stop.

When Archer finally pulled his lips from mine he beamed down at me. "Lavender. I'll *happily* help you when your heat comes."

Heat rose in my face, I probably looked like a tomato but I didn't care. I had no idea how to respond to someone telling me they'll happily fuck me through my heat. While part of me wanted to jump up and down with glee, part of me felt nervous.

For months I had imagined Archer, and it seemed like he had also been imagining me.

What if I'm a disappointment to him?

CHAPTER THIRTY-SEVEN
Lavender

My skin was starting to itch, and no matter what I wore the texture irritated my skin. I knew I didn't have twenty-four hours before I would be lost to the delirium, so I had to find Kane. The entire pack other than him was onboard with my heat, and while they would be able to satisfy me plenty —I was leaking an embarrassing amount of slick just thinking about it—something about not having Kane there didn't feel right.

He was in the most obvious place—the gym. To get abs like that you had to practically live at the gym, and be blessed genetically, and avoid most junk food. It sounded like a miserable experience to me, but whatever floats your boat.

He was lifting weights. Why did it have to be so damn sexy? I was holding on to my sanity by a thread and he was lifting weight sweaty and shirtless? It just wasn't fair. Between the buzz cut, and the many shirtless muscles he looked... sexy as fuck.

He noticed my entrance immediately. Anyone would because I was making the place smell like a goddamned florist. He faltered, resting the weights on the rack and sitting up to look at me.

"What do you want?" He grunted, leaning down to pick up his bottle of water.

"To talk."

"So talk."

"Do you hate me?" I asked, too pent up to beat around the bush.

"Don't ask things you don't want the answers to."

"Your answer would be bullshit I think."

His eyes widened at my words and he stopped what he was doing. "You're so hot and cold, it's insane. You're all grumpy and surly, yet you're constantly taking care of me. It was you who ensured I ate and took pain meds during my last heat."

He opened his mouth to reply but I cut him off.

"Don't even deny it. My brain may have been heat addled, but I recognised your scent easily. You're the one constantly cutting up fruit and putting it in front of me, and I'm pretty sure you're to blame for all the random veggie snacks I keep waking up to find on my bedside table!"

His face reddened. I was right.

"Lavender…"

"Why?" I reiterated.

"I don't hate you!" he snarled. "I like you—*too* much." He threw his metal water bottle roughly onto the floor, the clattering noise echoing throughout the gym.

I didn't react, didn't flinch, instead I just stared at him. A month or two ago I wouldn't have been able to look at him without shaking, but I knew there was no way he could hurt me. I had just listed the many ways this large, surly alpha had been caring and overprotective over the last few months.

Kane was like a teenager who had never really dated, and didn't know what to do with the big feelings he was having. I liked him a lot, despite his brutish nature—who was I kidding, I liked him *because* of his brutish yet caring nature.

He could toss me around a room and snuggle me after, what omega wouldn't want that?

"I like you as well," I admitted with a shrug. He stilled, looking at me with wide, wild eyes. "Talk to me. What's stopping you from actually talking to me?"

"We kidnapped you."

"Yes, I am aware of that," I replied simply, ignoring his bewildered look.

"You're not safe with us."

"I am, you've made that clear several times in fact," I shrugged. Just batting down his questions felt like the best method for dealing with him.

"Lavender..."

"Kane."

His mouth opened and closed several times as he attempted to find the words.

I sighed, walking closer to him, his dark leathery smell growing in intensity with every inch I got closer. He was the tallest of the pack so he towered over me. Up close I could make out the little flecks of amber in his green eyes.

This alpha had been so growly and grumpy at me, yet in his presence I didn't feel in danger—I felt safe.

"Forget about packs for a moment, Kane. If this is just about you and me, what would you want?"

Kane grumbled. "You know full well what I want."

"No, use your words, grumpy. Talk to me," I said gently. Of all the guys, Kane was the hardest to talk to, he maintained such a stoic attitude, it was infuriating at times.

"You! Isn't that obvious? I've said I like you a lot—why are you so stubborn about this?" He growled.

"Me, stubborn?!" I asked incredulously. "*You* have been a stubborn ass when it comes to your feelings. Ugh! Why do I feel like we're talking in circles? You like me, I like you—so why are you so mad? Because you like me *too* much?"

"You're fucking the whole pack," Kane said as he looked around the room. His face held no anger. "You just *fit*. You fit in a way my sister never would have. She wouldn't have spent hours with Theo discussing how to dispose of a body, or gone toe to toe with Gage when he was being an ass. You fit, Lavender, better than I ever thought anyone could and frankly that scares the shit out of me."

"I'm fucking *your* pack, Kane. I know you don't want to admit it, but they are." I sighed, running my hand through my hair before placing my hand on Kane's forearm. I expected him to flinch, to back away, but he didn't. His words held a lot of truth, I had slotted into life with this pack in a way I had never expected. "I'm going into heat now, and yes I fully intend to spend it with the pack—and I want you to be included in that. If you're not ready I won't be mad, but just know I want you there despite everything we've been through. Don't join unless you're serious about your place in the pack, that'll just be cruel to them—you're many things Kane, but you're not cruel."

I lifted up onto my tiptoes and placed a gentle peck on Kane's cheek while he looked at me, startled.

"Also this room smells like sex on a stick thanks to you getting all workout sweaty, so I can't really stick around unless you plan on fucking me senseless, because this shit is potent." I waved my arm around the room.

Kane's eyes darkened at my words, and I resisted the urge to grin in triumph at the impact my words had on him.

I needed to find an alpha willing to satisfy my impending heat—luckily there were a few of those around.

After leaving Kane to his own devices and giving him time to think things through, I padded through the house on the hunt for Theo.

The cramps were increasing in intensity, and the urge to grab the nearest alpha and drag him onto the nearest flat surface to fulfil an urge was only getting stronger. I didn't bother to knock as I strode into Theo's room—I was on a mission. Only an hour earlier I had been grumbling about being sore and tired out. The last thing I had wanted was more sex. Now the heat hormones were kicking in and I was clamouring for more orgasms and knots.

The faint sound of water running alerted me to Theo showering. *Naked, wet alpha. Perfect.* Sitting on the bed I waited patiently—I could behave myself. Occasionally.

Luckily I didn't have to wait long before Theo made his way out of the bathroom without a stitch of clothing on or even a towel to protect his modesty. The lack of hair only served to make him look longer. Being the least hairy, baby faced member of the pack didn't detract from the thick, wiry muscles that covered his torso. Droplets of water ran down his chest and I resisted the urge to lick them up.

Theo's eyes widened and his nostrils flared. Just my presence in his room was making it smell like a florist before Valentine's Day.

"Hello Princess—my eyes are up here," Theo laughed.

"But you're naked," I pouted, "and needed."

"Hmm, I think I can help with that," he said as he stalked over to the bed. I expected him to kiss me, or maybe just get straight to it. I was more than ready—there was already slick on the bedspread because I was leaking through the tiny lacy panties I had put on under my dress.

When he got on his knees at the end of the bed I raised my brows, curiosity peaked. His hand grabbed my thighs and dragged me to the edge of the bed with ease. Lifting up my skirt he smirked at me before lowering his head, taking a deep breath and raking his tongue over my lace covered clit.

Oh shit. The moan I let out was downright pornographic, and I was still clothed, my dress bunched up around my waist so Theo could get all the access he wanted.

He wasted no time in pushing the thin scrap of lace to the side, diving in. He teased me with soft flicks of his tongue, taunting me with what I really wanted. My heart stuttered with desperation and my hands fisted the blankets beneath me, their soft texture grounding me.

"Theo," I snarled as my hand clenched in his hair.

"Princess, I like to take my time, you're just going to have to be patient. I'm dying to have a taste of you." His voice held a smirk and part of me wanted to kick him in frustration if he didn't make me come soon. I was fit to burst and he was teasing me.

"Please!" I whined, a low keening sound.

"Since you asked so nicely." Rough, repeated strokes on my clit made me see stars. Just as I felt myself starting to reach that edge one of his hands left my thigh and two fingers filled me with zero resistance.

"Fuck me, so slick, so sweet," Theo panted, never letting up on his assault.

His hands gripped my thighs so hard there would probably be bruising, but that only heightened the pleasure for me. Marking. I wanted to be marked. Bitten. Claimed. Three quick flicks of that sweet spot inside me had me hurtling off the ledge. My vision blurred as I spasmed with the intensity of my release.

I panted, staring at the ceiling as I tried to gain my bearings.

Theo clambered up the bed, hovering over me with a boyish grin on his face which was coated it slick. Capturing my lips in his, I moaned at our combined taste. Floral and fresh, it was addictive.

"Did that take the edge off?" Theo asked as he pulled back. His face was free of any frown lines and he looked content with heavy lids giving him a lazy appearance.

While the orgasm had been mighty fine, already my midsection was starting to feel tight and I could feel my body screaming out for what it needed. Knots. Lots of knots. Four knots to be precise.

Embarrassment washed over me. A sudden feeling of insecurity. Was I going to be a bother over the next few days, constantly hounding them for sex? I knew that seventy-five percent of the pack had given me an enthusiastic yes when it came to joining my heat, but doubt still crept in.

"A little," I told him, biting my lip, but he could tell I wasn't being honest with him.

"You need more?" he asked, ever perceptive. I nodded, shyness overwhelming me. I never felt shy with Theo, we had done all manner of things, but something just felt different.

Tears gathered in my eyes and Theo looked startled for a brief second before sitting up and pulling me in for a hug.

"I-I'm sorry," I hiccuped. What had come over me? My emotions were more turbulent than when I had first been kidnapped. I felt hollow and horny, not the most logical combination. Seconds ago I had been gleefully ready to get knotted repeatedly and now all I wanted was cuddles.

"Don't apologise princess, you're in heat. How about we get you to your nest? The others will be around soon I bet," he soothed.

At the mention of my nest I pulled away, sitting up straight and looking at him hopefully. "Nest," I agreed, nodding enthusiastically.

Next thing I knew I was airborne. Theo swung me into his arms bridal style, while standing on the bed, jumping down with me still in his arms and bounding out of the room. "To the nest!"

CHAPTER THIRTY-EIGHT
Archer

I had just finished my third test of the security system. It was infuriating to me, sometimes it worked perfectly, sometimes it crapped out for no obvious reason. While I had been doing my best to hide how stressed I was, I knew Gage had noticed how late I'd been staying up working.

Rubbing my eyes, I closed my laptop. Staring at the screen so much wasn't good for my eyesight in the slightest. I was about to amble to the bathroom and grab a shower when my phone started ringing, the vibrations loud on the metal worktop of my desk. With a sigh I turned back to the desk to read the text from Theo.

> THEO:
>
> Heat time! I'm having all the fun, join if you want Archie!

It was time? My desire to sleep was forgotten. I threw my phone in the general direction of the bed, practically sprinting out of the room and taking the stairs two at a time to Lavender's room.

The moaning was clear from down the hallway. I didn't bother to knock, opening the door and striding right in. The cloud of perfume hit me first, so potent it nearly knocked me off my feet. Sweet vanilla and lavender was all I could inhale, and the smell alone made me rock hard.

Then I noticed what was happening on the bed, and I wondered if it was possible for me to get so hard my cock would explode.

Theo was sprawled on his back in the nest, hands behind his head as he gazed up at Lavender almost reverently.

I would be looking the same if I had a naked omega bouncing on my dick.

Lavender's hands bushed over Theo's chest as she rose and fell, her chest flushed. Her head was thrown back and eyes were closed like she was in rapture. The position pushed her breasts out. Watching them bob up and down as she took what she wanted from Theo was beautiful.

"You joining in or just watching, Archie?"

I glanced over to see Theo smirking at me.

At his words Lavender slowed down, opening her eyes to look at me. Her gaze was hazy, she was deep into her heat fog now.

"Alpha," she whined in excitement, holding her hand out to me. A blissful, almost serene look adorned her face.

Powerless to resist I joined her on the bed, claiming her lips with my own with hunger. I couldn't get enough of her sweet floral taste. It was like the sweetest drug, it simultaneously calmed me down and got my blood pumping.

Theo gently lifted her off him ignoring her pained whine at the loss. "No, *knot*," she hissed.

"Yes, knot. Archer's going to knot you while you give me that pretty mouth, how does that sound?" I resisted the urge to groan at that idea, I was more than up for that.

Lavender nodded eagerly, looking between the two of us. Her hair was a wild mess—combing that out was going to be a nightmare by the end of her heat. Without another word Theo shuffled back until his back was against the headboard, cock standing at full attention. Lavender wasted no time adjusting herself so she could get her mouth on it.

On her knees, bent over in front of Theo gave me a spectacular view of her slick drenched lips. My mouth watered at the sight, she was practically presenting for me, and that called to my hindbrain.

While part of me wanted to talk to Lavender about it, I knew she wanted this, she had made that crystal clear and I doubted anything I said would sink in while she was deep into the heat haze.

A low, keening whine emanated from Lavender's chest and Theo chuckled before breaking off into a moan at whatever sorcery Lavender was performing on his cock. "If you don't fucking fill her up soon, she's going to get bitey, and considering where my cock is right now I would like to avoid that."

"Bite?" Lavender gasped, looking up at Theo with what I could only describe as unbridled glee in her voice.

"No, no bite," Theo tutted.

"Why?!" Lavender whined pitifully. Theo gave a look that said *hurry up and knot her you idiot.*

Running my hands over the globes of her ass, I took a moment to appreciate the sight as she thrust back into my hands, leaning down to play with Theo again. The movement made her legs spread open even further and I couldn't resist letting my finger trail over her slick soaked slit. She was drenched thanks to riding Theo.

Pumping my cock a few times I lined myself up with Lavender and sank in slowly, inch by mind blowing inch.

Fuck. Slick-wet heat practically strangled my cock, the muscles clamping down on me so tightly I could already feel the need for release starting at the base of my spine. My hands gripped her hips tightly as I watched my cock disappear inside her.

Lavender's moans were increasing in intensity and pitch. She was getting close. From *my* cock. I had been so fascinated watching her slick pussy swallow my cock repeatedly I hadn't realised Theo had finished, and she had swallowed it down, until he was moving, his hand reaching down to tweak her nipples.

I was close, too close. I didn't want to finish too soon, and I could already feel my knot starting to inflate. Pulling out, I flipped her onto her back, climbing over her so her leg was over my hip and sinking straight back into her depths before she could complain. Her hands gripped my neck as I increased my pace.

"Knot me alpha, please!" Lavender begged in a breathless voice. Those words from her mouth almost made me finish right then and there. The power this small omega held over my body was insane.

"I want to feel you come on my cock *then* I'll give you my knot, okay?" I asked, smirking down at her as my hand found her clit, flicking it firmly in time with my thrusts. Lavender threw her head back as she came, her body convulsing with the strength of her release while her walls clamped down on me, demanding every drop of cum I had.

When she was at the height of her orgasm I thrust harder,

bottoming out, lodging my knot firmly inside her. Her howl of pleasure made me come even harder.

Locked together I turned us so I was on my back with her sprawled over me while she caught her breath. Sweaty and flushed, she was freshly fucked and beautiful.

"Fuck..." Lavender muttered.

"Yeah..." I echoed the sentiment.

"When I'm more lucid I want to see if your cum tastes like gummy bears," she mumbled against my chest as she dozed off, clearly exhausted. My cock stiffened at her words.

I was going to be knotted in her for a while—and I wouldn't have dreamt of complaining.

I had intended to stay awake while Lavender slept on me, but the exhaustion overtook me quickly. The warm content feeling was like a sedative, I'd never felt so comfortable and content as I did with Lavender like that.

Out of all the omegas I'd seen when I'd hacked into the Haven, I had picked the perfect omega for us by some stroke of luck.

Warmth enveloped me, pulling me back to reality. Opening my eyes I looked down and groaned at the sight of Lavender swallowing my cock. What a fucking perfect way to wake up— I planned to return the favour a few times before her heat ended. If her slick tasted as sweet as she smelled, well I would be falling headlong into an obsession. The moment I saw what she was up to my cock went from semi hard to granite. For someone who had no experience with alphas she was a professional with her mouth. Just a few licks and she could have me speaking tongues.

Once she was happy with my hardness she clambered over me, wasting no time in sinking down on my cock and riding me with abandon. She threw herself down on my knot with a snarl of pleasure and I was hurtling over the edge, pumping her impossibly full of cum despite only having been awake two minutes.

Lavender hummed happily, gyrating on my knot, exploring the feel of it in an almost lazy manner.

"She needs to drink soon," a voice said from the doorway. Gage was holding several bottles of water and granola bars. He placed them in a basket next to the nest he had clearly been filling with snacks and hydration for the duration of Lavender's heat.

Lavender grinned over at Gage lazily. "You're really gone aren't you, darling?"

"Knot," Lavender declared happily, grinding down on me harder, making Gage laugh.

CHAPTER THIRTY-NINE
Lavender

Theo held me in his arms, holding my legs open as Gage lapped at me, sending me to maddening heights. It was amazing, his rough tongue making several long almost leisurely passes over my clit.

"Fuck me," I whined, a low, pitiful sound. It was nice and all, but I needed knots, they were the only thing that could quell the pain radiating through my core.

"Hush darling, you need to learn some patience," Gage laughed, his voice teasing.

If only I had a lamp, I would have whacked him upside the head.

"Asshole!" I snarled.

Archer was exhausted, dozing on his stomach, arm outstretched above him.

I had tired him out.

But I needed *more*.

"Do you want me to stop?" Gage asked, pulling back, his face covered in the glistening evidence of my arousal.

"No! No, please."

"Please what? What do you want me to do?"

"Make me come," I pleaded.

Theo chuckled gently in my ear. "I think you forget who's in charge of this little adventure, you don't come until Gage says so. He could make you wait, leave you wet and begging for our cocks." His arms held me firmly in place. Throwing my head back onto his shoulder I looked him dead in the eye and whined.

"Please, fuck, please make me come," I looked back at Gage who was smirking up at me. "I need it, I need your mouth, your cock, your knots, please *alpha*."

"How the fuck can you resist that?" Theo moaned. "I want to knot her myself now."

I ground my ass down on Theo's erection, but Gage's glare stopped me.

"Behave, sweet girl or I won't let you come."

"I'll behave."

"Good girl," he rumbled. "Fuck, she likes praise, her walls just clamped down on my fingers when I said that."

Thankfully he returned to his ministrations, his fingers increasing in tempo as his tongue flicked over my clit.

"Fuck, so close, alpha, please, close," I babbled.

Theo lightly bit my ear lobe, making me jolt. "Do you like having Gage licking your sweet pussy? I'm jealous, I've tasted you several times but I'll never get enough. Maybe I'll indulge in that sweet cream whenever I want. Maybe when you're in the kitchen grabbing a snack I'll just throw you on the counter and have my fill. Or I'll wake you up with my tongue buried deep inside you, would you like that?"

"Yes!" I panted as Theo's hand reached up to gently roll my nipple between his fingers.

It was too much.

I needed more.

"You're so close, aren't you, princess?" I nodded, my back arching off the bed with the intensity of it. Theo hummed. "Then cover your alpha's face in your cum, do it now!" He bit down gently on my shoulder and I exploded with a keening whine.

Gage didn't ease up until he had wrung every last tremor from my body, looking up at me triumphantly.

My mind drifted, it felt like everything was in a haze. There were moments of clarity followed by moments of delirium. My body warred between exhaustion and the need for knots.

I hadn't realised I had closed my eyes until I felt the plastic lip of a water bottle on my mouth.

"Drink." Gage's voice held no room for complaint, he had thrown his alpha weight behind the word so I complied, chugging the cool liquid until Gage was happy. "Good girl," he cooed.

I warmed at the praise. Exhausted, I slumped in Theo's arms, letting him pet me gently, his hands running through my hair, lulling me into rest.

Something didn't feel right. Sitting up, I rubbed my eyes blearily looking at the alphas asleep in my nest, Gage and Theo were with me, Archer was probably showering or getting food. I didn't like that he wasn't with me. They were exhausted, heck I was exhausted as well but that didn't stop the thrumming deep in my core, begging for knots.

I grabbed the first item of clothing I could find, a shirt off the floor. A quick sniff and I could tell it was Gages. Slipping it on, I surveyed my nest with a gentle whine.

The blankets were sticky, and rumpled in a way I didn't like. Irritation irked at me, and I couldn't control the urge to get up and start moving the blankets.

"It's wrong," I muttered to myself, pulling at the blankets like a woman possessed. My actions disturbed the sleeping alphas. Gage sat up with a groan, his face going from sleepy to concerned when he took in my dishevelled state.

"Lavender, baby, what's wrong?" he asked in a gentle voice, clambering over to where I stood at the end of the bed, tears gathering in my eyes.

"It's wrong! All wrong!" I cried pulling at the blanket, but Theo was laying on one corner and didn't budge.

Gage looked at Theo, leaning over and thumping him in the leg, making him jolt up, his expression still asleep.

"Huh? What?" Theo mumbled.

"Get out of the nest. Lavender needs to fix it," Gage ordered, his voice firm. It had the desired impact, Theo ambled out of the bed and walked past me, kissing the top of my head as he wandered over to the armchair and sank into it.

"Not right," I mumbled, pulling the blanket off the bed and throwing it towards the door. It didn't go very far, but at least it was away from my nest.

"What do you need?" Gage asked, lightly touching my back and he searched my face for the answer.

"Things that smell like you," I admitted, tears streaming down my face.

Gage nodded, relief washing over his face—probably because this was a request he could fulfil.

"Do you want me to go get you our bedding?" he asked.

I nodded.

Theo stood up, scratching his stubble as he meandered out of the room. "I'll go grab mine."

The pair of them acquired a lot of bedding, Archer's as well as their own. Wasting no time I had started arranging their various pillows and sheets so I would be encompassed by all their scents as I lay in my nest.

Sweet sugar. Lemon, whisky. Every scent blended together in a lovely way—but something was still missing.

"It's still not right," I cried as large, broken sobs escaped my chest. I hugged myself as I sat in the nest, looking around at the crumpled pillows and blankets. I turned to Gage. "I uh... I—"

"Talk to me, darling."

"Kane," I said simply.

Gage's face lit up in realisation. "You want his scent as well?"

I nodded, still sobbing. "He doesn't want me though, he rejected me."

"No! Kane didn't reject you, darling. He's just dealing with his own problems right now."

"He *did* reject me though, he isn't here. I told him I wanted him here!" I sobbed angrily. "It doesn't feel right without him!"

Gage and Theo shared a look, I didn't pay too close attention to it, until Gage stepped away from the bed practically running out of the room. The loss of him made me whine loudly, but Theo filled his spot seconds later, clambering onto the bed and pulling me in close, tucking my head under his chin.

"Let's have a cuddle, Princess. Gage'll be back soon," he soothed. "Do you wanna cry, cuddle or fuck?"

"Rest," I mumbled into his naked chest. The throbbing

ache wasn't dominating my every thought at that moment so I inhaled the clean lemon and pine scent of Theo. My hands wound around his back as we laid on our sides. I sobbed gently, unable to shake the feeling that something wasn't right.

I was so hot. Theo was the only thing grounding me. If I didn't get more knots soon I would probably spontaneously combust.

A deep rumble emanated from Theo's chest and I melted against him. It sang to my every sense, turning me into a pile of relaxed goo. Theo was purring for me, and its effect was immediate, relaxing me and lulling me into calmness.

Footsteps indicated that someone had entered my room, maybe two someones, but I was too lethargic to care.

"Lavender?" A gravelly voice spoke from the edge of the nest.

Kane.

Sitting up so fast my head span, I took in the hulking man at the edge of my nest. Gage stood behind him, arms crossed and concern evident on his face.

Kane looked like shit. I doubted he had slept a wink since my heat started. The bags under his eyes were a dark purple, and his face looked pale and slightly gaunt. It was a punch to my gut to see him in that state.

Why was he here? Did Gage force him? I didn't want him here if it was against his will.

Theo slid off the nest and out of sight but I could still smell him, he wasn't far away. Kane hesitated, his face more open than I had ever seen it as I reached out my hand to him. His warm leathery scent was potent and he was only on the edge of the nest. I wanted him in there with me.

"Don't make her fucking wait," Gage snarled from behind

Kane. "If you're in you're in. Don't you dare drag it out and hurt her."

Kane nodded, clambering into the nest. "Hey, nuisance," his voice was gravelly and breathless.

I squeaked in glee, throwing myself into his chest. He rolled onto his back so I was sprawled all over his front. "Hello," I beamed at him before leaning down for a quick kiss. Kane's hand flew to the back of my head, deepening it.

He tasted dark and smoky. His lips were demanding, rough but also surprisingly soft. I clawed at his clothes, demanding he take his shirt off. I wanted his skin on mine.

"Are you sure?" he asked, pulling his lips from mine, ignoring my whine of protest.

My hand snaked up to his neck, my nails digging in.

"Fuck me, alpha," I snarled. "I want your knot, Kane."

The use of his name spurred him to action. I was airborne for a brief moment before being pressed into the mattress with every delicious ridge of Kane's body pressed up against mine. The sheer size of him compared to me wasn't intimidating, it was exhilarating. I wanted him to *own* me.

Hot breath tickled my neck as he nipped my earlobe, only stopping to rip his T-shirt off, throwing it across the room and returning to me.

"Knot! Please," I moaned, panting with need.

"I'll knot you when you're good and ready, omega," Kane warned.

"I'm ready, so ready. Wet. Ready. Please. See for yourself," I babbled mindlessly as Kane's teeth raked along my neck, teasing me.

The hand that wasn't holding him up trailed down, and upon feeling the sheer amount of slick his eyes widened before a feral, hungry look crossed over his face.

"You *are* ready, aren't you?" he asked, fingers flitting over my clit.

"Yes! Please, it *hurts,*" I whimpered as another cramp hit. It had been too long since I had been knotted.

Hoisting my leg over his hip, Kane spread me open, the tip of his cock pressing against me in the most maddening way. I was slightly sad that I didn't get a chance to touch it, or taste it first, but all that could come later when my body wasn't screaming with the need to be knotted.

He stilled, hesitating a moment. Doubt flashed across his face. "You're sure?" he asked gently.

"Kane!" My fingernails dug into his neck. "If you aren't fucking me in the next three seconds I will go insane."

He listened to me.

Oh holy fuck he listened.

Kane didn't hesitate this time, slamming his entire length until his hips were flush with mine.

So full.

Kanes strangled moan was music to my ears.

"Fuck, you're like a vise on my cock. I'm not going to last."

"Move," I pleaded.

He did as I begged, his hips moving agonisingly slow at first, gathering speed until he set a frantic pace. The tip of his cock brushing against that sensitive spot inside me with every thrust making me feral with need.

"Bite me! "I demanded, "Please, *alpha*!"

"Not today, little nuisance," Kane ground out. "Stop asking or I'll find something else for that mouth to do."

Was that meant to be a threat?

I wanted that!

I was quickly hurtling toward the ledge, but I wanted to come on his knot. My teeth found the juncture between his neck and shoulder and I bit down, hard but not enough to break the skin.

It had the desired reaction.

With a roar Kane slammed home, his knot expanding.

Holy shit. I was being split in two. It was impossible to feel *that* full. The intensity made me detonate, coming with a keening cry, nails digging into Kane's forearms as he trailed soft kisses along my shoulder, whispering reassuring words.

We collapsed together, Kane rolling us onto our sides so I wasn't squished under the sheer weight of him. We both panted, trying to regain our breath. I was sweaty and flushed, but Kane looked serene, a lazy smile on his face as he looked down at me.

Our moment was ruined by Theo jumping on the bed and flopping down next to me.

"Welcome to pack Rowe," he smirked at Kane.

Kane's face didn't fall, in fact his smile widened as he kissed my forehead.

By joining the others in my heat, he had accepted his place in their pack.

If only I could be part of that pack.

CHAPTER FORTY
Lavender

The pack had come bounding up to the nest in the morning, filthy, covered head to toe in dirt and grinning. I was doing my best to rest and recover as several of my muscles were still screaming from our athletic pursuits, but they were clearly excited about something.

"Did you fall into a mud pit?" I asked Archer with a giggle, looking him over. "Don't you dare enter this nest—I just got it clean!"

"Almost...but come see!" Archer grinned, practically pulling me out of the nest and out the door. How the hell did he have so much energy when we had just spent several days in a constant state of fucking? I wanted to nap for a year.

"Wait! I can't go outside—Rouche," I started to protest.

"Yes you can." Gage grinned, he was in a similar state to Archer, covered in streaks of mud. Wearing a tight T-shirt that made his biceps look a little too prominent for my liking.

"Why?" I asked.

"As of this morning the whole property is now fenced in, ten foot high solid fencing, so you can wander and explore the property as much as you want!" Gage beamed at me. "We wanted to give you a bit more freedom without having to worry about Detective Dickbag."

"Seriously!?" I asked, looking at Kane who was walking our way, shirtless despite the late season. Why was he always shirtless, and why did I still get so damn turned on by it?

Kane smiled. "I'm completely serious, little nuisance, you're free to roam, though maybe stay close or take one of us with you, these woods can be dense at times."

"Of course!" I squealed, jumping at Kane who picked me up with ease, my legs wrapping around his hips as I latched on to him and placed a kiss on his mouth in thanks. "I want to look around!"

"Maybe after I shower?" Kane asked, looking down at his muddy self.

"Well, maybe we can explore together... then shower together," I grinned, grinding down on Kane's growing erection.

"Fucking minx," he growled, pressing me closer to him and nipping me on the shoulder, making me perfume like crazy. You would think after such an aggressive heat I wouldn't still get horny at the drop of the hat, but one grumble or growl from these alphas and I was thinking about presenting and begging for knots.

"No! None of that yet! I want to explore before you defile me." I giggled, clambering down so my feet were on solid ground. "You told me there was a pond on this property, with ducks! C'mon, *please*!" I asked, looking up at him pleadingly.

He leaned down and gave me a quick kiss. "Okay, but I'm getting you clean after we've been outside."

"Deal."

After an hour of exploring, and at least twenty minutes of that spent cooing over the ducks, Kane, having had enough, swept me up into his arm and carried me over his shoulder back into the house, straight up the stairs and dragged me into the shower.

"Eager, are we?" I had taunted while he fireman carried me up the stairs, lightly smacking his ass as we went.

Any taunts were quickly silenced though when he pulled me into the shower fully dressed, pressing me against the tiles, letting his teeth scrape against my neck in that gesture that made me perfume profusely.

By the time Kane was done with me I was reduced to a puddle of slick, boneless and unable to stand on my own. Kane, pleased with his work, had carried me to his bed, carefully drying every inch of me before laying on the bed, and pulling me to sprawl over him.

CHAPTER FORTY-ONE
Lavender

It was such a lovely day, the sun was bright and the air was warm. The leaves were starting to fall, and I wanted to take advantage of it. After a quick breakfast of cinnamon apple overnight oats that Kane had prepped the day before and left in the fridge for me, I grabbed some dry oats and peas and got dressed. I dressed in one of the pack's T-shirts, leggings and a light raincoat, just in case, before making my way into the gardens.

Archer was meant to be with me, but he had spent half the night working furiously on his laptop, trying to increase the security on the fences. When I woke up, I found him still dressed, sitting up in bed next to me, slumped over his laptop snoring lightly. He didn't wake when I moved the laptop, closing it and putting it on my bedside table and gently pushing him over so he was in a slightly less uncomfortable sleeping position.

Even when I kissed him gently on the forehead, inhaling that sweet, familiar scent of comfort, he didn't budge. So, I decided to let him sleep in.

I'd been assured many times by Kane that the security was now reinforced tenfold, and it should be technically safe for me to roam. He would be able to see my every movement through all the cameras he had dotted around the property. As such, I felt comfortable taking some oats and peas down to the pond for the ducks. After my first time feeding the ducks, I had returned the next day, delighted to find several baby ducklings added to the pond. I didn't know which of the alpha's had done it, but it meant the world to me.

We had fallen into a semi comfortable routine with the guys having to return to their various jobs. Kane had been taking calls about security clients and Archer had been working away on his laptop doing something I wasn't smart enough to understand. He had tried briefly to explain coding to me, but he could have been speaking French for all I understood.

The walk down to the pond was short, but beautiful. The air was crisp, but that just invigorated me. Crouching at the water's edge, I grinned as the baby ducklings, who now knew me, started swimming over. This place, these alphas, had become home in a way. The thought of returning to the Haven made my gut twist.

When did that happen? When did my feelings on my situation change? It had been gradual, but as I fed the ducks I got lost in thought.

I was in love with Pack Rowe.

Taking a deep breath I shoved my feelings down, my heart pounding in my chest. I wasn't ready to address all that yet. Grabbing my snacks I watched the ducks paddle closer to me. I was under no illusions, they associated me with food, that's why they liked me in the first place, but they made me happy either way. They nibbled at the water, trying to gobble up the oats and peas. I was just about to open the small bag of seeds Theo had ordered for me when the hairs on the back of my neck stood up, and a sickening sensation spread through my stomach.

"Well, hello there," A slick, deep voice said behind me. I knew immediately that this wasn't one of my men. *Stranger, outsider, enemy.*

Turning to stand, I saw a tall man, but not as large and imposing as my men. He was a thin, clean shaven beta wearing a blue police uniform with slicked back dirty blonde hair that looked too polished, too perfect. His dark eyes bored into my soul, I felt sick to my stomach. Everything about him set me on edge.

"W-who are you?" I asked, praying silently that he wasn't downwind of me and couldn't catch my scent.

"I'm Detective Alec Rouche, an old friend of Gage's." He smiled, but it wasn't warm or welcoming, it was dark, and sinister.

"I'm just a housekeeper. I'll go let Mr. Rowe know you're here," I spoke, taking great effort to hide the panicked stutter in my voice. Maybe he would believe I was just a beta maid? After all, omegas were rare, and no stranger would expect to come across one so easily.

How the heck did someone manage to come onto the grounds? Kane had used extreme measures to secure this place.

Taking in the oily beta in front of me I resisted the urge to shudder. Instead I took a small step back, towards the pond. He was mere feet away from me and I didn't like that at all.

"No need to lie, I know you're an omega. I'm sorry at how you've been treated by these brutes," he scoffed. "Alphas never know what to do with something precious." His eyes raked over me, the appreciative glances impossible to miss, even from a distance.

"I-uh, I don't know what you're talking about," I disagreed. "Let me go get Gage," I tried, turning toward the house, my eyes still darting back and forth from him and my exit.

"No!" Rouche shouted, and I stilled, it wasn't a bark, he didn't have the power to bark at me. He smelled like burnt mushrooms, hardly a pleasant smell and very clearly beta.

"I need to go get my boss, he'll be able to help you." I took a step toward the house.

A small prick of pain blossomed on my thigh. Turning back to Rouche I was surprised to see him holding a small gun, pointed at me. A split second later I looked down at my leg, noticing the dart that had pierced clean through my jeans. The ground underneath me began to feel unstable and I stumbled back. Rouche frowned, advancing towards me.

"No, no, no, petal. You'll fall in the pond." He rushed over to me, gently wrapping an arm around me while he cooed. My mouth felt thick, like it was full of cotton.

"I need to..." I mumbled. My feet slipped and I felt my thigh take the brunt of the fall, the muscle burst into pain and it felt cold. Blearily looking down I could make out the bright red stain. I was bleeding.

My thigh had scraped across one of the semi jagged stones outlining the pond, tearing the skin. My stomach turned at the sight.

"Oh no... Careful now. You look so pale, my lovely. Tsk. Alphas never can properly care for your kind. It was the same with my Juniper. I'll get you bandaged up."

I tried to step away, but he was there, easily holding me in place.

"J-Juniper?" I asked, sleepily. My eyelids felt so damn heavy, and I didn't know how to stop it.

"You'll see her soon, don't worry lovely," he soothed, as my eyelids lost the battle and I slipped into darkness.

CHAPTER FORTY-TWO
Archer

I woke up late. The sun was already blasting through the windows and Lavender's side of the nest was made nicely with multiple pillows piled up. Stretching, I sat up, looking around for Lavender. She had probably gone to get breakfast and was curled up somewhere reading. She was usually up and about long before this time. I had been up so late, I didn't even remember falling asleep.

Going downstairs in nothing more than a loose pair of joggers, I ran my hand sleepily through my hair while I sought out Lavender. My stomach was protesting, demanding breakfast, but I could get food once I located my omega.

The bedroom and bathroom were both empty. She had clearly been in the kitchen because one of the jars that Kane put the oats in was empty and sitting by the sink. I checked the sunroom and the den, but still no luck—my nose wasn't leading me to her, either.

Frowning, I pulled my phone out of my pocket. If I

couldn't find her, I could just track her movements on the cameras. After spending hours updating and ensuring they were top of the line, I could track every little thing in our house.

I could see her in the kitchen about an hour ago, leaning against the counter while she ate her overnight oats straight from the jar, at one point pausing to add some chocolate chips from the cupboard. No matter how many fruits and toppings Theo added, she always added some chocolate. It made me smile as I watched her disappear back into her room, and come out dressed, with a jacket on. Had she gone to see the ducks? I switched over to the outside security cameras. Sure enough there she was, crouched by the water, playing with those ducklings Kane had acquired for her.

Watching with a smile I started walking back to my room to grab a shirt and some shoes to join her, watching my phone screen the entire time. I had just made it to the top floor landing when I noticed a second figure entering the screen. Rouche. I would recognise that bastard anywhere. The terror that gripped me when I saw them exchange words, Lavender doing her best to back away, and Rouche pulling out a tranquilliser gun and shooting Lavender in the leg, gently bundling her up into his arms as she clearly swayed and stumbled under the effects of the drugs.

Despite the time stamp on the footage indicating this happened over an hour ago, I ran out to the grounds, shirt be damned. The pond was desolate, even the ducks had gone into hiding. Lavender's scent was still clinging to the plants. The scent of her terror and panic, that dark, burnt floral sweetness that burnt the back of my throat as I drank it in. Frantically dialling Kane I put my phone to my ear, shaking violently with both panic and rage.

The second the dial tone indicated that Kane had picked up, I didn't even wait for him to say hello.

"Lavender's been taken," I panted.

"What?!" He snapped.

"Rouche, that asshole came and drugged her while I was asleep, I was fucking asleep Kane!"

"We will be back in ten, no five minutes. Where's Theo? He should be there! Check the cameras." I did just that, following Theo from the moment he left his bedroom. He went to the kitchen and added fresh berries to the oats he had let soak overnight, ensuring they were ready for Lavender when she woke up. He even prepared a baggy of oats and peas for Lavender to take to the pond later. He knew her routine so well. We all got a great sense of pleasure at looking after Lavender, predicting her needs and meeting them pre-emptively. Her joy and happiness were like a drug.

I watched in horror on the camera as Theo looked up from what he was doing, as if he heard something. He moved through the house, searching for the source of the sound. When he came through the hallways and poked his head outside the front door he was met by Rouche, holding a weapon, possibly another tranq gun? I fucking prayed it was a tranquilliser. Theo didn't stand a chance.

Rouche dragged him into a bush off screen, so I followed the path, finding Theo passed out. I knelt, checking his pulse, letting out a sigh of relief when I found it to be weak but steady. I gently shook him, trying to wake him up. He was breathing, which was good. After a few moments of shaking he started to stir, groaning.

"Lavender?" he asked in a deep, lethargic voice. He dragged open eyes that were hazed with the effects of the drug. "Lav?" he asked again.

"Theo? Wake up."

As I shook my friend awake an SUV came barreling up the path to the front of the house. Kane was out of the passenger side before the car came to a full stop, seeing his packmates and rushing towards us.

"Is he okay?" Kane asked, kneeling by us, his eyes raking over Theo's groggy form.

"I think so, just a little out of it," I confirmed. "Did you see the footage?"

"We watched it in the car," Gage confirmed, jogging over.

"It's that fucker Rouche, isn't it?" I could have sworn it was him.

"That was definitely Rouche," Gage growled, looking thunderous. "I knew something was off when he turned up here with no warning the other day. He seemed too keen on the scent he picked up."

"How did a beta manage to get onto our lands and kidnap our omega?" Kane asked with a growl.

"*Our* omega?" I asked, grinning despite the situation. Kane seemed fully accepting of Lavender's place with us.

"Yes, our omega. Rouche needs to die for this," he snarled.

"He still lives in the same house he grew up in," Gage confirmed.

"Let's go get our girl," Kane growled.

CHAPTER FORTY-THREE
Lavender

Why *does it feel like I've been hit by a truck?*
My head throbbed while my body felt heavy and sore. A sharp piercing pain radiated behind my eyeballs when I tried to open them, even the dim light was too bright. This wasn't the first time I had found myself in such a situation, but my recollection was hazy and I didn't recall being this uncomfortable last time.

I turned over, my bare arms scraping across a scratchy fabric I lay on. Where was my jacket? I could have sworn I was wearing one.

"Hey," a sweet, soft voice said as a soft hand gently touched my forehead. Taking a deep breath I could recognise the sweet strawberry scent. Omega. "Are you okay? Can you try to sit up?"

I had been drugged. Again. Was there a goddamned sign above me that said 'super druggable omega'? Because it was starting to feel like it. Prying my eyes open I gathered my senses together enough to realise I was lying on a bed covered in possibly the least comfortable bedding I had ever experienced, and there was an omega crouching by the side of my bed, looking me over with wide, worried green eyes.

The omega was tiny compared to me, with masses of dark waves and skin so pale it was downright sickly. She wore a pink and frilly garment with a matching headband. Her face was so emaciated that it made her eyes look comically large.

"Lavender? That's your name, isn't it?" she asked in a soft voice.

"Y-yeah," I confirmed groggily. "Who are you?"

"My name's Juniper," she whispered. "Your leg was pretty badly cut, I bandaged it the best I could with an old shirt, but I didn't really have anything to clean it with. I'm so sorry."

Despite my foggy head my right thigh burned with a vengeance. It was crudely wrapped in some pink fabric, but spots of blood were visible.

Juniper. That grabbed my attention, sitting up I ignored the pounding in my skull and the desperate need to vomit. I looked at this dainty omega. Those eyes were so familiar—of course they were.

"Are you Kane's sister?"

Juniper's eyes widened "You know Kane?! How?"

"Sort of a long story, but we're... close. He told me about you. Where are we?"

"Home," Juniper said simply, giving me a sad smile that didn't reach her eyes. I took a moment to look around the room, horrified. It was as if a six year old, princess obsessed little girl had vomited all over every surface. Everything was pink, frilly, and covered in bows. Even the uncomfortable bedding I was sleeping on was abysmally girly, and it had little dainty pink ribbons all over it.

"Do you know where exactly we are?" I asked again, looking at our surroundings and noting the tea sets, nail polish, and glitter pens. It was a preteen Barbie princess room.

There were no windows, and the artificial light coming from the single bulb on the ceiling and a pink lamp next to the bed. The whole place smelled... wrong. Chemical.

I turned to the frail omega, horrified. "How long have you been here? You've been missing for almost five years."

Juniper bit her lip, tears filling her eyes. "In that case, I've been here for five years."

Shit.

"Who did this? Everyone thought you were kidnapped by a rogue alpha?" I swung my legs over the bed, but the action made my head spin. Juniper reached out, her hand pressing down on my shoulder to make me stay put.

"Stay sitting down, I think he drugged you with something strong."

I stared at Juniper, what sort of serial killer lair had we been tossed into? I thought about various long term kidnapping victims. Jaycee Lee Dugard, Elizabeth Smart, The Fritzl family. None of those stories had a particularly happy ending—and Juniper had been here for *years.*

"Was it an alpha that did this?" I asked again as she hadn't answered.

"No!" Juniper gasped, sitting on the edge of the bed now that I was sitting up as well. Next to me we were almost on eye level. "It was never an alpha—it was Alec all along. He took me, he's obsessed with omegas." She looked around briefly. "There's cameras in this room, but they don't record sound so he'll be watching us."

I subtly observed the room, noticing the CCTV cameras in

every corner of the room, the blinking light a taunt, letting me know I was being watched.

"Holy shit... Alec is the cop in charge of your missing persons investigation, and you've been with him the entire time?"

"He's good at covering things up." Juniper grimaced.

No one deserved this. My face must have shown my horror, because she bit her lip and nodded her head, like she was trying to clear her tears. If anyone had a right to cry it was her.

"He's never *really* hurt me. Just a few bruises and injuries when I misbehaved, he's convinced he's really an alpha and once my heat hits we're meant for one another."

So he was a nut job, good to know. Something rang untrue in Juniper's words though, and I had the sinking feeling that she had been hurt—a lot. "Once your heat hits?" I asked. "You're not that much younger than me, surely you've had several heats since you came here?" I had experienced at least twelve heats by this point, so it stood to reason she had experienced a similar amount.

Juniper shook her head, gulping. "I've never had one at all. I managed to convince Alec it was simply because I wasn't mature yet—but I think it's because of fear."

I nodded, racking my brain to think of various things I'd learned at the Haven. "Yeah, extreme stress or fear can sometimes stop your heat. Omega instincts won't allow you to be in such a vulnerable situation, not always though because it didn't work for me."

"Yeah, that's what he wants," Juniper confirmed.

"So let me get this straight. He's just kept you hostage, waiting on you to 'mature' so you can bond?" Juniper nodded "What's with all this, then?" I waved my hand around the room.

"He's obsessed with this idea of the pretty little, docile omega. This room wasn't my choice at all—far too pink." She looked around the room with a grimace. "This is *his* idea of what an omega wants. I fought him a lot in the beginning, but I quickly learned it wasn't worth it, he gets angry when I don't cooperate. But when I behave, I'm fed well, and he treats me like a princess, only I'm not allowed to leave."

"Oh god," I muttered, looking around the room again as if a way out would have magically appeared in the last twenty seconds. "We need to get out of here."

"I've tried, trust me the only way out of here is through that heavy, reinforced door. The first year I was here I threw so much at that thing and never even made a dent."

Pushing my hair away from my face I noticed just how shaky my hands were. I wasn't cold. *Probably the drugs,* I surmised. "He—Alec, he's never forced you... right?" I asked, trying to be tactful, but struggling to get a grip on the right words. Just how badly had this omega suffered? She should have been safe behind the Haven walls, where her biggest concern was who did she fancy chatting to that day and not whether or not she would ever see daylight again.

Juniper shook her head. "No. He's kissed me a few times, light groping and he sometimes insists on sleeping in the same bed as me—but he always goes on about how our first time will be perfect. He wants it to be when I'm in heat and he would never risk ruining that. He's *obsessed* with the idea of heats. Like it's the ultimate alpha thing."

"Oh that's gross." I gagged. "Why did he take *me*?"

If he had his omega captive in this freak show basement, why did he need me? Gage despised Rouche, that much was obvious, but he had zero clue he had anything to do with Juniper's disappearance.

"I don't know, do you have heats? Also how did he find you, you know Kane?"

"Yeah, Kane and his... well, his pack."

"His pack?!" Juniper asked in a whispered shout. "He formed a pack, with who?!"

"With Gage, Archer and Theo, they've been together for a few years, but he's only just made the decision to officially be a pack member, I think. They've been looking for you since you were taken."

Juniper's eyes filled with tears and she quickly wiped them away. "I assumed they would have moved on, I don't know how I feel about them still missing me. And you... are you their omega?" Her eyes lit up and she grinned.

"That's a complicated story. Technically your brother kidnapped me from a Haven a few months ago because they thought I had overheard something that could have stopped them from taking down the man they thought took you. I was just a captive for a while, but we all became close. The pack is amazing—you should know, you grew up with them."

"You sound like you love them." Juniper smiled softly.

"I do. They're fantastic people. I haven't exactly told them how I feel yet. They *did* kidnap me and we've never discussed what's going to happen long term. Plus Kane was pretty convinced that you would be forming a pack with Gage, Theo and Archer. He was trying to keep himself apart from the pack for when you came back. It's taken him some time to adjust to that."

Juniper chuckled lightly "Kane is such a martyr—they're not my pack. Did I have a passing interest in Gage when I was a young girl? Of course I did, you've seen those eyes!" She laughed and I nodded, they were pretty stunning eyes. "But now? I couldn't be less interested, all I want is my freedom, maybe if I'm free I'll go to a Haven." She frowned "If I ever get out of here, it's been so long. You said Kane didn't even know who took me?"

"They were sure it was an alpha who has been trafficking omegas for a few years now—they assumed that you were one of them because he had expressed interest in you to your parents not long before you were taken."

"I think I remember who you mean. My parents kept me out of it, but some gangbanger did try to talk to them about me and was quickly shown the door. They honestly never suspected Alec?"

"Not at all, he's just a beta. I think he only got me because I went outside unaccompanied, otherwise he never would have made it through the security and my alphas. He's spent the last few years, from what I understand, blaming Gage's pack for your disappearance, and I'm guessing everyone thought he just missed you terribly. I doubted anyone thought a beta would take an omega, so they never looked into it."

"That's what I did—went out alone. I was mad at Kane for being overprotective so I went for a walk alone, to prove I could... well. He was right."

"He's going to be so smug, I can see it now," I chuckled weakly.

"He's not changed much then, has he?" Juniper's smile was sad.

"They'll find us, I'm sure of it. Plus there's two of us now—and Alec is only a beta, we can overpower him."

Juniper frowned. "I'm not so sure, he's strong and he's usually got drugs on him in some form to make me more... docile. At least that's how it was in the beginning until I started doing what he wanted. He never feeds me much, he loves the idea of me being smaller than him, like an alpha and omega."

She was tiny, her arms held next to no muscle. My stomach turned when I realised she had been starved regularly over the last few years.

"But... what does he want from me?" I asked, voice croaky.

"I don't know. Do you need the bathroom? I have one behind that screen, there's a camera though so he'll probably be watching." She shuddered.

"Oh god no," I blanched. "I'll hold it." I didn't know how long I could do that for, but I wasn't going to have a pervert watching me take a whizz—that was disgusting.

How many times had he watched Juniper? As terrified as I was, my heart broke for the omega whose privacy had clearly been non-existent for almost half a decade.

Juniper opened her mouth to speak but the sounds of a lock turning distracted us.

"Just go with it, it'll be better for us!" Juniper whispered, panicked as she looked at me with wide, pleading eyes. As much as I wanted to fight and scream, Juniper probably knew better in this situation.

Alec entered the room, holding a bottle of water and a sports drink. Wearing a T-shirt and a pair of jeans he looked far more relaxed than when I'd last seen him.

"You're awake!" He cooed happily, walking over to us, ignoring my flinch as I tried to shuffle away from him. He placed the drinks on the bedside table, looking me over.

"I bet you don't feel great, Petal, you need to drink. I see you've met my little bluebird." He gently stroked Juniper's hair, and she gave him a smile that didn't reach her eyes, but he couldn't tell. He revelled in her smile.

"Do you like your new friend?" he asked her.

"Yes, I do." Juniper kept the smile on. "Is that why she's here? To be my friend?"

"Yes, she wasn't being taken care of by other mean alphas. I thought she would make a nice addition to our family."

I felt sick at his words, simply looking between the pair of them.

He turned to Juniper. "I've been speaking to a friend of mine, he's got some lovely medication for you."

That sounded ominous.

"Medication?" Juniper asked sweetly.

"To bring on your heat! I know we wanted to wait, but with Lavender here I thought it best if you go through your heats at the same time." He leered at me, and I refused to let my disgust show on my face. Like I would ever spend my heat with such a vile, disgusting creature? "I've got to go to work, bluebird, take care of your friend and make sure she rests, okay?" Smiling down at Juniper, he petted her like a fucking dog. I wished I had some sort of utensil I could shove in this Bundy wannabe's eyes.

"Of course, I will," Juniper smiled back but her eyes still had no light in them. How did he not see that? I guess delusion was a powerful thing. I remained silent as they conversed, opting to simply watch their interaction.

"I think Petal will fit in very well." He smiled, looking over at me. "Make sure she gets some clean clothes, those are too dark and dirty for you pretty little girls."

He grinned sadistically before turning to leave, the telltale sound of a door locking let us know he had penned us in.

"What the fuck?" I croaked, trying to make sense of what I had just seen.

"If I play along, he doesn't hurt me." Juniper gulped. "He's going to bring on my heat," she whispered, her voice tiny and broken.

"We'll get out of here before then. I won't let that happen. Kane won't let that happen either."

Juniper stared vacantly at me, her eyes filling with tears. She was so pale, I worried she was going to keel over.

Pulling herself together she shook her head and wiped away the tears. "I'm so sorry, we need to get you a change of clothes. He loves all this girly stuff. Drink this first, the seal is still intact." She passed me the bottle of sports drink, and looking closer, I could see it was unopened. I snapped it open and chugged it.

"Deja vu," I muttered.

"Excuse me?" Juniper asked.

"Not my first time being drugged, though last time it was Archer and Gage taking care of me."

Juniper smiled sadly. "I've not spoken about them in years. How are they doing? Did Gage finally take over his dad's shop?"

"They haven't been focused on their own things, they've been preoccupied with finding you." I shrugged sheepishly.

Juniper's eyes watered. "They didn't put their whole lives on hold did they? I always imagined them happy, free." She quickly wiped a tear as it fell.

"I'm sorry, I won't lie to you—your brother loves you dearly and couldn't go on without finding you first."

"But he may never find us!" she sobbed.

"Well, they'll know who took me," I said, and Juniper stilled.

"How?" she asked, a touch of excitement entering her voice.

"He took me off the pack lands, and they've installed security cameras everywhere so he's bound to show up in the footage. He didn't cover his face or anything, so I would bet my favourite pillow that he was caught by at least one of the cameras. You said they grew up together?"

"Yeah, Alec lived on the same street as us and he used to hang around Gage and Kane a lot. He always thought he would be an alpha one day, he was distraught when that never happened."

"I think he lost his mind a little, if this situation is anything to go by," I said, gesturing to the overly pink room. "Do you even have a nest?"

"You're in it," Juniper grimaced. I couldn't hide my shock... It was an *appalling* nest. The pillows were made of a scratchy material and there was no way an omega could be comfortable there. Even the bows were made from a cheap disgusting feeling ribbon that would be a pain to lie on.

"I tried telling him early on... he punished me for it." She looked at the ground. "I learned to just accept whatever he gave me and to act thankful for it. After a while he mellowed out a bit. I despised every time I had to touch him. Overtime, I think I became kind of broken—like my inner omega is numb or in hibernation. I haven't had heats, I'm terrified of touch, well his touch. Yours is different," she admitted.

I reached out to grab Juniper's hand. "I'm so fucking sorry this happened. It's not okay at all and you *will* be getting out of here."

Omegas were unique creatures, and there were few hard and fast rules. Alec had clearly suppressed Juniper's omega side without even realising it.

Juniper gave me a tear filled nod. "If I ever get out of here Kane's probably going to lock me away again."

"He won't. Not if he ever wants to get laid again," I

snorted. Juniper's face fell in shock before breaking into a shit eating grin.

"So you and him, tell me more about that!"

"Yes, I have been very... active with the pack, but they haven't claimed me, I was their captive—though the conditions were a *lot* better than this. "

"How did they even kidnap you?" Juniper asked.

"They broke into a Haven, drugged me, and I woke up in their home and was not allowed to leave."

"My brother actually did that?!" Juniper asked, horrified.

"He did," I laughed. "But it was because they were trying to find you, and they genuinely cared for me. They kept their distance so our instincts wouldn't take over, and honestly were pretty respectful, giving me space and freedom to wander—well, at least when they were convinced I wasn't going to club Theo with a lamp again."

Juniper looked confused so I explained my now-regrettable encounter with the alpha. "When I first woke up, Theo bought me food... I kind of knocked him out with a lamp and made a break for it—it was working until Kane rugby tackled me. Don't blame him though, he didn't want to risk any chance he had of finding you. In time we all started to trust one another and the thought of going back to the Haven was... Painful. I couldn't picture leaving their sides."

"You love them." Juniper repeated her earlier statement.

"I do." I smiled, then hissed as a cramp ripped through my midsection.

"Are you okay?" Juniper's hand flew to my upper arm as she looked me over, trying to find the source of my pain.

"Yeah, I only just finished a heat so I'm feeling sort of rough. My hormones are all over the place right now. I've had two heats in the last three months."

"Fuck," Juniper whispered. "I don't know what Alec will do if you go into a heat here..."

"I think we both know what he'll do," I gulped. "You said he's obsessed with heats."

"He is. He says they're the ultimate bonding experience, but if you have a heat before me, he may decide I'm not worth the wait and just get rid of me."

"No, I don't think so. He's been obsessed with you for *years*, and let's face it, he's no alpha. An alpha is loyal to their mate and would physically hurt themselves before harming them. DNA changes with a bond. Alec isn't like that, I think *he'll* think having two omegas will make him a bigger and better alpha than those that didn't form a pack with him."

Juniper nodded. "Yeah, that does sound like him—but if you go into heat..."

"He wouldn't be able to satisfy a heat. I would be in pain, and with all the hormones and stuff I would probably get nasty. How would he react to that?" I asked. "You know him best."

"It will make him angry, he's violent when angry." She gulped. "In the early days he beat me a lot, left me chained up for days, doing anything he could to break my spirit and make me his perfect little doll. He tried to bark at me to get me into heat when he was impatient. It didn't work of course, it only reminded him of what he wasn't... I have never seen him so angry, and he took it out on me." More tears trickled out.

I gripped her hand tighter, looking her in the eye. "Listen to me, we are getting out of here. I don't care how many times I need to tell you that, but you *will* be home soon. If your brother doesn't come for us, we'll find a way out ourselves. He's one beta and we are two intelligent omegas."

Juniper nodded, wiping away the tears. Instinctively, I

pulled her in for a hug. Juniper stilled for a moment before sinking into the hug, sobbing, taking deep, ragged breaths.

"It's been so long since anyone but him has touched me." Her body-wracked with sobs that she did her best to conceal from the camera that still watched our every move.

Tears gathered in my own eyes as I stroked my hand over Juniper's hair. While I had been living my life complaining about dating annoying packs, or not being able to get a particular flavour of gummy bear, Juniper had been living a type of hell no one deserved.

I vowed to myself that I would get her out, that she would go home, and never have to wear goddamned pink ever again.

CHAPTER FORTY-FOUR
Lavender

Whatever had been in that tranquilliser dart had done a number on me, and it took a while for it to wear off. Juniper insisted I take the bed as I was recovering and Alec hadn't had the forethought to bring a second bed into the room before dumping me here. It felt wrong taking the bed from someone who was skin and bones, but I couldn't stop the blackness creeping in at the corners of my vision.

The last thing I wanted to do was sleep, but the drugs ultimately won that battle. My sleep was fitful, and my mind kept running through various ways to escape. Most true crime stories I knew of had people escaping out of cars or when being transported. Usually when someone was stuck underground with no windows the outlook was bleak.

When I woke up, neither of us knew how much time had passed. There were no clocks, and no natural light sources so it was impossible to tell.

Juniper showed me around the room, the wardrobe, the

bathroom I had zero intention of ever using. "What do you do all day?" I had asked her, hobbling around after her.

"Not much," she had admitted with a wince. "Just sit here and look pretty for him—he occasionally brings me sketch pads and charcoal. I used to sew before this, but he won't let me near any needles."

"I wish I had a real weapon," I mumbled. "Asshole needs a lamp to the head—if yours wasn't so small I would use that."

"It's super glued down, I tried that." Juniper smiled weakly. I chuckled, it was hard to truly ascertain Juniper's character and personality while locked in a basement by a mad man, but something about her just seemed so steely and strong, and I admired that about her.

"Drat." I turned back to the bed with a wobble. The light-headedness was only getting worse, surely the drugs had to be leaving my system.

"You're burning up," Juniper said, touching my face. "You need to rest. I'll make Alec bring some Tylenol next time, okay? Don't wear yourself out."

"I won't."

"I'm so happy to have someone else to talk to, even if I hate that he's brought you here against your will," Juniper admitted with a frown.

"I know, I hardly saw the guys for the first two weeks I was with them and I started to go insane from the lack of human contact, I don't know how you've managed to cope so well,"

"I really haven't managed to cope at all, I just put on a good face because that's what I need to survive."

"I understand that—Sage said something similar after she was taken."

"Sage?"

"An omega friend of mine. She came to my Haven after she

had been kidnapped by a criminal pack. She came to us for sanctuary for a few days until her mates could come and get her."

"She still wanted to be with a pack, after all that?"

"She told me it was totally different. That the pain she went through was still there, burning under her skin but being with her pack helped to soothe that feeling... Her alphas build her up, make her feel strong. That's what a true partnership does."

"Did my brother do that for you?" Juniper asked.

"He did, in his own way. He's a little overprotective given what happened to you. But I've watched too much true crime, and I've picked up a thing or two. I even scratched Kane up real good in the early days. I bet it's easier to take down a beta..." I trailed off, looking toward the locked door.

"You think we could really hurt him?"

"I think we could. Is there a blank spot on the cameras?"

"Not really." She grimaced.

"I watched a documentary a while back, where a girl who was in prison made a weapon by filing a toothbrush handle down."

"I have nail files!" Juniper said happily. "He likes my nails to look pretty and manicured," she said, flashing her sparkly pink nails. "He's watching us though, and would notice us getting the file out... unless... Why, Lavender, I think you need a manicure!" She grinned at me, her voice dripping in over enthusiastic sarcasm. "I mean, just look at your poor bitten nails. I am just being a good girl getting you pretty," she smiled, and I could see through her words immediately.

"Why Juniper, I would love it if you did my nails!" I smiled back, and we went over to the table. I ignored the burning pain in my thigh. My walk was more of a hobble now. I sat on one of the tiny padded chairs while Juniper got her nail supplies out.

She started filing my nails, making them neat and tidy. "I've had a lot of practice," she laughed without humour.

"When we leave here, we never have to do our nails again," I said. Juniper gave me a genuine smile of happiness.

"That sounds like heaven. I dream about just running through the forest, digging dirt with my hands, that sort of thing." She sighed. "Would a lavender colour be too on the nose for you? I only have pretty pastels because darker colours don't fit into his picture of how omega's should behave."

"Let's go with the lavender," I smiled. Halfway through the first hand, I felt the nail file slip easily under my hand, and up my sleeve. Juniper was good at this, she must have perfected being sneaky after years of being watched by cameras.

"How long do you think it will take?" she asked.

"Give me twenty-four hours, and I should have a weapon."

"I'm scared," Juniper admitted, keeping her focus on my nails.

"I would be scared if you weren't worried. You're not alone anymore, remember that. Whatever happens, we'll face it together. If he tries to separate us just say we're pair bonded or some shit and he can't separate us. That will make him panic."

"Is that a thing?" Juniper asked with a frown.

"Kind of. If an omega is super attached to someone they can suffer negative side effects when taken from them. Pain, and this horrible deep sense of wrong takes over."

"That's how I felt when I first came here, then I just became... numb. For the first time in a long time, I think I'm starting to feel again. Hope feels like a dangerous thing."

"Your brother held onto hope for years. When Archer suggested that you might be dead I had never seen Kane so pissed. Both Theo and Archer struggled to restrain him—it was honestly quite scary, but I know he would never turn that anger on me so I wasn't worried. Kane's always been so gentle with me."

"He has? I always said he would be a softie with an omega."

"He accidently barked at me once," I admitted. Juniper's eyes went wide. "I had dropped a glass, and in a panic, he shouted at me to not move, because I had nothing on my feet. He was so worried he barked without even realising it—and he felt so bad about it afterwards. He hadn't warmed to me entirely by then, but he could see I was shaken up. Barks can be brutal."

"I guess I've been lucky in that regard that Alec can't actually bark," Juniper admitted.

"Yeah, when it's not from someone you trust completely it is horrible. The whole pack was pissed at him, but that night I couldn't sleep and he snuck in just to comfort me and didn't say a word."

Juniper sighed wistfully. "I miss him."

"Me too."

CHAPTER FORTY-FIVE
Lavender

The paleness of Juniper's face was starting to concern me. Ever since Alec had made it clear he intended to be a part of my heat and chemically kickstart Juniper's, she had become withdrawn, looking off into the distance and hardly speaking. She had managed to stave off his advances for so long that she didn't fully comprehend what was happening anymore.

When we were sure we were alone, Juniper unwrapped my leg, using water from the bottle to rinse it. The cut was several inches long and still weeping blood whenever I moved. Juniper sacrificed another of her pink shirts to bandage it, but when I apologised she snorted, insisting she was happy to be rid of the frilly monstrosity.

"How will we do it?" Juniper asked into the darkness as we curled up on the bed together. We were meant to be sleeping, but rest evaded us both.

"I'll go for his neck. It's the best place to cause maximum damage. If you get the chance to run, you do it. Don't wait for me."

"Wait, no," Juniper protested. "We—"

"*Yes.* You've been here for years. Get free and find help. Kane will find you and with any luck I'll be right behind you," I assured her. "And if not, you know where I am."

Would I be right behind her? My leg was bad, and I was feeling sicker by the hour.

"Okay. When?"

"In the morning when he brings breakfast."

"Okay. Lavender?"

"Yeah?"

"Thank you," Juniper choked out tearfully as we reached for one another, clinging to each other in the pitiful excuse for a nest.

The makeshift weapon was up the sleeve of my silly, frilly pastel pink blouse I wore with a white pair of trousers. It wasn't the worst outfit; Juniper's Lolita style dresses were a lot more difficult to work with. At least with the trousers I had the space to move and run.

We sat at the table, trying to act relaxed but our spines were ramrod straight as we waited.

Alec was a creature of habit, so he turned up for breakfast promptly at 8am, just as Juniper said he would. He smiled at us.

"My girls," he smiled at us, hugging us both tightly, kissing the top of my head.

"Hello," I greeted, shyly. I needed to remember that I needed to be meek and docile. Not bold, and not like a weirdo who had watched so much true crime that they knew the best methods for escaping a psychopath. "What's for breakfast?" I asked.

"Waffles! Today feels special, I got a parcel today from a friend of mine for our sweet Juniper. He got me the medications to kick off your heat. I know we agreed that natural was best, but I know better now." He grinned at Juniper. "We'll be together like we always wanted, only better, because now we have Lavender to join us!" He laid out the plates, piling the waffles from Styrofoam take out containers onto them. As he bent over the table to place a waffle on Juniper's plate, I saw my opportunity. The way his neck was exposed was too good an opportunity to miss.

Letting the shiv fall into my hand I pounced, aiming straight for the jugular and sunk the makeshift knife in with as much force as I could muster. The resistance of his skin was gut churning but I kept pushing with all of my might. He let out a strangled sound which came out sounding... wet.

It lasted maybe three seconds before Alec grabbed me by the arm, throwing me clean across the table.

"Go! Juniper!" I yelled, righting myself and looking at Alec, he was clutching his neck, eyes bulging in shock. There was blood leaking from the wound. He stood between me and the door, which Juniper had already fled out of. The look in his eyes had faded from shock, to pure unadulterated anger.

I felt like I had been doused in freezing cold water, his look of hatred chilled me to the bone. He looked like he wanted to murder me. He staggered towards me, and I attempted to dart by him, but he grabbed me by the shoulder with one hand, throwing me against the wall. His other hand was pressed firmly against his neck, attempting to stop the flow of blood. My shoulder burned in pain from the impact. Scrambling to my feet and keeping low I darted away from him and towards the door.

"You bitch!" He gurgled. "I'll fucking kill you."

I thought fast. I wanted him to chase me, not Juniper. I would be slower and Juniper had a head start, but I wanted to be sure—so in a moment of stupidity, I decided to taunt him.

"Ha! Maybe if you were an alpha, but you're a pathetic beta—do you really think you would have a chance with an omega like me? Pitiful," I snarled, before turning on my heel and fleeing, making it to the door before he could stop me. My movements were fast but jerky. My leg screamed in pain with every step and my vision spun. I couldn't let that stop me, I needed to escape and this was my only window. I darted down the hallway, up the stairs and out of the front door to... woodland? Where was I? My nose told me that Juniper had run dead ahead of where I stood, down the winding road that likely led to civilisation.

I ran down a small footpath, panting with the effort. The crashing sound of the blundering beta following me was loud. He roared, with pain or anger—I couldn't tell. The ground was strewn with twigs, leaves, and rocks, I kept tripping and nearly falling.

"You fucking bitch!" he roared behind me. *Shit.* He was getting closer.

"Help!" I screeched as loudly as I could while still running. If I ever made it out of this mess I was going to do an hour on the treadmill every day to ensure I was prepared for this horrible situation, should it ever arise again.

A fist grasped at the back of my shirt, pulling me to the ground. My skin burned from the impact, a sharp pain and a popping sensation in my shoulder. Alec's dark shadow loomed over me.

Fuck.

CHAPTER FORTY-SIX
Gage

Alec's house had been a bust, it was desolate, and long empty judging by the dust coating everything. I had torn through the house, taking out my rage on the dust covered furniture before screaming at my packmates that we had to keep searching.

It had taken Archer almost twenty-four hours to locate a property that Alec had bought with a shell company a few years back. He strode into the den where I was pacing with a tablet in hand, a dark look on his face. His usually light stubble was a lot darker and his eyes were bloodshot, hair dishevelled. We all looked like a mess.

"You'll never guess where that fucker purchased property."

"Where?" I asked.

"Alberta Street."

We all sat up straighter at Archer's announcement.

"*What*?" I snarled. Alberta Street was the street we had all grown up on, including Juniper. What the fuck was he doing there?

"What number?" Kane asked, his voice dark and dangerous.

"Twenty."

Next door to the house Juniper had grown up in. I wanted to vomit. We hadn't returned since Juniper had gone missing, it just didn't feel right. The small town an hour away hadn't been home in a long time. Our families still lived there, but we had hardly spoken to them in years.

"I guess we're going home," I said.

"Time to get our omega back from that fucker." Theo twiddled a blade with his thumb.

"As a pack," Kane said, meeting my eye with a look of determination.

"We're in agreement," Theo said, looking up from the knife in his hand. "Once we get Lavender back we are never letting her go. None of this bullshit about kidnapping her—she's ours. She's Pack Rowe's omega."

"She's ours," Archer croaked.

I nodded before looking at Kane. He nodded at me with a gaze that held a lot of meaning.

"The moment we get her back, we bite her—if she wants it," Kane said.

"Fuck I'm tempted to do it wether she wants it or not. I won't though, consent is king and all that jazz," Theo said, raising his hands in surrender.

We were a pack, but we weren't complete without Lavender.

The drive to our hometown was tense, we were all wound tightly. What if Rocuhe wasn't at this property? He was a fucking cop and could get away with shit. Who knew how many tricks he had up his sleeve? Rain pelted the windshield in the dark while we sped through the night. We weren't going to wait for daylight. Every one of us were armed and ready to fight for our omega.

There were no lights on in the small Victorian property. We parked close, intending to sneak up to various entry points and break in quietly.

That plan was shattered when we heard the loud roar from the woodland at the back of the house. Alec. I would bet money on it.

"Theo with me, Kane and Archer go from the left side," I commanded quickly before taking off in a run towards the scream.

I followed the sounds of scuffling. Mere feet off the trail, I made out the shape of a figure crouched over someone. The darkness made it hard to discern their figures, and the rain was washing away smells alarmingly fast, but I could tell what was unfolding in front of me. Alec was on top of Lavender, his hand at her throat.

I saw red. Reaching forward my hands grabbed Alec by the back of his shirt and his hair, ripping him away from Lavender so hard he flew several feet away.

"Get rid of him!" I snarled to the others, turning my attention to Lavender.

I sat Lavender up, checking her over. Every inch of her body was covered in cuts and bruises from running through the forest. There was a startling amount of blood covering her torso, but from one glance at Alec, it was obvious the wound on his neck was the culprit. Had she done that? If I hadn't been so terrified for her I would have been damn proud.

"Lavender? I called her name as she drifted in and out of consciousness.

"Gage?" Her voice was low and hoarse, the red, ugly bruises on her neck clearly the culprit. Her right eye was red, like a blood vessel had burst. Lavender whimpered in pain as I rearranged her. Clutching my shirt in her fists she burrowed close to me, inhaling deeply.

"She's hurt," I called over to Kane, who was still pummelling the unconscious Alec. His face looked almost caved in. The words immediately stopped Kane's intense focus on ending Alec, and instead he came and knelt by us, gently reaching his hand out to stroke Lavender's hair out of her face, looking upon her injuries himself.

"We need to call an ambulance," Archer demanded.

"We need to take her home—if we call an ambulance she'll be taken away and we'll be arrested," Kane said, looking around. He frowned. "Something smells... odd about her."

"Of course she smells odd!" Archer thundered. "She stinks of fear, blood and dirt, of course she doesn't smell normal."

"No... something sweet." Kane shook his head, "Never mind..."

"Let's get her back to the SUV. Kane, are you happy to transport our friend here down to the basement?"

"He shouldn't even be on the same grounds as her," Kane snarled, looking over at the crumpled, bloody mess of a beta.

"Agreed. He won't be there long. We need Lavender to see the doc as soon as possible though, and I am not waiting around because we need to take that twat somewhere else." I slid my arms under Lavender's legs and around her back. "Now this may hurt, Darling. Just hold on to me," I soothed as I gently lifted her.

She whimpered as she tried to adjust her position, letting out a low whine that hurt every alpha there to hear.

"I'm sorry, Lavvy girl, we'll be home soon," Archer soothed as he led the way back to the SUV. He drove home while I stayed in the back, Lavender's head on my lap. Archer could see this was tearing me up inside. I was meant to be their leader, but I was doubting my ability to lead now. If I couldn't keep our omega safe I was a pitiful excuse for an alpha, and my pack deserved better than that.

"She'll be okay," Archer soothed from the front seat, trying to calm his own nerves. If he had never hacked into that damn firewall out of curiosity one evening, Lavender never would have been tangled up in our mess. She didn't deserve this. She was good and pure, sweet and kind: the opposite to our brutish and boisterous pack.

The doctor was waiting for us at the compound. Theo must have called him while he was helping Kane move Alec into the van so we could transport him. I wasted no time in sweeping Lavender back into my arms and carrying her though the house to her bedroom, her nest. Gently placing her down despite her whimpering protests. The doctor had followed us without a word, and was immediately putting his bag down, grabbing a stethoscope, a blood pressure monitor, and a little clip he attached to her finger.

"What happened to her?" he asked as he started checking her over.

"A beta who probably won't be breathing much longer," Archer growled.

"Hmmm, I hope you'll be taking care of that?"

"We will be," I assured him.

"Well, make yourself useful, go grab a few wash cloths and a bowl of clean water, clean her up gently so we can see how much of this blood is hers."

"Lavender stabbed him in the neck, so it's probably mostly his," I confirmed. "Good, seems like you have a spitfire on your hands," the doc said as Archer returned with the washcloths, handing one to me.

"We do," I nodded, starting with her hand I started rubbing gentle circles on the skin, getting rid of any grime or blood and revealing the bruises underneath.

"Her shoulder is messed up," Kane told the doctor, looking at her left shoulder. It was the one that had looked out of place when we had first found her on the floor of the forest, Alec on top of her.

"It looks like it's been dislocated. Besides that she's got a lot of scratches, a broken finger, and the bruises on her throat from being choked. It's not pleasant, but she should recover nicely. Omega's heal really well, which is good because I don't have any antibiotics I can give her—all my stuff is oral or low grade, she needs stronger stuff," the doctor confessed.

"Why can't you get them?" I growled.

"If I try to get my hands on what she needs it'll attract far too much attention to me, she needs proper, high strength IV antibiotics to fight the infection."

"Is there nothing else you can give her?"

Doc sighed. "She's got an infection from that mess on her leg. You can wait it out and see if the weaker stuff I've got works, but I wouldn't be hopeful. I don't want to give her anything that could mess with her kidneys—a hospital will have everything she needs."

"She'll get better," Archer insisted, never looking up from the section of forearm he was gently dabbing clean.

Lavender didn't get better. Within hours of arriving home she had started to burn up. The doctor had taken up permanent residence in her bedroom, keeping a watchful eye on her. Kane was doing the same, watching over her like a statue, eerily unmoving. He refused to leave her side as she tossed and turned. Despite the good painkillers, she was restless. Kane had growled at the doctor to give her more pain relief, unhappy at her whines every time she moved. They were grating at Kane's self-restraint. I could tell by the look in his eyes he wanted to throw a table through a wall. He was so angry, so desolate. He was tormented when Juniper was taken, but if he lost Lavender? I doubted Kane would survive such a blow. So he stood watch, if he had any choice in the matter he would never leave her again.

When Archer had brought her here I'd had doubts, but the daft little omega had worked her way under my skin. My soul was hers, my body was hers and my heart was completely and forever hers.

I was in love with Lavender.

Watching her writhe in pain felt like a special level of torment, like I was being punished for all the shitty things I had ever done in his life.

Three days. It had been three days since we had brought Lavender home, and she showed no improvement. She hadn't woken up for more than a few seconds and every time she did wake she would only mutter something unintelligible before slipping into unconsciousness. We had taken to sleeping in her room, on the floor. We didn't want to crowd the nest while she was injured, she needed space to heal. Kane hadn't left the room to eat or shower in those three days either. He was starting to smell a bit ripe, but no one mentioned it. We were all in need of a little self-care, but it was the farthest thing from our minds while watching Lavender toss and turn, her hair sticking to her damp forehead.

"She needs a hospital," I broke the silence, my tone sombre.

"She needs the Haven medical staff," Kane replied. His eyes were empty, almost shell shocked.

"We can't take her there," Archer said. "We would never see her again,"

"This isn't working," I sighed, running my hand through my hair, "She'll die if we keep her here—you know it."

We *did* know it, but none of us wanted to admit that the way to heal Lavender was obvious, only it would mean we would lose her, possibly forever.

"They would never let her out, not without a pack, and we would never be allowed within a hundred feet of an omega." Theo sighed, looking over at Lavender longingly.

"We vote," I said. "I can't make this decision for us. I say yes, she needs the Haven,"

"I say yes, but I fucking hate it," Archer added.

"Yes," Theo's voice was empty, lost.

"Kane?" I asked.

"I can't lose her," Kane said. "So... yes."

It was unanimous. We were going to take Lavender back home. To her home.

CHAPTER FORTY-SEVEN
Lavender

A steady, rhythmic beeping disturbed me. I ached, and my body was so tired that even opening my eyes felt like a monumental chore. So I didn't, opting to let myself drift into sweet oblivion once more.

The next time I woke, opening my eyes, while difficult, wasn't impossible. Cracking my eyes open I took in the familiar sight of a hospital room. A luxury hospital room. I was laying on expensive, high thread count sheets on a hospital bed that felt like a cloud. The room didn't smell like cleaner, or antiseptic, instead it smelled like freshly cut grass and sea air, so relaxing and calming.

I knew where I was.

I was at the Haven.

Looking around the room, my eyes fell on Donovan standing by my door. The guard who used to regularly guard the floor that I lived on was sitting on a chair in the corner of the room, watching the door. Guarding me. He looked exactly the same, his hair cropped short and his face clean shaven.

At the sound of me moving, his head whipped around to look at me, eyes widening. "You're awake!" He smiled. "I'll get the doctor, she'll be so happy to see you're awake, it's good to have you home."

He stuck his head out of the door, talking to someone in hushed tones that I couldn't hear. A second later, a beautiful woman with red hair in a sleek bun and a white medical coat came into the room, smiling at the sight of me.

"Miss Lavender! How are you feeling?"

"Sore… how did I get here?" I asked, looking around the room again. Where were my alphas? I couldn't detect their scents anywhere.

"A good Samaritan dropped you off at our gates, you had clearly been through hell. Do you know who took you?" she asked kindly as she tapped a few buttons on the medical monitor next to her.

"Uh…his name was Alec. He wanted an omega. He's a policeman, or a detective, I don't know," I lied.

"Don't worry, security has been tripled. How someone got into the walls of the Haven is beyond us, but we won't allow it to happen again. There are three extra security guards per dormitory now, almost one guard to each omega."

I cringed internally. We hardly had any freedom as it was living there. Having a guard on your ass at all times would easily get stifling.

"Fawn has been pacing the halls outside, by the way, she really wants to see you, but we told her she had to wait until you were up for visitors."

"How am I… What happened?" I asked groggily. The pain

meds I was on were potent and I was struggling to think straight.

"You had a nasty infection from a cut on your leg. Your throat was bruised pretty badly and you even burst a blood vessel in your eye. It also looks like you had a nasty shoulder dislocation. You really have been through the wars, haven't you? I'm glad you're safe now."

"Yeah," I nodded. "Can you let Fawn in?"

"Fawn went to get food, just moments ago—there is someone else here who would love to see you, if that's okay."

Assuming it was another omega friend, I nodded. The doctor walked out the room and a moment later Sage walked in. I hadn't seen the pretty blonde beta-turned-omega since she had left to be with her pack several months ago.

Her eyes were rimmed red, her hair piled haphazardly on top of her head.

"Lavender!" she cried, making her way over to my bedside. "I came as soon as I heard you were back. Are you okay?" She sat in the chair next to my bed, gently gripping one of my hands. "The doctor said you were pretty hurt, but are you making a full recovery? Who took you?" Sage asked, eyes wide. "Callan and the rest of Pack Rivers are at your disposal."

I looked over at Donovan. Sage understood my meaning immediately. Glancing over at him she cleared her throat. "Would you mind terribly letting us girls talk alone, just for a bit? You can wait outside."

"I'm not sure I'm allowed." Donovan frowned.

"I would much rather just talk with a fellow omega..." I said, peering down. Donovan got the message, stuttering that he would simply wait outside to let us have our peace and quiet.

"Okay, now he's gone, tell me."

"I was kidnapped by a pack, but then I fell in love with them…" The whole tale spilled out of me as I spoke with her. Sage understood me. She had an unconventional relationship with her pack as well, and she had also been kidnapped by an alpha intent on trafficking her several months prior. Looking at her now though, it was hard to believe, she looked so happy, radiant even.

"And there is no way the Haven would consider letting them court you, officially?"

I grimaced. "They're suspected criminals, linked to drug smuggling and human trafficking. They would shoot them if they came within a mile of this place."

"I'm so sorry—why on earth did they bring you back? If you were so close? You said they admitted they loved you?"

"They must have found Juniper," I said, heart sinking in realisation. "If they found Juniper—maybe they chose her?" Tears formed in the corners of my eyes. They abandoned me the moment they had her back, cutting me off from them for good.

Large, ugly sobs burst from my chest, and I practically wailed in distress. Sage sat on the edge of the bed, pulling me in for a hug and holding me as I let my tears flow freely.

Two weeks later I had been given a clean bill of health by the doctors, but nothing felt right. My days were spent holed up in my nest staring vacantly at my tablet. I didn't fully want to admit to myself that I was waiting for Archer to call me like he used to.

I didn't know what day it was, but I had a packed day of moping, crying and maybe a good session of self-pity.

Fawn had other ideas.

"Get up," she said, pulling the blankets off me. Why was she so awake? Couldn't she just leave me to wallow?

"I've got a meeting, and I want you to join me." She folded the blanket neatly before returning to me, grabbing me by the arm and pulling me into a sitting position. Next to me she looked even more polished and proper than usual in her floral blouse and slacks.

"No, I don't want to," I grumbled.

"For me?" Fawn asked. "I don't really want to do it solo, I could use a friend."

Normally I would have called bullshit on that. Fawn could deal with packs with her eyes closed, but I was too tired to fight her so I let her shove me into the shower. I didn't wash my hair, and when I turned off the shower Fawn shouted from the hallway. "Get your pert ass back in there and wash your hair or I swear to god I will get a hose and do it myself, don't test me Lavender!"

"How can you possibly know I've not washed my hair?" I shouted back, gaping at the door, wearing only a towel.

"It takes you ages to wash that mass of fluff on your head. Also do a damn hair mask. It'll make you feel better.

"Fine!" I glared at the door before shucking the towel and getting back in the shower.

Once out of the shower I threw on the first clothes Fawn passed me, not even paying attention to them.

"You're an ass," I grumbled as I put on a pair of leggings.

"I'm your friend," Fawn said as she leaned daintily against the vanity. "Come on, I missed you. I gave you a few days to mope, but this has to stop. Plus the Keepers are going to get extra worried soon if you don't at least make an effort."

I wanted to snarl at her but she was right, the Keepers had

started hovering, and their incessant questions were getting irritating. With a sigh I threw my hair up—there was no way I could get a brush through it.

"Come on, let's go see your fanboys," I sighed.

"Thank you." Fawn smiled sweetly.

CHAPTER FORTY-EIGHT
Kane

After we dropped Lavender off near the Haven and waited just long enough to ensure she was picked up, things started to move very fast.

We threw ourselves into finding all possible evidence we could pointing to Alec Rouche being a crooked cop. It didn't take long. Once we started shaking that tree everything fell out. He had done all manner of things: bribery, imprisonment, excessive violence. For some reason he kept getting away with it.

I felt like my life was on autopilot. Every time I closed my eyes, I could see Lavender's limp body being carried into the Haven, through the walls, and away from us forever. Every time I got close to someone they were ripped away from me. Bringing down Rouche was the only thing pushing me to move forward.

Once Archer got a hold of his computer we learned that he had been using police resources to tap into our security system.

All those nights Archer had hardly slept trying to keep us secure was rendered moot by a jackass with the power of a police department behind him.

We also found a shitload of evidence that proved that Rouche had been fabricating stories about my pack to make us seem like hardened criminals. In fact, if it wasn't for him we would have a spotless record. Our chasing omega traders, much to our shock, was totally off the police's radar.

Gage in his position as our pack leader—yes, I was officially part of the pack now—took the mountain of evidence we had collected and strode straight to the police commissioner. He refused to take no for an answer and they saw everything.

Alec Rouche was unfortunately still alive. I had pummelled his face in but somehow he survived that and the blood loss. His jaw would never work properly again, and he had significant damage to his cognitive function due to lack of blood because our omega was a resourceful spitfire.

Despite our decision to stay away, Archer did hack back into the Haven's system one last time to ensure that Lavender was on the mend. Within a week she was back in her nest and the doctors reported that she was healing well.

If she had suffered permanent damage because of us I doubted I would be able to live with myself. She had become a point of light in my very bleak existence and I would happily spend the rest of my life on the outskirts ensuring her happiness.

Two weeks after that night back home we found ourselves in the last place we ever imagined we would be—in an interview room at the Clearmont Haven.

It wasn't because we were being accused of a crime, far from it. With Rouche being sent away for a long, long time it became apparent all the stuff on our record was fabricated by him, and we were given a heartfelt apology from the boys in blue, as well as a clean record. He had been pinned with Lavender's kidnapping—the original one *we* committed, so our names were clear of that.

"Well, all your paperwork looks pristine," the brunette beta with polka-dot glasses said as she flicked through our files. "It's not often we get packs looking to find their forever partner with a recommendation from the police commissioner!"

That had been a stroke of brilliance from Gage to ask for one.

"Thank you, Anna." Gage smiled at her easily as he leaned back in his chair. All four of us were gathered around the beta's desk. She was the guardian of sorts, the woman who would give us final approval for what we wanted.

"All your finances look pristine as well. I think you would make an excellent addition to our Haven."

"Now your profile will be added to our system, and if any of our omegas are interested in you they'll send you a message —you can't message them first."

We all nodded and made noises of confirmation.

Our plan had been to do everything as legitimately as possible. Join the Haven, pay the fees, and then pray that Lavender saw our profile.

Surely she wouldn't isolate herself for too long?

I had voted for Archer to hack in again and make her talk to us so we could explain, but apparently the Haven had figured out how he got in before and beefed up their security. The only thing he managed to find out was that Lavender was out of the infirmary.

So we had to wait.

That night we gathered around the kitchen island eating a simple meal of chicken and vegetables.

"Have you heard anything about Rouche's house?" Theo asked, pushing his food around the plate.

Gage shook his head. The police had been all over the house by the time we went back after getting Lavender home safely so we had no idea what actually went down in the building or what our omega had endured.

"He's got a list of charges a mile long, the fucker was so crooked," Archer said. "I've been watching the police file on him as it's updated with every new charge. There's multiple kidnapping charges."

Theo put his fork down with a sigh. "So that fucker has done it before? Ugh! This place feels empty, stupid asshole ruined everything for us."

He was right. Our home felt cold, like all the sunlight had been taken out of it. Theo hadn't even stepped foot in his rage room, and his nightmares were back without the calming influence of Lavender.

"We need to give her time and she'll come back to us. She knows we wouldn't just leave her."

"Does she?" I asked, raising my eyebrows. None of us had really let her know how we felt, how much we wanted her to stay with us.

Heck, we didn't even know if *she* wanted to stay with us.

"We can—" Gage's phone buzzed, cutting off his words. With a huff he picked his phone up off the counter, stilling when he checked it.

"What is it?" I asked.

"We have a message from the Haven—but it's not from Lavender."

"Well ignore it, we aren't interested in any omega other than Lavender." Theo frowned.

"Who's it from?" Archer asked.

"It's from someone called Fawn," Gage replied.

"That's Lavender's friend! She lives in the same dorm as Lavender, they've been friends for years."

"Well what does her message say?!" I asked forcefully.

Gage turned the phone screen so we could all see it.

FAWN:

> What the fuck are YOU doing on here? I know who you are.

"What do I reply to that?" Gage asked, looking between us with a lost expression.

"She's a good friend of Lavender's—tell her the truth!" Archer insisted.

Taking a deep breath he started to type.

ROWE:

> We're looking for Lavender and hoping she'll see us.

FAWN:

> Are you legitimately on my roster or pulling some bullshit like before?

ROWE:

> 100% Legit. What happened wasn't our choice. We need to talk to her. Please.

We went back and forth for several minutes, being very

careful with our wording—we didn't want to admit to anything criminal because these messages were likely recorded.

We sat around the kitchen, food forgotten while we waited for the final reply from Fawn.

> FAWN:
> Fuck. Come in tomorrow. I'll see you. You better be for real or I'll stab you myself.

That was how we found ourselves in a meeting room at the Haven. Nerves ate at me as I paced the small room filled with armchairs, staring at the glass partition. On the other side was a drink cart, a comfortable looking armchair and a small coffee table.

Fawn had responded to us, but she had been prickly at first. It wasn't until we got onto a call with her and explained everything, who we were to Lavender—well maybe not everything, that could have easily led to our arrest and ruined all of our work to destroy our tarnished reputation.

"She's late," Theo grumbled, his foot bouncing nervously.

"She can be as late as she wants, we'll wait," I said.

It was twenty minutes later that we heard footsteps at the door behind the glass and two people walked through.

The first person I assumed to be Fawn, but the other was unmistakable. She had lost weight in the last two weeks, and she was far too pale with bags under her eyes but Lavender was unmistakable.

"Lavvy girl!" Archer jumped out of his armchair.

The other omega glared at Gage while Lavender stood gaping at us. "You lot need to talk, but don't take too long, the guards will be coming around soon. If you're mean to her I'll find someone to chop your cock off, okay? All of your cocks."

The icy steel of her gaze made even my balls shrivel up as

she turned and glided out of the room, with her head held high.

"H-how are you here?" Lavender asked, staggering forward and sinking into the armchair in front of us.

"We just got approval to start courting omegas, we had to see you—the right way." Gage grinned at her as he spoke, pure happiness on his face at seeing Lavender again.

"We couldn't leave you Lavender, we are fucking in love with you, and we want to court you, properly," Archer said.

"How are you even allowed in here?" Confusion was plastered across her face.

"We signed up and paid the fees—it turns out we had been falsely accused for many years by a member of the police department, so once that was cleared up we decided it was time to make our family whole." Gage couldn't take his eyes off her as he spoke.

"But you guys found Juniper?" Lavender whispered in a small voice. "That's why you left me here, wasn't it?"

Juniper?

"What on earth makes you think we found Juniper?" I asked, my voice more terse than I intended.

"Why the fuck did you bring me back here?" Lavender asked, sitting up ramrod straight.

"You were sick," Gage whispered. "We didn't want to."

"And you didn't find Juniper?"

"No, Lavender, are you okay? Rouche was an ass, but he wasn't a trafficker."

Lavender shot up and started pacing, mumbling to herself. Her head whipped to us, looking between us with wide eyes. "After Alec kidnapped me I woke up in a basement, Juniper was there with me—she's been there for years!"

My heart stuttered in my chest. Surely not? A cold sensation radiated through my body, turning my bones to ice as my vision blurred.

"How?" I asked, my voice strangled. My chest felt impossibly tight. *Is this what a heart attack feels like?*

"Alec kidnapped her, it was never traffickers—oh god. You idiots! She escaped the same time as me, ran out into those woods alone. *Fuck.* You need to go find her, now!" Lavender pointed at the door as she spoke.

That sweet smell that had clung to Lavender when we found her had been so familiar. How had I not recognised my sister's scent? What kind of brother was I? My stomach turned and I sank into one of the seats.

Juniper was alive.

"Holy fuck," Gage cursed, looking between me and Lavender. "Are you sure it was Juniper?"

"Of course I am!"

Archer pulled his phone out and started typing away. "I'm searching for any reports in that area on the night we found Lavender."

"Was Juniper okay?" I asked quietly. My sister was out there, she had been for two weeks and I had no clue.

"All things considered. She's malnourished, definitely traumatised, but she's not as bad as I'd have expected for someone in captivity that long. Didn't you guys check out the basement of Alec's house?"

"We heard him yell and got distracted from the house. Our focus was getting you home—we didn't realise."

I stood up, taking a few measured steps to look at Lavender who was glancing between us all, her hand clutched to her chest.

She wasn't eating properly. Her face was somehow even more gaunt than when we had dropped her off. Her upper arms looked frail and the T-shirt she was wearing was far too large. We need to get our omega home and safe. Then we could hunt for my sister.

"We will be finding my sister soon, but that wasn't why we came, Lavender."

"Why did you come then?" she snapped.

"To bring you home!" I thundered

Lavender blinked and took a step back. "To bring me home?" she asked in a small voice.

Gage kept his voice level, but I could smell the anxiety rolling off him. "We love you, Lavender and we want to do this the right way, through the Haven. Bring you home as Pack Rowe's official omega."

"Why?" Lavender's response was simple.

"*Why?*" Archer repeated in a strangled voice.

"Yeah, why? Because if I am coming back with you *willingly*," she hissed the last word quietly. "Then you'd better tell me why you love me."

"Because you are a stubborn ass. You regularly go toe to toe with us even though that's basically a chihuahua going up against a rottweiler," Gage babbled, all his words rushing out. I didn't know if I should stop him or not.

"That's *very* complimentary," Lavender snarked, crossing her arms.

"Shut up, you know you're beautiful. We want to do this the right way because we want to spend the rest of our lives listening to you and Theo debate how best to dispose of a body over dinner, or listening to you prattle on about how a planet is in the microwave somehow—"

"Retrograde," Lavender interjected.

"You know what I mean." Gage levelled her with a playful glare.

"Home isn't the same without you, Lavender," Archer said. "The house is empty and cold. We can't even go near your rooms because we hate you not being there."

"You clubbed me with a lamp so you know I adore you." Theo smirked.

"As for me," I started to speak. "I owe you everything."

Her face softened as she pushed a strand of hair behind her ear. "Kane..."

"Without you I never would have accepted that I was part of this pack, I would have stayed cold and distant. You..." I paused trying to find the words. "You helped free my sister, Lavender—I fucking owe you *everything*. I shouldn't be asking you for anything, but I still want more. I want you in our home, as part of our family. But it's your choice, Lavender. I refuse to let anyone make that decision for you."

Lavender looked between us for a moment, her face softening further. Taking a deep breath, she stepped closer to the glass between us. We were inches apart and I wanted to reach out and touch her so badly.

"In that case... I think I better talk to the Keepers." She smirked. "You lot better get your courting gifts ready, because I'm worth *a lot* of gummy bears. If I'm not in a diabetic coma from the sheer sugar overdose then you're not doing it right!"

CHAPTER FORTY-NINE
Lavender

I tiptoed down the corridor toward the den, hiding my surprise behind my back. Everyone was in the den waiting for takeout to arrive, so it was the perfect opportunity for me.

Settling into pack life had been far easier than I'd ever imagined. It had taken a few weeks to do everything the appropriate way. I had spent a week with them visiting me daily bringing me all manner of gifts and candy. It had been wonderful but every night I had cried at how lonely I felt without them in bed with me. The moment they signed all the paperwork and brought me home we had hunkered down in the nest and refused to leave for several days.

The ease of every day was shocking in a new way. There was no jealousy. I was never worried about giving too much or too little attention to any pack members—everything just flowed and meshed easily.

The sex was also completely mind blowing and I had

become a bit of a nymphomaniac. At any time of the day, on any and all surfaces, everything was game.

Archer and Kane were sitting opposite each other, a chess board between them, Kane had been annihilating Archer lately and he was stubbornly trying to regain his title as chess champion of the house. Gage was sitting on the sofa scrolling through his phone. He looked up to smirk at me, knowing full well what I was about to do—he was the one who helped me obtain my little surprise.

Theo, the intended recipient, was lounging on the sofa, his attention firmly on whatever game he was playing on the TV.

"Hey Princess," he murmured, only looking away from the screen briefly.

"Heya," I did my best to keep my voice casual.

When he went to open his mouth again, I moved before he could speak. Pulling my surprise from behind my back I plopped the tiny Ragdoll kitten on his chest.

Theo's immediate reaction was to go completely still. "Is that a cat?" he asked.

I chuckled. "I'd hope you know what that is. You're the one that went to school to be a veterinarian."

"Whose is it?" he asked, gently sitting up and cradling the kitten to his chest, scratching behind its ear and grinning when it rewarded him with a purr.

"Yours," I smirked.

His head whipped up to look at me with disbelief. "No, I—"

"I got him for you. You said you wanted a pet."

"B-but the brain injury," he stammered.

"When's the last time you were unstable?" I asked pointedly. He had been the picture of calm and reasonable for months. Anytime he felt even slightly off he would seek me out for comfort and would feel normal after a few moments between my scent and purr. He would always suggest some sexual therapy, and sometimes I indulged the request, because who doesn't love copious orgasms?

"I don't want to hurt him," Theo whispered, looking at the tiny animal with pure adoration in his eyes.

"You won't, I trust you—we all do." I sank onto the couch next to him and rested my head on his shoulder, watching the kitten as it played with the string of Theo's sweatshirt.

"He's beautiful," Theo kept his voice quiet, unable to take his eyes off his new pet. "Is he a Ragdoll?" he asked.

"Uh, I think so?" I bit my lip. "He's cute and fluffy. That's all I needed to know."

"Can't you get DNA test kits for pets?" Archer asked, smiling over from the chess game.

Theo's face somehow broke into an even bigger grin. "You can!" he cried. "I'll order one right away, I want to see *exactly* what this little guy is. My bet is mostly Ragdoll, just look at these fluffy little ears!"

"I'm glad you like him," I grinned.

"I love him—how the fuck did you get a cat without me knowing?!" He turned to me, confusion evident.

"Gage drove me to town to pick him up early this morning. You were still dead to the world."

Theo smirked. "Is that why you were so intent on tiring me out yesterday?"

"It wasn't, but I'm not complaining." I plucked the kitten who was wriggling out of Theo's grasp and gave him a quick cuddle myself before letting him down on the couch.

"He's going to scratch up all the furniture, isn't he?" Kane asked, with a shake of his head.

"Oh for sure." I laughed. "But it'll be worth it, just look how cute he is!"

"We needed a mascot around here," Gage laughed from the other end of the sofa. "What are you going to call it?"

"Dahmer!" Theo exclaimed, looking between me and the kitten eagerly.

"As in *Jeffery Dahmer*?" I cried with a laugh.

"Of course, it suits this family!"

"I don't know true crime, but I do know who Dahmer was—I like it." Kane said, moving a chess piece.

I laughed, leaning up and pecking Theo lightly on the lips. "Dahmer it is. I've ordered all the bits you'll need for him and they'll be arriving later today."

"You're pretty perfect, you know that, right?" Theo asked, looking at me with pure, unadulterated happiness in his face.

"I'm far from perfect, but I *am* perfect for this family." I beamed.

"You know what this means?" Archer asked with a smirk.

"What?"

"That we get more snuggle time with Lavender—I mean it's only fair seeing as you have a new cuddle partner…"

"No!" Theo exclaimed, grabbing me by the hips and dragging me onto his lap before gently depositing the fluffball on my lap.

His hand circled the back of my neck, his thumb gliding over the bite mark he had put there during my last heat. Lemon and lavender filled the air as he drew me in for a hungry kiss as I squirmed in his lap. I had been marked by every single one of my alphas and it felt perfect, they had each taken their turn during my heat.

We hadn't given up on finding Juniper. Weeks after escaping the basement we hadn't gotten far, but we were making progress. Alec was locked away and physically mangled so he posed no threat. Juniper had escaped, we just needed to figure out where she ended up.

We were settling into the den for the evening, wrapping up in blankets and putting on a movie when Kane's phone rang.

He remained mostly silent throughout the call, but his face turned white, then broke into a smile and then fell again.

"Kane?" I asked, clambering off Theo and tossing the blanket to go check on him. He looked up at me, his breathing ragged.

"They found Juniper—and she's gone and shacked up with a bunch of alphas!"

Also by Melissa Huxley

Havenverse Series

Knot Their Burden

Knot For Keeps

Knot That Delicate (Coming soon!)

Pucking Alphas Duet

Packed in the Penalty Box

Pack Power Play

Pucking Pregnant

Pack Plus Three (Coming soon!)

Printed in Great Britain
by Amazon